In Death's Keep

Book One: The Dominion Wars

J. A. Beix

authorHOUSE®

AuthorHouse™
1663 Liberty Drive
Bloomington, IN 47403
www.authorhouse.com
Phone: 1-800-839-8640

First published by AuthorHouse   11/13/2009

ISBN: 978-1-4490-4531-9 (e)
ISBN: 978-1-4490-4532-6 (sc)
ISBN: 978-1-4490-4533-3 (hc)

Printed in the United States of America
Bloomington, Indiana

This book is printed on acid-free paper.

For Alexis, thank you for helping me realize a dream.

List of major characters, places and things:

Aedulica: Remote city located in the forest of Nemorosus.

Aegrus Sea: Sea creating the Eastern border of Silexunatra.

Aliondrae Desenya: Countess of Arxsolum, first cousin to the King.

Andwer: Edward Ardenon's first lieutenant, career military man for Arxsolum.

Artrin Keydon: Historical figure, ancestor to Aliondrae.

Arxsolum: Ancient keep located in the Southern Dominion.

Barawal: Large City located at the junction of the Ferox River and the Aegrus Sea.

Caellestus: Ancient wizard with godlike powers widely blamed for the War of the Dominions.

Caoudrol: Elven leader.

Cedric Stamwin: Historical figure, hero of the War of Dominions.

Deyecuisinawel: Elven sword fighting technique, meaning liquid sword.

Dey Syalin: Royal city of the Northern Dominion.

Discere: Court wizard of Arxsolum.

Edward Ardenon: Second husband to Countess Aliondrae Desenya.

Evanidus: Forest home of the Elven Nation.

Ferox River: River separating the Northern and Southern Dominions, primarily used for trade.

Gryffyn: Weapon's master of Arxsolum.

Irritum Sea: Stagnant body of water located south of Arxsolum.

Jaxen Desenya: Son of Aliondrae, heir to Arxsolum.

Lanhana: A historian for the council of wizards.

Lexis: Member of the shade unit, protégé of Phillos.

Lineaus: Arxsolum's court healer.

Lockstan: Stragess' second in command, captain of enemy forces.

Marhran: Large fighter, member of shade unit.

Nemorosus: Forest dominating large portion of the Southern Dominion.

Perata: Amnesiac man taken in by the Desenya twins.

Phillos: Assassin recruited to be member of shade unit.

Quinvium: Major crossroad city in the Southern Dominion.

Rammel: Dwarf, mason who lived in the Voro Mountains, member of shade unit.

Reynil: Royal city of Southern Dominion.

Shade unit: Perata's elite team of spies.

Silnac: Large city midway between Arxsolum and Barawal.

Sorcia Desenya: Daughter of Aliondrae, powerful wizard, leader of shade unit.

Stragess: Invading General - favored of Caellestus.

Tallox: King of Southern Dominion, self proclaimed General of Eastern Alliance.

Tonagal: Eccentric thief, member of shade unit.

Voro Mountains: Mountain range running from the Elvin nation of Evanidus to the Irritum Sea creating the natural border between the East and the West.

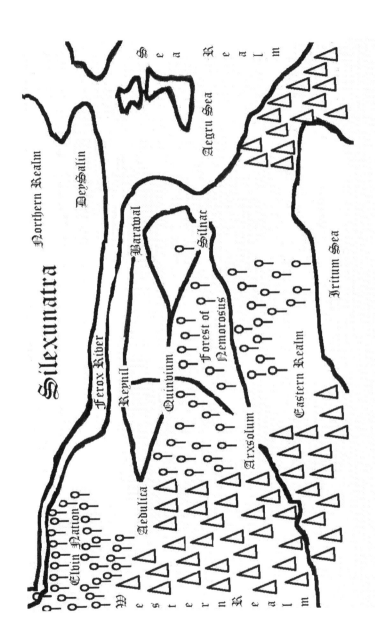

PROLOGUE
Staggered Existence

The night grew incredibly still as all the world suddenly stopped moving. Nothing made a sound, no wind, no animals, nothing. The old wizard awoke with a start, his dreams disturbed him on a level he had never before encountered. His heart was racing as he leapt from his bed simultaneously wiping the inordinate amount of sweat from his brow. He hastened to the balcony in an effort to get some fresh air. As he opened the doors and entered the night he was stopped dead in his tracks by an unseen force. His ancient muscles tightened without his consent, rooting the mage in an agonizing stance. If he had been allowed, the intense pain would have dropped him to the hard stone floor. The very fiber of his being was drawn in all directions at once. Discere understood many things, more things than any one man had the right, but at that moment he was nothing more than a newborn entering a strange world far beyond his comprehension.

In his countless years, the old wizard witnessed some of the greatest feats of magic, but this dwarfed all of those combined, something was happening, something outside his knowledge, something different from known magic. He felt the fabric of existence being ripped open by an immense power. Time no longer registered as the pressure that bore down on him wore heavily on his soul. All Discere knew was that he could not stand anymore, and then it was gone.

Minutes, hours or even days could have transpired as far as Discere knew; he was too disoriented and too relieved to care. His sweat-matted beard slowly began to whip in a howling wind. He chanced a glance out into the countryside, his breathe still ragged. The departure of power left a void that was quickly filling with a chorus of commotion and confusion of a bewildered world. Chaos tore through Silexunatra like a furious tempest determined to make its presence known. Erratic lightning raced across the sky amidst the downpour of rain and hail. Booming thunder and the ensuing vibrations rocked the foundations of the primeval keep. Discere clutched the thick stone wall desperate to share its strength. Lightning flashed half a dozen more times before he found the will to pull himself away and stagger back to bed. The toll of the experience was such that he could do nothing more than return to a nightmare-laden sleep.

Chapter One:
Storm Remains

"Sorcia, slow down!" pleaded an exasperated Jaxen while using all his riding skills to catch up to his overly spirited sister. "You know that our mother would be upset if she knew how far we have gone without escort!"

Sorcia sighed and slowed her mount down to a canter. With an innocent voice that was only betrayed by her mischievous blue eyes she responded, "I just wanted to see the extent of damage from that storm last night, besides the Countess will be too preoccupied with state affairs to worry about us." Even though she said it she knew that her mother would be concerned about them, she was always concerned about them.

Jaxen took the opportunity to look at the so called damage his sister was using as an excuse so that he could refute it and for the first time noticed the forest was truly in a state of disarray after the devastating storm. He scolded himself for not being aware of his surroundings at all regardless of the fact that he was concentrating his efforts on Sorcia. "Gryffyn would tan my hide." He said under his breath while continuing his inspection. He marked several uprooted ancient trees that had stood since before the War of The Dominions, ripped from the ground as if they were saplings. Small craters remained where intense lighting had struck and ravaged the ground. The massive quantity of rain was flooding the lowlands, laying waste to many of the farmer's crops. Even the animals of the forest were reluctant to continue on with their everyday routines, they just looked around as if they were in a different world.

As Jaxen reached his twin sister he could see the look on her face. It was not one of fear but of excitement, a look that Jaxen knew all to well. A look that bespoke trouble and no amount of guilt would stop her from acting on it. Although Sorcia was barely past five foot tall, she was afraid of nothing and faced life like it was one grand adventure that needed to be taken. In fact, she reveled in it. If people did not want to follow her, she cared little. She would do with out them and she could do with out them. Being naturally gifted in most things and even more so when it came to magic was enough to make her quite a formidable individual. Her only weakness, if it could be called a weakness, was her inability to focus. Her attention span was nearly nonexistent, which very much frustrated her mother, her teacher, and at this moment her brother.

He was the polar opposite of Sorcia, dark-eyed and the very definition of focus. He took every day as if it was his duty, his job to be alive and he was very serious about it. At an early age the realization that life would happen whether he wanted it to or not was thrust upon him. As heir to Arxsolum he was allowed very little free time and less room for error. He looked around one last time and shook his head realizing that at this time there were a multitude of more important things he should be doing than wandering through the forest of Nemorosus looking at uprooted trees and frightened woodland creatures.

Sorcia steeled her bright blue eyes on her brother, "Jax, you just do not understand," her voice was almost cryptic, "last night I felt that storm, I mean actually felt it. It was no ordinary storm… it, it means something." She looked around the forest as if something were going to jump out at any moment. "I just don't know what."

"You are just being a silly little girl," returned Jaxen feigning to be unimpressed, "you would use any excuse to get out of the castle, and oh look a big scary storm…better check it out." He chuckled, "Do not forget Sorc, I know you."

Sorcia continued to stare directly at her brother and in an unyielding voice said, "Well, if you know me, then you know that I am not lying to you right now. That was no ordinary storm, I know it and oh…did you see Master Discere's face today? He knows it as well."

Jaxen knew that Sorcia was not lying, she never lied. She was far to brazen for that, she truly believed that last night's storm was unnatural and when it came to anything magical, he just had to take her word for it. The more he thought about it he did notice the court wizard this morning; he looked extremely exhausted and very old. Jaxen turned his gaze back toward the city while he wondered if that was enough to go against their mother's wishes, besides he was still annoyed for letting his sister get him out here in the first place. Her excuse was to make sure everything was secure, which as far as he could tell was. The line needed to be drawn somewhere and that meant at least countering some of his sister's nonsense. "Sorcia, Master Discere is an old man, not just by our standards but by old men's standards. I think after so many years you just start to look like that." He was not nearly as convincing as she; in fact, he could not even convince himself. He may not have the gift of magic, but the damage wrought to the forest was far worse than any caused by even the severest of storms and he had no other explanations.

"Jax, you know better than that, Master Discere will probably out live both of us! Besides he just wasn't himself, I think the storm spooked him. I think he felt what I felt, and what I felt was eerie."

Jaxen lowered his head knowing he was not going to win the argument and tried a different strategy to rein her in, "Well, maybe then we should be talking to him about what happened last night. I mean, you are always telling me that he is considered one of the most powerful wizards in the council and that he has probably experienced, studied or examined pretty much everything imaginable. So, why don't you just ask him, instead of gallivanting halfway to Reynil?"

She swept the dark, untamed hair out of her face before positioning herself into her most defying stance. She was not about to be taken back to the city just so she could listen to the petty troubles of the townspeople. As far as she was concerned they were already too much of an annoyance. "First of all!" returned Sorcia, "I never said he was one of the most powerful wizards in the council, the most knowledgeable sure, but he is not that powerful. Secondly," she continued, "I am his apprentice don't you think it would occur to me to ask him first?"

"Well..." started an impatient Jaxen.

Sorcia kept on talking "I did ask him you fool and he refused to answer. Not in his typical 'you're not ready' type of refusal, but something more like 'I have no idea and I am a little concerned over it' type of answer. So even if he did know, well, he's not sharing, so you see, I have to find out about this storm on my own." She gave him her crooked smile. "So you can come with me or run back to the castle and listen to the farmers complain about their crops. You are old enough to make your own decisions."

Jaxen knew he could not make her go back; she was far too stubborn when she set her mind. He also knew that his mother would be even more upset if he let her go on alone. "All right," he said hoping that he could appease her curiosity, "but you have to promise that we go no further than the lake."

"We?" questioned Sorcia feigning surprise. "I did not know you were coming along," Her smile widened more with each word and her pace quickening with each breath. "We should go this way. Try to keep up."

"So," said Jaxen changing the subject, actually glad he was not dealing with the responsibility of his civic duties, "what are you looking for exactly?" He continued his study of the landscape and was truly amazed at the remnants of last night's storm, which were quite strange indeed. Some very large trees seemed to be cut in half while other smaller trees that stood less than a couple of feet away were unaffected.

"I guess we won't know until…" Sorcia stopped suddenly her eyes staring to the north. "Maybe…"

Jaxen followed her gaze and saw what it was she was looking at. He lunged to grab a hold of Sorcia's mount before she could rush over to what appeared to be a man lying under a tree. "We do not know who that is!" cautioned Jaxen, "stay with me and be alert, it could be a trap."

Sorcia hated and liked the way her brother always tried to protect her. "Well," she mocked, "I feel sorry for any bandits who mess with my big brother." She tore away from his grip and headed straight over, all the while still taunting him, "I hear he is going to be the greatest swordsman in all the Dominions."

Jaxen swore and followed suit. It was clear from a distance that it was a human underneath the tree, although the man's coloring was unusual. Fair skin and light hair were usually only seen on elves or sometimes on the northern mountain dwarves. But this man was far too large to be a dwarf and too heavily muscled to be an elf. In fact, he would be considered large even for a human.

"Do you think he's dead?" questioned Sorcia who had approached close enough to notice that the man was completely naked. "Hey you there," she said. "Are you in need of help?"

Both of them dismounted from their horses. "Sorcia, he looks like he is hurt badly, burned or…or…something," stammered a puzzled Jaxen as he reached the stranger. He stopped and whispered, "I think he may be dead." He took a closer look, "No wait, I think he is breathing." He turned his attention to his sister, "Do you think you could heal him?" he questioned without concealing his doubt. He knew that she would be a powerful wizard one day, if she ever took it seriously, but this could be beyond her current ability.

She answered his question without saying a word and gave him a wink that was supposed to be reassuring, "I happen to be rather good at healing. Jax, could you sit him up so his back is against the tree?"

Jaxen was always amazed when he saw his sister work her magic. Wizardry was a thing that no matter how hard he tried he just did not have the gift. It is not something you can work at, you either can or you cannot. He watched as she sprinkled some powder on the strange looking man's head while she touched him with her other hand. She then started chanting her arcane words that sounded like gibberish to Jaxen but he knew well enough not to interrupt.

Sorcia had done this spell many times and the words came unbidden to her lips. She summoned her internal magic and began her connection with the injured man's life-force. Everything began as normal and then in a flash a flood of energy dwarfed and engulfed her own. She tried to release the bond, but was unable pull loose. She had never encountered anything like this, even when attempting to heal other wizards. The very connection was completely foreign to her, nothing was being forced upon her but neither was she able to influence anything, she was trapped in a sea of energy. She tried to understand what was happening but it was all too overwhelming. She believed that she saw into the man's mind for a brief second but what she saw made absolutely no sense. As fast as his thoughts appeared they disappeared but still she could not release. The strain of the bond was such that she was beginning to lose consciousness. For the first time in her life Sorcia knew what fear was.

After a couple of moments, Jaxen started to get a little nervous. He did not expect the man to jump to his feet and start dancing but he did expect something. His sister just kept her hand on the man's head and remained perfectly still. To Jaxen, it looked as if his sister were in some kind of trance. He knew that he was not supposed to bother her while she worked her magic, but this was taking far too long, something had to be done. "Sorcia, Sorcia," he repeated tentatively, "how's it going?"

There was no response, only the silence, only the stillness. When her breathing grew labored he got worried. He tried to reassure himself by telling his inner voice that Sorcia knew her craft well, but it was not helping, he could not shake the feeling that something was wrong. He knew his sister; he knew that she had the audacity to try a spell that she was not familiar with and this might be such a situation.

Sorcia's face beaded with sweat and her eyes rolled into the back of her head. It looked as though she would lose consciousness any second. Disregarding the potential of angering his sister for interrupting, Jaxen grabbed a hold of Sorcia and pulled her away from the stranger. The result was immediate.

"Jax?" asked a startled Sorcia looking into her brother's face "what happened?" Her breaths came in gasps, as though she just finished one of Gryffyn's toughest drills. "I couldn't reach him, but..." she started, "I, ah, I couldn't seem to let go. I've never had that happen before."

Jaxen noticed a strange expression on her face. Was it fear? Before he could be sure, she replaced it with her usual curiosity, and asked, "Did he respond in anyway, any reaction at all?"

"No, nothing, he just laid there." answered Jaxen, irritated that his sister could be so obtuse. "Don't worry about him, how are you?" he said the last a bit rougher than intended.

"Me," she said as if nothing happened. "I'm fine; I'm just surprised that he would not respond to my spell...nothing more."

Jaxen was not convinced by any means but he did not want to infer that perhaps the spell was beyond her ability and said, "Do you think maybe he is too far gone for you to help?"

Sorcia looked at him knowing what he was actually thinking and shook her head, "No...no, Master Discere actually made me attempt to heal a corpse before, just so I would know how it feels." She shook her head in an effort to get rid of the memory and spoke gravely. "It was creepy...like trying to fill a bottomless pit, but I could release at any moment. No, this... this was different. My magic started to work," she paused, looking almost scared again "but then was stopped by something, and in doing so, trapped it...

trapped me." She trailed off into her own thoughts. "So do you think I should try again?" she asked a shocked Jaxen.

"Are you insane? No, no…you should not try again, that would be completely foolish!" Jaxen's look allowed no room for a contest. Without knowing what else to say Jaxen decided to act, "If this man is alive then we are responsible for him. What we need to do is take him to Master Discere, if he dies along the way, well we tried, and if not… we can at least get him food and shelter and some clothes until we have a better solution. Do you agree?" He may have asked Sorcia, but it was more of a statement than a question.

Sorcia shook her head in agreement; not knowing if she would have the courage to try another spell anyway, the thought of it gave her the chills, which was a very odd feeling for her. "We should probably cover him with something, don't you think?" she asked trying to get her mind occupied. "We might make quite a sight hauling a strange looking naked man through the city!"

The two teens worked together to hoist the stricken man over Jaxen's large mount. As Sorcia wrapped her saddle blanket around the man she noticed a strange marking on the man's arm. "Hey Jax, what do you make of this?"

"I have never seen its like, maybe he is from the Sea Dominion or something. I bet Master Discere would know."

The ride back to the castle was very quiet as neither spoke another word; Jaxen began investigating his own thoughts as to the events in the forest. How had this man come to be lying there naked and what happened to Sorcia's spell? Was she actually afraid or was that just his imagination? It occurred to Jaxen that Sorcia's whole demeanor seemed different today, almost as if she was beginning to grow up a bit.

Sorcia meanwhile replayed the event in the forest in an effort to better understand her failure to heal the man. She had done that spell many times and knew that she did it perfectly, she always did it perfectly. She had summoned the magic and began her connection with the injured man. Everything seemed normal and then in a flash it all fell apart. She tried to remember what she saw, but the only thing she could compare it too was catching a glimpse of insanity itself. It did not help that it was only a fleeting moment and to be honest she was not even sure she saw anything, it just happened too fast. She tried to focus her thoughts to begin to piece together this puzzle, but they quickly turned to how she and Jax would get through the city without drawing an overabundance of attention to the extraordinary man strapped on her brother's horse.

Her fears were for naught, people for the most part left them alone. The townspeople had their own problems and concerns to deal with. The unusual storm created a host of work, yet Arxsolum would survive this storm as it has always survived. Sorcia's thoughts wandered as she recalled some history lessons of her homeland. Once considered a great city, Arxsolum was located directly in front of what was the only pass through the Voro Mountains. The epicenter of trade between the Dominions, business thrived and interesting travelers arrived daily. She scoffed as she concluded that Arxsolum was now the epicenter of nothing. It had been relegated to the status of a mere border-town since no people have utilized the pass or even crossed the mountains in hundreds of years. The War of the Dominions made sure of that. Her history lessons tell of the many powerful wizards that were defending the city, tired of the ceaseless attacks during the war and came up with a plan; a plan that would protect them from invaders forever. They recruited all the engineers and masons the city held and with an unrivaled display of unity and power, collapsed the pass. Once closed, the whole reason of being for Arxsolum was gone.

She sighed once more imaging what it would be like to live in that time, a time of growth, visitors and excitement. She switched her vision to the five foot thick slanted stone walls that reached nearly forty feet high. Her teacher once told her that Arxsolum's original construction was intended to be the first wall of defense against invaders, and it presumably did its job well. She did agree that the city itself is more of a keep than anything else.

She noted the defensive towers that ran the length of the wall at 100 yard intervals with passageways connecting them and the double-angled slits every 5 feet under a protective covering. She began to imagine the advantage Arxsolum's bowmen would have while launching arrows at invaders attempting to scramble up the uneven rise toward the massive gates. She surmised that even if they survived the deadly arrows they would still have to navigate a series of three gates that protected the only entrance into the city. Each gate was a giant portcullis backed by large solid doors made of wood and steel construction that locked into the walls and the ground. Above the three gates sat a large gate house that could store men and weapons, as well as two large murder-holes. These simple but devious holes would allow defenders to attack the enemy from directly above with whatever weapons they had on hand, or whatever their imaginations allowed. It was the perfect killing ground.

Even though Sorcia had entered and exited these gates all her life she had never given thought to the purpose of them or the ingenuity of the builders. Inside the walls the buildings were laid out to create choke points all the way to the castle. In fact there was no direct route to the castle from the gates. An invading army would find it difficult to move quickly or aggressively forward and would most likely end up lost. Like most of the inhabitants of Arxsolum that had lived there all of their lives, Sorcia assumed it was that way because that is the way it was. She spun around and looked at the mountains that surrounded the countryside and marveled at how right those wizards were. Without the pass no one has attacked Arxsolum since and she could not imagine why anyone would.

Sorcia brought her attention back to the city, instead of trade and travelers she was stuck with a farming community full of peasants and those who chose to live in the middle of nowhere. What she did not understand was why her mother paid so much gold to keep such a large standing army when a smaller civil force would be sufficient. The only answer she ever received was that it was more out of tradition than any practical purpose, since they have not had any real enemies in more than 100 years. Still she had to admit she was impressed with the quality of the army and had to give credit to Gryffyn for that and even some to her annoying stepfather who found the money to support such a capable force. Her reverie was interrupted as they reached the inner castle gates.

Chapter Two:
Of Unknown Origin

"You there," Jaxen commanded the guard as he deftly hopped of his mount, "have someone take these horses to the stable and give me a hand with this man."

The Sergeant of the guard reacted instinctively to his young lord's order. "Yes my liege." He took in the wounded man with a quick glance and then inquired, "Are we to take him to the healer's quarters?"

"No!" Answered Sorcia quickly, while throwing Jaxen a look that asked him to back her up, "take him to the guest suite for now and retrieve Master Discere without haste. Tell him it is an emergency."

The Sergeant delegated the needed instructions to a nearby page and personally helped retrieve the injured man from the horse. If he noticed how the man looked, he kept it to himself. It was not his place to question the orders of his future lord, especially in his position. With the rest of the army being sent north he was promoted young and if he wished to keep his post upon their return he would need to make sure he did not offend the heir apparent or Arxsolum's favorite child. 'Of course,' he thought to himself while they hustled the strange man through the keep, 'that also meant covering his ass with the person who made the decisions currently.'

No sooner did they position the injured man on the empty bed than Master Discere burst through the door almost knocking over the exiting Sergeant. With only a muttering of an apology he quickly scanned his two young wards looking for any signs of damage. "What is this I hear about an emergency?" He then added in a more cheerful voice as he could tell they were unharmed, "your mother would have my head if I ever allowed anything to happen to you two."

The twins smiled at each other, the old wizard was more like a grandfather to them than a teacher. "For once, Master Discere, it is not us. It…" Jaxen hesitated because he did not know how to explain exactly, he opted to point toward the man on the nearby bed, "ah…we did, however, find this man about two leagues into the forest and he is not doing very well, we are not quite sure what ails him."

Master Discere started to chastise Jaxen, "two leagues into the forest? What were you …?" He never completed his sentence as his eyes began to register how the man looked. "How curious, how very curious," he mumbled to himself.

Jaxen and Sorcia could tell that aged wizard was in deep thought as he examined the stranger but began to barrage him with questions anyway. "Who do you think he might be and what do you think he was doing in the forest without clothes?" which was immediately followed by Sorcia asking, "more importantly, what do you think is wrong with him?"

Master Discere looked at them as if he finally realized they were in the room. He then raised his hands to silence there questioning, "well, as for what is wrong with him I would say he has had some very traumatic experience, but as to who, or should I say 'what' he is, well, that is a different story altogether. Ha," he chuckled, "…I cannot believe I am saying this." He hesitated making sure what he was about to say was plausible, "but I would venture to guess that this man is a Perata." He looked at the twins thinking that he just stated something utterly amazing, but all he got in return were blank stares. In an effort to clarify his statement he continued, "I am saying that I think he is indigenous of Peratus!" But again the twins merely shook their heads without the faintest recognition.

"I don't recall the land of Peratus in my studies, or Perata or anything remotely like that," responded Sorcia.

"It does sound vaguely familiar," followed Jaxen. "I think I read about it or seen it on a map or something, but we never went into much detail. It must be a pretty small place." He scratched his head attempting to recall where he had heard that name before, but nothing more came to him.

The look on Master Discere's face was a mixture of annoyance and sadness. "How is it possible that two individuals, who have been given the very best education, have never learned their history? Peratus is, or should I say, was a region bordering the northern most part of the Dominions. Perata is just what a person born to that region is called; they are above average size, fair-skinned, and have a light coloring to their hair, similar to how this man looks." Master Discere stopped to see if this was sparking any sort of recognition. He then continued on in his didactic voice "The Perata were legendary for their fighting skills, they were just naturally tough. They had to be with such an inhospitable environment; freezing cold winters, unfertile ground, not to mention being surrounded on all sides by enemies, principally the Northern Barbarians…"

Sorcia, who felt she was being teased, interrupted him "Barbarians, like children's stories barbarians…?"

"Yes barbarians," returned Discere, "however, do not think for a second that they are merely children's stories. They exist…a race much larger than humans; you might have heard them called hill giants, which is where they live, in mountainous regions. Of course, they do not exist nearly in the numbers they once did. You see…hill giants are a very warlike being and at one time they numbered in the tens of thousands. Believe me when I tell you that just one of them is far more than enough. You can imagine with such a large populace that they were in need of plenty of land, their own region being overpopulated as it was. The only way to grow would be to head south. The problem was that just to the south was already occupied." He paused for effect, "As I said earlier, the Perata were very capable fighters. The battles between these groups must have been incredibly horrific. Barbarians for example, are exceedingly strong and considerably vicious. They have been known to devour the remains of their enemies, sometimes while they were still alive." Master Discere saw the look of disgust upon the twin's faces and continued to explain. "They believe it intones them with whatever strength that person had in life. Well, anyway…since they felt it was time to expand their domain, they headed south in force. The first land they entered was Peratus; it was also their last. Because even though the hill giants outnumbered them, the Perata were fierce. Everyone was trained to fight as soon as they could grasp a weapon, including women. Oh and they were a proud people, there was no way they were going to allow these mountain nomads to take their land. In fact they would fight to the last person if…"

He was cut short by an enchanting voice from the hallway, "rumor has it they did fight to the last person, and that is why Peratus is no longer. If I recall properly they were wiped out by that invasion. Others, well, most people in fact, consider the whole thing to be nothing more than myth, a bedtime story to frighten children." The Countess laughed, "The story then goes on to say that the barbarians were so weakened in number by their invasion that they no longer had need of more land and moved back into the mountains. Like I said though, many believed that there never was a land of Peratus, and that the first and only time that hill giants ever ventured south was when the God Caellestus bid them to fight in the War of the Dominions. I think they just do not want to admit that the hill giants were capable of such large numbers, especially after the damage they caused in the war with so few." She smiled to herself for remembering such obscure history. "Am I right?" she asked Discere already knowing she was.

He responded, "As long as you realize that those who believe that Peratus never existed are fools. The historians in the council of wizards are far more accurate than those in Reynil."

"Of course," she said with a grin shifting her gaze to the sick man, "so what do we have here?" Her regal bearing allowed nothing in the form of shock or amazement. "Well, he certainly does have strange coloring. I can see how the guard mistook him for a wounded elf."

"Yes, of course my lady," answered the wizard, more than happy to return to the problem. "The situation is that we have a sick or injured man, I can assure you he is no elf… but he is definitely not from any land around here, which is why the history lesson."

"That is all very interesting, as are all your lessons," replied the Countess quickly, "but do you not think we should take care of him before he dies in our midst?"

"As a matter of fact, I have sent word to Lineaus on my way up here. He should be here momentarily."

Sorcia winced a little upon hearing the healer's name. Lineaus was a wizard who decided to dedicate his entire magical study in the pursuit of healing. Wizards who specialize in a single area have little magical ability other than in their field. Most wizards learn to heal but not to the extent of those that reach the rank of healer. Discere never focused on one aspect of wizardry but instead devoted his life to study the widest array possible. In doing so, he is capable of spells that most wizards have never seen, but it also means he may not have mastered any one area such as healing, which is why he sent for Lineaus as a matter of precaution and he was glad he did. Upon seeing the strange man's appearance, he could tell that whatever it was that ailed this man was far from ordinary.

In an attempt to prevent Lineaus from the same fate as she, Sorcia interjected, "I…ah… already used a healing spell on him Master, which is why I didn't take him to the infirmary right off." Not wanting to disclose the full account in front of her mother, she just gave Master Discere her most serious look. "So I don't think we should use another on him quite yet, we don't know how his body will respond."

Master Discere, a bit confused, stepped back and looked into Sorcia's eyes and then seeing a confirming look coming from Jaxen said, "Yes of course." He knew already that something was odd when Sorcia sent for him because of a sick man, her being more capable with healing than he. But since she was an intelligent person and if she believed it best not to heal this man presently than he would respect her judgment even if he did not understand. His mind raced through a multitude of reasons why she would not want to heal this man and decided it had something to do with her mother being in the room. This Master Discere did understand; ever since Aliondrae lost her first husband, she had became incredibly protective of her children, so it was probably best not to mention anything that could be considered a danger to them, no matter how small. That, of course, did not mean he would refrain from a proper interrogation when she was not around.

Before anything else could be said on the subject, the court healer whisked into the room and made his way to the patient without hesitation. He looked up from the sick man after a quick diagnosis. "My lady," he said speaking directly to Aliondrae, "this man is in fever, I need to bring his temperature down. It shouldn't take much, a quick healing session, but he will have to gain consciousness on his own. Of course, once his body is healed, he should respond soon after. Although I must say that I am not sure what exactly is going on with these…" he indicated the strange burn marks on the man's body. "These burns are not natural; perhaps magical…I'm not sure, I have never seen such lesions." He motioned toward Sorcia, "Well since you are here this would be a good time for a lesson young lady. Why don't you go ahead and begin, and I will assist you."

It was obvious to Discere that Sorcia really did not know how to handle the situation so he stepped in on her behalf. "Actually, Lineaus, a healing spell has already been attempted and due to the nature of this man's wounds it would be better if we could heal him naturally. You know… the usual procedure in cases like this." He hoped that Lineaus would trust him and not ask questions. At least not while Aliondrae was in the room, of course, it was silly to think the Countess was not aware of such things, but if Sorcia wanted to keep what happened from her mother then he would respect her wishes, for now anyway.

Lineaus looked at the wizard to make sure he had heard properly. First of all, if the man had already been healed, then he would not be in this state. Second, there was no usual procedure for this sort of thing. It was clear that his friend did not want this man healed and he was not giving out any explanations. It was against his nature to not heal a sick man but he and Discere went back a long way; they were friends and had mutual respect for one another. He looked down at the patient who was definitely unconscious but his trained eye could see that the man's body was taking care of itself so there was no real harm in waiting. He decided he would play along, "Yes, of course, well…we just need to keep him comfortable and I can probably whip up a salve to help his wounds. We also need to keep some food ready for when he wakes, he will need it to regain his strength. Otherwise all we can do is wait until we know more." He added the last for Discere.

"I consider him under your care, Lineaus," Aliondrae said to the healer. "Report to me if his condition changes." Then in a strained voice she said to the others in the room, "You three; come with me." She then added, "I am glad your father isn't here."

Sorcia, sardonic as always when Count Edward was mentioned, asked "Mother, are you talking about our father, or your husband? Because Edward isn't our father, and I could understand why you wouldn't want him here, but to say that you're glad our father isn't here is…" Aliondrae did not let her finish before she cut her off with a scathing look.

"Do not try to change the subject young lady. You know that I would never say anything bad about your father, and do not use this as an excuse to be disrespectful to your step-father." Her tone made it perfectly clear that she was not in the mood for any of Sorcia's usual insults.

Count Edward was not born into royalty; it was Aliondrae who was of royal lineage. Edward just happened to be a prominent businessman who was around when the twin's father caught ill and passed away. He was not a bad ruler by any sense. In fact he was excellent with finances, which helped Arxsolum run smoothly and the main reason that Aliondrae married him. It was love of her city and not a love for him that kept the marriage strong, he was definitely good for Arxsolum. This is not to say that Edward did not have his share of faults. After acquiring a vast fortune in the trade business he then found his way into royalty. Now he had money, power, and an army to back him up. These things would be enough for most people, but Edward was ever so ambitious.

Recently these ambitions had taken the bulk of Arxsolum's army north to support the King. It seemed Edward most desperately needed to prove himself in battle, as he had done in business. Once the rumors of an impending war reached his ears, he jumped at the opportunity to fulfill his quest for glory. Of course he would tell everyone that it was his civic duty to help defend the Southern Dominion, which his city, Arxsolum lies within. That means it is ruled and protected by the King, and in time of need must answer the call of the King. The truth of the matter is that Arxsolum is so far away from everything that mainly only traders and adventurers would travel this far south, other than that Arxsolum is pretty much left to its own devices. In fact the majority of other cities barely even know that Arxsolum exists and do not care. So when Count Edward announced that he was taking the army north to help bolster the ranks of Tallox's forces, many people, including the Countess, were shocked. The goings on of other cities had very little to do with them. Aliondrae had probably only seen her cousin, the King, a handful of times, and talked to him only once, and that was long before he assumed the throne. She knew the truth of it, it was only Edward's ego that led him north with her city's defenses, but at the same time it was nice having him gone for at least a short while.

"We're not here to talk about your fa... my husband." She corrected herself. "But now I would like some answers. Do you three really think I am that big of a fool? Did you really think that

I would not catch that bit about not being able to use magic to help that man? Honestly! I have been ruling this city for two decades and in that time I have dealt with far more cunning individuals than you three. So start talking. What is the real reason you do not want this man healed? Did he hurt you? Is he dangerous? Should he be under guard?" Towards Discere she demanded "And what's your part in this? You need to remember to whom you are employed." She felt bad about this last remark. She understood that he would never do anything that would in any way hurt her family, but she wanted answers.

The old wizard started to respond, "My lady, I had no intention…"

His words were quickly cut off by Sorcia, "It wasn't him mother, I…I actually did attempt to use a healing spell on that man. Something strange occurred, something… I don't know exactly but I just didn't want to worry you or subject anyone else to it without more information."

Aliondrae was taken aback, "what are you talking about… 'didn't want me to worry?' Why would that worry me? You know that I am always willing to listen to you about anything. You should not have to feel the need to lie or keep secrets. So please, tell me what happened."

As the twins relayed the story of their encounter with the stranger, both Aliondrae and Discere listened intently. At certain points the wizard made Sorcia repeat the story with as much detail as possible. He seemed especially concerned about the feeling of not being able to let go during her spell.

Knowing Sorcia's propensity to rush things he had to ask the obvious question, "Are you sure you did the spell correctly?"

"Yes! Master, you know that I can complete a healing spell even better than you." After a deep breath she continued on self-assuredly, "I know I did it properly, in fact I did it perfectly." Then towards her mother she said, "I am sorry for keeping this from you it's just that sometimes you overreact and it seemed the right thing to do under these circumstances so that I could avoid this very conversation."

Aliondrae remembered what it was like to be a young girl, trying to get by without other people's help. She also remembered how her mother treated her in similar situations and knew that would not be helpful. "Listen, both of you," she said to her children. "I will always be here for you for whatever reason, and if I sometimes over-react like you say, it is just because I love you. Even you old man, sorry for that comment earlier."

The wizard mumbled in return, "no offense taken my lady and now if you excuse me I will return to my study. I must have something that explains this." As he turned to leave the room, "you two," he said to the twins, "Do not forget your lessons tonight and do not be late; it seems we have been neglecting our history."

Chapter Three:
Just Names

"My lady," Lineaus interrupted the Countess who was sitting in the library reading, "you wanted to know when he came around, well he ah…he seems to be lucid again, but… well…he is difficult to understand."

Aliondrae looked at the court healer knowing of whom he was speaking, "Exactly what do you mean he is difficult to understand? Is it as we thought…that his mind is not right?" It had occurred to her that the stranger may be more than just physically sick. The little time she had spent in the guest quarters she could hear him shouting incoherent phrases that made her believe he might be mad and the fact that he was found without clothes in the middle of a forest did not escape her attention either.

Lineaus attempted to word his next statement in the best way possible and decided instead to ask a question, "Well… I am guessing you are referring to all those things we have heard him muttering while he was asleep?"

"Yes, you had said it was probably just due to the fever, right? Have you changed your mind" ventured Aliondrae, who tried to recall even a bit of the strange things she heard. It was during one of his more vocal episodes that she began to think that maybe this individual was beyond their ability to help.

The balding old healer started to get very animated and spurted out excitedly, "That's just it my lady, Master Discere and I think that it may not be nonsense, but perhaps some kind of language, the likes of which neither of us have heard before."

"Some kind of language?" repeated a confused Aliondrae. "Are you telling me that Master Discere hasn't an idea as to what language it is?" Dubious, she stood to face the healer and said as a matter of fact, "Master Discere has traveled throughout all the Dominions and I would bet to places best not talked about. He would know if it were a language or just babble."

"That's just it, He…nobody knows what it is, but that's not all…" The healer paused to take a breath and continued, "It would seem that he does understand our language, he is just not… well… he is not very good at it. I would guess that it is not his first language, but one he has learned. I admit it sounds strange with his accent, but with a little patience it is definitely understandable. So you can see our difficulty in trying to communicate. Between his confusion, the language barrier and him dropping in and out of consciousness, well it is very slow going."

"This all sounds very interesting; perhaps I shall go see our guest for myself." She had planned on finishing her book before she had to return to her duties, but this could be a good diversion, besides it had been a few days since she last checked on him. "How is healing going otherwise? I noticed his burns looked much better last time I saw him, but I am guessing there will be some scarring."

Lineaus gave a quick laugh, "actually he is healing exceptionally fast considering the fact that we have not attempted to use magic on him as you instructed, and getting stronger daily.

The moment they entered the room it was clear that Master Discere was attempting to speak to the stranger. She smiled as she saw Sorcia sitting in a chair with her writing utensils; it appeared as if she were taking notes. 'There is a sight worth remembering,' thought Aliondrae, her daughter actually willingly paying attention to something. Usually her interests would go from one thing to another in the blink of an eye. 'Well, we will see how long this project lasts.' Thoughts of her daughter's unnaturally studious behavior were interrupted by Master Discere's raspy voice. "It looks as though he is going to go out again, it would probably be best if we give him a moment to rest." The wizard was speaking to no one in particular, just stating an observation.

Upon seeing her mother enter the room, Sorcia excitedly jumped up and said, "Mother, you won't believe this, but Perata here," nodding her head toward the stranger, "doesn't seem to know how he ended up here, he doesn't even know his own name. It is as if his life started here in the castle a few days ago."

"Perata," Aliondrae seemed confused about the use of the title, "is that what he told you to call him?"

"Well, since he does not have a name…I mean one that he remembers at any rate, I … I figured Perata is as good as any." Sorcia replied proudly, "besides, Master Discere said it is a just name, and Perata said he didn't mind."

"Yes, I actually think it is an excellent name," said the wizard, "Although, I am beginning to think I may have been wrong in my initial assessment about him being from Peratus. It did seem rather farfetched at the time. However, we did not have much to go on. Now we have a little more." He reached over to a table near the bed and pulled out a large book.

The Countess recognized it immediately, 'The Known Lands: A Study.' She thought back almost fondly, 'how many hours had I studied that book as a child?' She just smiled a quick smile, of course, Master Discere would do some research, it is his very nature. It is man's very nature; he has an affinity for learning, believing that it would be man's only salvation.

"After brushing up on a little history…" Discere said as he flipped to a certain page "Ah, yes, here it is" he started to read from the battered text. "As I have found something interesting about the amazing hardiness of the humans in this region…" He stopped so he could explain what he was reading. "The author is Lanhana, a historian long ago, and she is talking about Peratus." He continued with his narrative "no, no, yes, here it is…it seems odd, then that they are so susceptible to magic. One would think that their physical hardiness would be an indicator of mental toughness, which would give them some defense against magical properties. As it turns out, they are easily manipulated by magical force, as if they were children. It would be my guess that this weakness could lead to their downfall." He looked toward Aliondrae as if what he just read would explain everything, but it had an opposite effect, it caused a look of confusion on her face.

"I do not see how that would change your mind, Sorcia said herself that the magic had a strange effect upon this man. If anything I think it would further your thinking, most probably the magic was too much for him…" she was going to continue but stopped when she saw Sorcia had something to say.

"About that" said Sorcia her eyes glowing with excitement, "Master Discere and I have been experimenting with the effects of magic upon this man…and," She smiled at her Master, "We have decided that magic has no affect upon him whatsoever, completely opposite of what that books says. So you see, he most likely…" She never completed her statement as she saw the growing consternation on her mother's face.

Aliondrae was shocked and stared wide eyed at her daughter, "You 'experimented' with this man?" She did not like the sound of one of her guests being the subject of experiments. She would not even allow prisoners to be ill-treated. "I gave implicit instructions that magic was not to be used to heal this man. I would like to believe that you would have enough respect for my wishes that you would realize any sort of magical experimentation would be included within that order."

Before the confusion could get out of control, Master Discere assured her that the experiments were mostly simple in nature and that they always took precautions. They had tried, under safe conditions, to speed his recovery, but to no avail. They did notice, however, that the man healed exceptionally fast without the help of magic. He also clarified that only one spell was potentially dangerous and they had Perata's consent for that. The moment they realized the man was not able to remember anything, Discere mentioned that he could search the man's mind; however, whatever secrets the man had would be open. He would never do it to another person unless it was consensual. In this, Perata was willing to try, anything that would help solve the mystery of who he was.

The wizard went on to explain to Aliondrae that what happened was very strange. Whatever it was lasted for less than a second, but it was staggering. The old wizard could not understand anything of what he saw. He said it was far too complex, beyond the scope of his imagination. It was a rush of something, maybe power, or Perata's thoughts, but it was so vast as to be completely overwhelming. But since it happened so quickly, he could not be sure of anything. He recounted that he saw this flash or surge or whatever it was and then nothing. It was as if the mind realized it was being opened and defended itself.

"Is it possible that he," Aliondrae alluded to Perata, "did something to prevent you from gleaning the information from his mind?"

Discere scratched his beard, "It would be possible for a trained wizard to block me out, but there would have been some sort of struggle. For him to shut me out so completely would mean that he is by far the most powerful wizard I have ever met, because I as much as I hate to admit it, I am quite good at that spell. I have yet to meet anyone that even if they were resisting from the beginning could do such without at least a little struggle. In this case there was no engagement, no struggle for control, just a glimpse and then nothingness. What's more the next couple times I attempted any type of spell nothing happened at all, not even in the least. I must say that although I thoroughly dismayed that we were unable to gather any more information, the implications of someone who is resistant to magic are staggering, but I do not think he is resistant to magic." He realized that his last words had captured his audience so he continued to speak as he simultaneously pulled out his pipe from somewhere deep within his robes. "My initial theory is that spells of persuasion that are directed at him have very little effect. Spells like healing, or my mind probe are much different than if I were to launch a fireball at him." He paused long enough to light his pipe and take a lengthy pull. "I am confident that would have an effect. This tells me that this man has very strong mental abilities, possibly a wizard himself, although he does not have the look. Anyway, this is contradictory to what Lanhana recorded of the Perata, which is why I no longer believe this man is a descendant of Peratus." He gave a little chuckle, "which also means that not only are we at a loss to what his name is; now we have no idea from where he came. A very intriguing riddle, I would say."

They all turned when they heard Perata begin to stir. He looked around the room settling his focus on the Countess. He then asked in his strange accent, "Did I go out again?"

"No, well perhaps for a second but that is all right, you need your rest, but if you're feeling up to it could you," responded Discere, "Can you tell us all that you remember to this point?"

"Of course," began Perata in his broken speech, "you are called Discere," he looked around the room and seeing Sorcia said, "and her name is Sorcia. The serious looking dark eyed young man, who I don't see here at the moment, is Jaxen." He stared at Aliondrae for a moment more and sighed, "But I must apologize because I do not recall your name and I still have no idea who I am."

The man's frustration was obvious to everyone in the room. For the most part they all believed that under the circumstances he was dealing with it rather well. Aliondrae took this chance to make her introduction and extended her hand in greeting, "Do not be too hard on yourself, we have yet to meet, my name is Aliondrae Desenya."

"This," added Discere nonchalantly as he motioned around the room, "is the Countess's home,"

"Countess," repeated Perata, "I am not familiar with that term."

The others all shared a wondering look and Master Discere explained, "Well, countess is a title of royalty, Countess Aliondrae is cousin to the King of the Southern Dominion." He paused, looking for any signs of recognition. "Does any of this make sense to you?"

There was an accepting look on Perata's face, "Well, I know what a King is, but beyond that nothing else is any more familiar than the rest. So I will just have to take your word for it."

Discere nodded with understanding and offered, "Speaking of the Dominions, I thought maybe if I gave you some history, perhaps something would trigger." He looked down toward Perata's arm. "I thought I would start with the Sea Dominion, because of your inking."

At this Perata followed Discere's gaze and looked at the marking on his arm. He recognized it but could not recall its meaning or where he got it. "The Sea Dominion?" he questioned, trying to connect those words to the mark on his arm.

Sorcia took the opportunity to explain, "You see," referring to his arm, "it looks like some strange round ship, with a giant bird on it. We have never actually seen a ship that looks like that, but it has an anchor, so… we figured maybe you could be from one of the islands."

Master Discere continued on for her, "Yes, well… the Sea Dominion happens to be more of a chain of islands that lie within the Aegrus Sea. The nation itself is loosely ruled by a trading coalition, which, of course, handles the majority of shipping between cities of the Northern and Southern Dominions. There are also some independent types, but they usually stay within the river systems." He stopped talking to allow the information to be absorbed.

Sorcia and Aliondrae were quiet hoping to catch a glimpse of recognition when none was forthcoming Aliondrae then began, "Some of the cities that would be up in that region are Reynil, which is the royal city of The Southern Dominion. It is located right on the Ferox River. To the east there is Barawal and Silnac, both, which lie close to the sea."

"Dey Syalin is in the Northern Dominion," added Sorcia hopefully.

"Do any of these sound familiar?" asked Aliondrae, "Anything at all?"

"Nothing, just names," returned Perata.

"I will just go on with the history then." Discere went on giving an account of Silexunatra, "The Dominions as they are known today are the nations of the humans, which at one time was more of a group of independent sovereignties. It wasn't until a few centuries ago that they united. It was the war that changed everything; a war that has never been rivaled. Even though we now refer to it as the Dominion wars it not only involved humans, but all the races, including elves, dwarves, and many others.

The war started when humans on the western side of the Voro Mountains attempted, in the name of the God Caellestus, to conquer all of Silexunatra. They somehow managed to unite goblins, giants, and even some factions of dwarves to their cause. The West invaded the Elven nation of Evanidus, which lies just north of the Voro Mountains. Such was the might of their army that the West was able to quickly overwhelm the elves. I say this because elves are very formidable especially in their own forest. Many attribute the invader's success to the fact that the attack came without warning and without provocation." The old wizard paused for a moment looking for the proper way to convey the rest of his thoughts. "A few believe that there were other factors involved in that attack, but that is not a discussion for this time. As for what happened to the elves, those that remained of their race had to take shelter deep in their forest. Their losses were significant and in truth still hurt their numbers today."

Discere expression was solemn as he recounted the attack. "Anyway, after their success in the Elven Nation the Western Army then turned its sights on the lands to the East. They split and attacked through Evanidus and also through the Southern Pass, which actually lays less than a league from Arxsolum. Since the small, independent kingdoms would not be able to stand against such a mighty force, many believed that their only course for survival would be to band together. They were united under two great generals, Artrin Keydon and Cedric Stamwin.

Stamwin controlled the armies in the North and Keydon controlled the armies to the South. Artrin Keydon was actually the great, great grandfather of our very own Countess Aliondrae and he was one of the architects involved in the plan to destroy the Southern pass, which in time was realized. That action in turn allowed him to head north and bolster Stamwin's army.

With only one front and the remaining elves harassing them from their rear, the invading army's advance was stopped and eventually broken. Some say that their God abandon them, others say that the wizards found a way to take the war to the God. Truth be told, nobody knows for sure what actually happened, but since then there has been peace, albeit uneasy, between the lands."

Master Discere broke off from his history lesson. "I wonder if any of this means anything to you at all?" he question Perata. "Does anything sound familiar?"

Perata shook his head in denial, "I must confess that your story is intriguing but nothing more." He then questioned, "So is that where this city is now, in an uneasy peace with their neighbors to the west separated by a mountain range?"

"Yes and no to answer your question," returned the wizard. "After the Western Army broke apart, neither Keydon nor Stamwin were willing to give up their control. So to avoid more war, the east was divided into the Northern and Southern Dominions using the Ferox River as a boundary. As time passed, old hostilities were forgotten and trade flourished between all the lands. Well, until recently that is…lately there has been talk of war in the Western Dominion and the King in Reynil fears that someone is uniting the Western cities for another invasion. I too have heard the rumors of the West but as too an invasion I would need more information. So you can see that even though centuries have passed old threats are never truly forgotten regardless of the successful trade between the lands."

"I'm sorry, but this all seems like some strange dream to me, nothing more," responded Perata, looking at each person in turn. "I know this is off the subject, but by any chance, is there more of that food from earlier," referring to some stew that was brought to him for breakfast. "I'm feeling much hungrier now, and believe that some food would greatly improve my strength."

Aliondrae was only momentarily caught off guard by the change of subject, but quickly recovered, "Yes, yes of course." She began to send Sorcia to get some food, but Perata interceded, "actually, if you wouldn't mind, I would really like to get up and move about a bit, I do not know much, but I know I do not like lying around."

With that, Aliondrae and Sorcia offered to give Perata a tour of the estate, well at least down to the dining area, neither woman feeling that the stranger posed a threat.

The wise old mage was not quite as sure about the stranger. There was something about his movements and he seemed to be handling his situation fairly well. Of course, he had never actually met a person with a similar ailment and was not quite sure how they were supposed to act. He imagined he would be desperate and in a frenzy. Perhaps it was just in this man's nature to take discomfort as if it were an everyday occurrence. It was definitely a testament to this man's coping ability; of course he could just be deranged. "If that is the case, I wonder, how safe is he?" He continued to think on the matter and pondered, "What could we do to help recover this man's memory? Well, he is built like a warrior, so maybe if we got him down on the training field? For that matter, he could be an escaped slave or a mason, or even a blacksmith. Although that seems inappropriate as it is obvious he is an educated man. In the short time spent here, his speech has improved immensely." Master Discere paced back and forth in the guest room mumbling to himself. "I need to understand his ability to withstand my attempts at magic and what language is it that he was speaking? Definitely nothing I have ever heard." He continued to talk out loud to himself, a habit he had when trying to work out riddles, "Although... he does not seem the type that would be in opposition to keeping secrets, which means that there is a possibility that he knows more than he is saying. Then again, it could be a defense mechanism; I need to remember that wherever this man is from, it is not here making this place a foreign land, and if he is true with his words then he has no idea as to how or why he is here. Is he dangerous? That is the real concern. His eyes have the look of a very dangerous man, but I sense no hostility towards us. This is all very curious." He stopped pacing and headed for the door. "Well, I am not going to come up with answers here; perhaps I will join them on their walk after all."

Chapter Four:
Game of Kings

Each day both Jaxen and Sorcia visited their guest to check on his recovery and each day they found he was getting stronger. They felt a strange obligation towards the man since they were the ones who found him. There was also the fact that he was extremely fascinating; he had a natural charisma that made a person want to be in his presence.

As soon as Perata was strong enough the incorrigible Sorcia decided to give him a tour of the city. It was a beautiful day in Arxsolum, the air was crisp and the sun was shining. She was not surprised when Perata jumped at the chance to get out of the castle. She could tell that he was getting fidgety being cooped up all day.

"You know you can't tell my mother, she would kill me if she thought I was interfering with your healing, but, I think sometimes she can be a little over cautious."

Perata gave her a sly smile, "It can be our little secret, besides I think a little exercise will do me some good. Maybe something will trigger some memories"

The two walked out the castle's gate. While Sorcia was pulling her cloak out of her bag she began explaining to Perata how the city was laid out. "If you want to see merchants peddling their goods then we could head toward the west end and if we want to be bored out of our minds looking at people's homes then we could head north. But since you look like you could use a little adventure I thought we would head down to the lower quarter. Of course I will first show you around a bit, just so you can see our fair city." She finished putting on her cloak and quickly lifted her hood.

Perata felt the air around him and even though he knew the answer he still had to ask, "Are you expecting it to get cold?"

Sorcia threw him a sheepish grin and replied, "Well, let's just say that I don't always want to be recognized, due to my, ah, station. Today, I am just another traveler, walking with her...well, rather strange looking friend." She glanced around the city and said, "in fact, it wouldn't be a bad idea for you to do the same. Now, don't take this the wrong way, but your looks are kind of, how should I say, uncommon around here, and we really don't need attention."

Perata just smiled and pulled up his hood, "of course, we wouldn't want too much attention."

After about an hour of sightseeing Sorcia directed them to what Perata could only guess was the lower quarter, he noticed that the buildings, although in excellent shape, were becoming simpler and less expensive. He found that he was always looking at the details of everything he passed and how the buildings were laid out, which made him pause for split second.

Sorcia noticed his delay and said "I bet you are surprised about the smell down here?"

Perata was definitely surprised but more by the question. He did not notice any strange or different odors than from the castle. "Actually, Sorcia, I really do not smell anything."

Sorcia wondered again where this guy was from, "That is exactly what I am talking about, usually, the poorer quarters of cities smell like a mixture between feces, rot and decay, but not here. Our city may be old and ugly, but we have the best sewers in all the Dominions."

Perata really did not know how to respond so he just nodded in agreement. The city did smell fine.

Sorcia, without much of a delay, launched into a complex story about how Master Discere had incorporated a system of smaller and smaller pipes connected to the underground river to create pressure to clean the sewers. She explained that at certain times in the day the floodgates would open and water would rush through the sewers and clean out anything and everything that happened to be there finally ending up in the Irritum Sea.

Perata listened intently and questioned, "Arxsolum has an underground river?"

"Yea, it must come from somewhere in the mountains, I'm really not sure where, at least we have a constant supply of fresh drinking water, but I think the clean sewer system is more impressive," Replied Sorcia.

Perata was impressed because he had given no thought as to where the water he was using came from. "It is funny but I could have sworn that I overheard someone talking about a river outside of city, is that connected?"

Sorcia was looking elsewhere but still replied "no, it is not connected, a lot of the farmers use that water but here in the city the underground water is much cleaner; oh, here we are. Let me do all of the talking, your accent is still a little strange."

Perata watched as Sorcia entered a small building marked only with the picture of a kicking mule. He thought to himself, "Well, it beats staying in bed all day."

As they entered the simple tavern, Perata noticed that many of the people inside were not nearly as suspicious looking as Sorcia may have inclined. In fact the place looked as though it should be located in a better part of town. One person in particular was Jaxen; he was sitting at a table drinking a glass of wine with a box in front of him. He noticed them as soon as they walked in and waved Perata over.

Jaxen offered him a seat and said "I knew that she would eventually bring you here. This is her second favorite place." Noticing the look on Perata's face he added, "Don't look so shocked, this place is much nicer than its location would indicate, it is kind of a getaway for people with money who like slumming it without actually suffering too much."

Perata just smiled an understanding smile not questioning what Sorcia's favorite place was and looked down at the object in front of Jaxen, "what is this?"

"Well," returned an eager Jaxen, "this is the game I was telling you about the other day, it is called Kings, and I would like to teach it to you if you are inclined."

"My father taught me this game when I was a child, he was quite good, in fact he is the last person I can remember bettering me. I like to think that I am much more skilled now as I have taken it upon myself to continue my learning after he passed." Jaxen skillfully opened the box and with gentle hands that demonstrated a great care for the game deftly began removing the necessary pieces. "What I like most about this game is that due to the fact that each team is equal in strength and the rules are set it only the person's skill and their strategy that means the difference between a win and a loss. I have also noticed that what I have learned playing this game can be translated to some of Gryffyn's war scenarios, which is why I think it is more than just a game, it is a learning tool as well." Jaxen look up from the pieces on the board to see if Perata was interested. "I should tell you that I am pretty good at this game even though I don't play it as much anymore. It seems that I have reached the point where it is not much of a challenge anymore. So…do you want to give it a try?" While waiting for a response Jaxen thought to himself 'Perhaps, this man can give me a challenge.'

Perata looked around the room for Sorcia who seemed engaged in her own conversations. "That sounds great. So what is the objective of the game?" he asked while looking at the board Jaxen was setting up. It contained several smaller squares that alternated between gray and white so that the identical colors only touched at their corners. Perata instantly counted sixty-four squares in all.

"All right, the game is simple; the object is to capture the other man's king, which is this piece." He pulled up the two richly decorated pieces of opposite colors that had crowns on them. "Each side has identical pieces so the game is as I said even. This one is the wizard. He is, in my estimate, the most powerful piece on the battlefield because he can move anywhere on the board in any direction. These two here are your cavalries, which have to move this way." He demonstrated the way that the cavalry was able to move, "They don't affect anything except for the squares onto which they move. For example, it may pass over this foot soldier while moving but it doesn't capture him. You also have your archers, which can only move diagonally and your siege engines which can only move forward and back. These others are your foot soldiers; they can only move one space at a time, except for their first move, in which case they can move two. Also when they capture another piece they do it diagonally."

Perata looked over the board to which Jaxen referred to as the battlefield. The game seemed very simple in orientation; use your pieces to capture the opposing king, it seemed familiar. He then brought his gaze toward Jaxen, "Well, I think I know enough to get started, the rest I can learn along the way."

"All right, but don't expect me to take it easy on you just because you're a novice. Since you are new I will let you start." He then turned the battlefield so that Perata's pieces were in front of him.

He took very little time to make a decision and moved one of his foot soldiers forward. Jaxen smiled as if this was exactly the moved he had predicted and went instantly on the offensive. As the game wore on, Jaxen was picking off the majority of Perata's game pieces at will. It was a strange mixture of excitement and disappointment at the same time. He was excited that he was so easily beating this man, who for some reason he wanted his respect, but at the same time, he also expected more out of him. He tried to tell himself that this is the first time that the man had ever seen the game and to expect anymore from him would be ridiculous. Still, the man was almost giving the game away, not protecting his major pieces at all. Jaxen figured he might as well destroy them all.

As the game continued on, Perata left his wizard unguarded. Jaxen saw it instantly and was torn between telling his opponent or just taking the piece, the latter won out. "You really need to be careful with this piece, he is by far the most important piece on the field," he gave a little laugh; "you really might want to hold on to him."

Perata looked at Jaxen with a slight smile "I was under the impression that the king was the most important piece on the board, since it is he who decides the outcome of the game." He then moved his remaining cavalry piece into a position that compromised Jaxen's king. As Jaxen went to make his counter he noticed that Perata's archers had his king's retreat cut off and that one of his advancing foot soldiers had him blocked on his only way out. There was nowhere for his king to go and then he heard Perata say, "I believe that is the game."

Jaxen could not believe it; with less than a handful of pieces left on the field Perata captured his king. He had lost the game. He was definitely in control of the battlefield, yet he had lost. He never saw it coming.

"I was beating you the entire game, still you won. I don't know what happened," stammered Jaxen.

Perata looked at him with a quizzical look, "You were winning? How can you tell if you were winning?"

"You know what I mean, I was destroying your pieces left and right,"

Again Perata gave him the same questioning look, "Is not the object of the game to capture the opponent's king?"

"Yes, that is the goal of the game, to take the king."

"Then why would you feel like you were winning by capturing my other pieces?"

Jaxen looked confused at the question, "Well you need to capture the other pieces so that you can eventually capture the king."

"Yet I did not capture very many pieces and I won the game, so again, I ask why capturing my other pieces would make you feel as you were winning?"

Jaxen knew this type of questioning well. Both Master Discere and Master Gryffyn used it when they were trying to teach him how to figure out what he did wrong. He thought to himself, 'well, I obviously did something wrong, I lost.' He then responded, "So you are saying that I was too aggressive?"

Perata looked at Jaxen, "No, there is nothing wrong with being aggressive as long as the aggressiveness is working toward the proper objective. You were so wrapped up in destroying my pieces that you forgot your objective. If destroying my men were your main objective then you would have done excellently, but since it was not, well…I think you see where I am going with this."

"I have always played aggressively and I can beat everyone…"

Perata cut him off before he finished, "There is nothing wrong with being aggressive, and it is a means to an end. However, you must understand that the end is more important than the means. You got caught up in the small details and lost site of the bigger picture. In the future, I would recommend that you focus your attacks so that you eventually trap the king. You need to plan your moves to influence your opponent's reaction; eventually reaching your objective, whatever it may be." He said the last part in a very fatherly voice and Jaxen got the feeling he was talking about more than just the game.

"Well…let us play another game, and see how you do." The second game was completely different from the first. Jaxen attempted to be not quite so aggressive and it threw his game off. Perata on the other hand used almost the same strategy as Jaxen did in the first. He saw how Jaxen trapped many of his pieces in the first game and then used it against him in the second.

Perata's strategy kept Jaxen off balance and he quickly lost many of his major pieces. He had not been this far behind since he was a small boy and did not know how to play in such a situation.

41

After a few more moves Perata trapped his wizard and the king came shortly after.

Once the game was over Perata just looked at his young opponent and said, "You played this game worse than your first."

Jaxen returned his look and replied, "I don't understand, I tried not to be so aggressive and still I lost. I don't…"

"Jaxen, you still think it is about being aggressive, it is not. Being aggressive is your game and there is nothing wrong with that. What you need to work on is focusing your moves so as to accomplish your goal. But remember, you need to do it your way. You have excellent offensive tactics but you opted not to use them this time. I guess that is primarily my fault, I did not make myself clear earlier." He paused looking for the right words. "You need to work towards your goal. An easy way to do that is figure out what your goals are and set smaller, more easily achievable goals first. That is how you formulate a plan." He looked at the young man sensing that the boy was taking him very seriously and in an attempt to lighten the mood added "and perhaps work on your defense as well, in case you run into a player like yourself."

They both laughed at the last remark and when Perata stopped he looked again at Jaxen and said "not to totally confuse you, but in this game, as well as all matters where you will face an opponent, your plan will change very often but your objective will, for the most part, remain the same."

Perata could tell by the look on Jaxen's face that he was confused with his last words, and his belief was confirmed when he asked "but, you just said that setting goals is the way to make a plan. If your objective is the same, why would your plan change?"

Perata was not really ready for this question because he was not really sure how he knew that in the first place. He did not even know his true name but here he was giving advice to a young impressionable man. The words seemed logical though and therefore figured he would continue on. "Jaxen, you have to understand that the opponent that you are facing has his own plans and own goals. You can safely assume that they will be different than yours. Your first plan is for the situation at hand and can be kept until the situation changes."

Perata reached down and picked up a few of the pieces from the game and continued on. "For example, imagine that you are fighting a battle and you believe that your enemy only has foot soldiers." He put one of the foot soldiers on the battlefield. "So you formulate a plan so that you can use your archers to decimate their ranks until they reach you at which point your foot soldiers can engage them with an advantage in numbers. Your objective is to win and your plan is simple. The problem starts when the enemy shows up and they too have archers and attempt the same strategy as you. Now you have no advantage because just as many of your soldiers were wiped out and the odds in the battle are even. So you can keep to your original plan and hope that your fighters are the stronger, or you can alter your plan; either way your objective is still to win."

Jaxen never took his eyes off the pieces that Perata had laid on the battlefield and quickly said, "But what else could you possibly do? There is no other option in that scenario."

"Well, there is always another option, granted it may not be something that you want to do so it might be the right choice to stick with the plan. Then again, you could just change the situation again, such as retreating to a position which would give you the advantage once again."

Jaxen returned, "But you can't really retreat in this game. You can't change the field in the game of Kings, it has rules."

"Yes, the game Kings has rules, but remember the scenario I gave you was a battle. And I will tell you that in a battle, there are no rules whatsoever."

Chapter Five:
Considering Avenues

Sorcia came upon the two of them resetting the pieces of their game. Her face only offered the briefest glimpse of surprise upon learning that Perata was the winner, for he did not seem the type to lose. If asked why she was inclined to think that she would not have the ability to explain the feeling; perhaps it was just the confidence with which he presented himself. Whatever it was, he was far different from every person she had ever known and that was enough for her. She truly believed, as did her teacher Discere, that fate brought this man to Arxsolum for a reason and whatever that reason was, she wanted to be a part of it. Realizing that she let her gaze linger on him a bit longer than prudent she allowed herself a mischievous smile; never really caring much for prudence. Her presence kept both men from returning to their conversation and she took full advantage of the pause by grabbing Perata's hand. Facing Jaxen she said, "Sorry to interrupt your little game, Jax, but it is time for us to be leaving."

Jaxen just stared back at his sister trying to figure out what she was up to, but then again he was actually glad for the break, he felt like he needed to revisit everything he ever learned about the game of Kings. He did stand up to say goodbye to Perata and whispered, "try to stay out of trouble," then added in a sterner voice as he watched the two leave the room, "seriously, do not go too far away from the city."

Sorcia led Perata toward the back of the tavern into a stable where two horses were saddled and provisioned. As he watched Sorcia pay the groom he realized the horses were for them. Perata was not overly shocked that he knew what horses were and was feeling pretty good about the fact that he seemed comfortable around them. His memory loss made it difficult to know what he was and was not capable of, but it seemed riding was in the first category. He took his cue from Sorcia to mount and followed her out toward the gate. When the street widened enough to get side by side he asked, "Do you not have a stable with your own horses up at the castle?"

"We do have a stable at the castle, but sometimes it is just easier to use this one," she responded leaving much unsaid.

"Easier, how can this be easier than using your own stable?"

Sorcia let out a slight sigh and took a moment to choose her words carefully, "sometimes people who work in the castle feel obligated to report the comings and goings of other people, especially me. The place we just left doesn't really keep too many records, so it is easier in a sense that I don't have to explain myself as much. In this case someone might question my choice of a traveling companion, which is you." She laughed, "even though you may seem harmless enough my mother would not be overly pleased if she knew I was taking you outside the city."

Perata could understand that and he also understood that headstrong girl riding next to him would find a way to do what she wanted regardless of other's wishes. "Well, that makes sense, but if it is going to cause a problem to go outside the city walls why do we not just have others go with us, an escort of your mother's choosing. That would also alleviate any sort of explaining that you would have to do."

Sorcia never took her eyes off the road and said, "If all we were going to do was site seeing I would agree with you, however, I had something a little different in mind…something a little more interesting. Something I don't think my mother would approve of no matter the company we keep."

Perata was not quite sure if he liked the sound of that. Sorcia was definitely a fascinating individual but consequences did not seem to enter into her calculations when making decisions.

Sorcia continued on, "I got the idea from something Discere said and I thought it might help you regain yourself...you know... your memories."

Perata was more than a bit confused and questioned, "Exactly what are we going to be doing that could help me regain my memories?"

Sorcia looked over at him with a conspiratorial look and whispered, "I am going to teach you magic."

'Magic,' Perata thought to himself then spoke out loud, "I thought we ruled out magic in the early stages?"

"No, we came to the conclusion that magic doesn't work on you, that doesn't mean you can't work magic. Think about it, what could possibly be blocking our spells but stronger magic. It makes perfect sense; it is my guess that whatever can block out magic is probably the very same thing that is blocking your memories. So if we can get you back started again, maybe that will trigger something, something to help us figure you out."

"I guess that is a possibility and I am up for doing whatever I can to reclaim my identity, but why the secrecy? If you truly believe it will help why hide the fact we are doing it?"

Sorcia shook her head, "you sure ask a lot of questions. The truth of the matter is that I am only an apprentice myself and it would be frowned upon if I tried to teach another. The thinking is that a student would not have the necessary experience to teach another and the consequences of dealing with uncontrolled magic could be disastrous, besides Discere doesn't think you are a wizard of any sort. I, of course, think it is worth a try and I feel confident enough to do so because even though I am only a student myself, I happen to be a particularly gifted student."

Perata and Sorcia continued their ride in silence; he had to admit that he was definitely intrigued. He had witnessed some of the things that both Discere and Sorcia were capable of doing and was truly impressed. Sorcia may only be a student but he was willing to consider any avenues available, 'who knows,' he thought to himself, 'maybe I am a wizard, I guess at this point anything is possible.' Not one to get his hopes up he switched his attention to his surroundings amazed at the amount of thought put into the construction of the city. The series of gates that he was passing through were certainly made with defense in mind; an attacking force would be hard pressed to breach such an arrangement. He glanced over to Sorcia as they passed through the last gate and instantly noticed a change, although subtle, come over her. Intuitively he knew that this girl did not like to be confined. Her mood lightened and her eyes almost glowed as they passed through the surrounding areas into a nearby forest. Perata immediately understood that this was her favorite place. The trees themselves spoke a tale of history that made the ancient city seem young. He too liked the forest, felt at home there, perhaps another clue to his identity, although instead of answering any questions it only created more. His reverie was interrupted about an hour into the ride when Sorcia announced in a cheerful voice, "this looks like a good place."

They stopped at a glade maybe a half of a league away from the main trail, it was obvious to Perata that she knew this forest well and had led him to a place where they would not be disturbed. Sorcia quickly jumped down and started setting up the area by pulling out a myriad of different items and situating them in designated places. She looked at Perata who was waiting patiently and invited him to sit facing her. "I am going to teach you exactly how I was taught. You may catch on right away or it may take some time. Try not to get frustrated because that will only make it more difficult."

Perata asked, "So if this is something that can be taught, why is it that not everyone practices magic?"

Sorcia thought for a moment then explained, "Not everyone has the ability; it is not actually something that can be taught. The training is not to teach you magic, but to teach you control of the magic." She let out a little laugh. "Trust me if it were something that everyone could do then everyone would. For the most part wizards are mainly identified by the fact that they have the ability to make strange things happen. They are then apprenticed to a master for their training. Of course there are always some of the more optimistic parents, usually those with money, who will send a child to apprentice in hopes that they will have the gift. I guess sometimes they find individuals who have the gift, but most times not. Take Jaxen for example," she paused and smiled as she thought of her brother, "he undertook the same training I did with Master Discere. He would get so mad because I could do things that he could not. He would try though, in fact, he would probably still be trying today if Discere would let him, but that is just his nature." She paused, "I actually have a theory about that. I think the fact that he tried so hard blocked him from finding it, because that is all it is. If it was sheer strength of will then he would be the mightiest wizard ever but you cannot just will magic to do your bidding, you have to coax it. You have to understand that magic is all around us, in us, the gift is not having it; the gift is being able to touch it." She shrugged, "it is the easiest thing in the world for me, as natural as breathing, but I think that is because I know how to make things easy. I allow things to be easy; I don't overcomplicate things like most people. Does that make any sense?"

Perata nodded his head and said, "Actually it makes quite a bit of sense, I do have another question though. If magic is something you touch, how come sometimes you and Discere use other materials or speak words while doing magic?"

Sorcia thought it was a peculiar question because she had always taken her ability for granted, but she reminded herself that the person asking could not even remember his own name much less know the ins and outs of wizardry. She then searched for the best way to answer. "Well…let's talk about spells first. Remember that I said training was not about teaching you magic but teaching you to control the magic, basically making it do what you want it to do. In order for magic to do specifically what you want it to do, you need to have your mind set in the right way. Any interference whether from an outside source or even a stray thought could easily disrupt the intention of the user, sometimes with very unfortunate ends. A spell, or speaking words as you referred to it, focuses the user on the sole objective of the user. The thing about spells is that they can allow a less proficient magic user to achieve greater feats of magic then would otherwise be possible. Think of it as a map to find the best way to your destination. Of course writing spells is another story all together. I can attest that it is no easy feat. I have actually tried to write a few but to no avail. Now Master Discere, on the other hand, is quite adept at it and has written a multitude of spells. One thing to realize is that the more skilled a person is the less they would need to rely on a spell. I use spells for many things but in actuality, I now have enough control that I probably don't need them for the majority of the spells I cast. I guess it became habit from when I was younger. Components are similar in their use; they are not needed but they can improve the outcome of your desired spell. It has been found that some things in nature react differently when using magic then others, so basically a spell component can increase the strength of a spell if it is present at the time of the casting. A sleep spell, for example, can be greatly enhanced in the presence of fine sand. Without it the person may only get drowsy, but with sand incorporated into the casting that same target would fall into a deep sleep. Discere actually made me spend countless hours learning what components work with what type of spell. If you think about it the more wizards learn the more precise their art is and there is an entire section of the wizard's council who are dedicated to learning more. The more powerful the caster the less dependent he or she would need to be on components, but even then they could still enhance their spell with them. So basically a spell will help you focus your thoughts and spell components will enhance the outcome. Does that answer your question at least in some regard?"

"Yes, that helps," Perata replied, "so I take it you are going to teach me some spells to get me started or something like that?"

"Actually, the first step is for you to be able to identify the magic, to reach it, because without being able to do that all the spells in the world won't help you. So that is what I am going to try to teach you this week. The first thing I want you to do is clear your mind of all the noise, all thoughts, everything. Concentrate on what you feel when you are not distracted, it is a feeling unto itself. This takes practice but it will become easier with time. Watch me."

Perata watched as Sorcia shut her eyes and took a breath. It was obvious to him that she became instantly relaxed, then without warning a blue flame sprung from her palm. She opened her eyes and began to explain, "I, in the most basic of descriptions, cleared my mind until only the magic was left, then I just sort of asked it to form this flame and it did. I am not, nor is anybody else able to tell you exactly how to do that, which is why we use spells to help focus our objective. Obviously some people are better at it than others." She took a breath, "once you can achieve the proper state I will guide you as best I can, of course, reaching that state may take a couple of sessions." She looked at him to see if he understood enough to get started and asked, "Are you ready to give it a shot?"

At this point Perata was not only willing but even a little excited to get started. Shutting his eyes, he tried to silence all the thoughts in his head. He concentrated on his breathing, which allowed him to block out the outside noises then tried to follow Sorcia's advice and look for the magic. The problem remained that he was not exactly sure what he was looking for or even if he was doing it correctly. Perata was a patient man and he could be methodical, but this was a completely different situation than doing something physically. He focused inward searching for any feeling that was even the slightest bit unusual. He also reached out to everything around him in an effort to catch even the vaguest of difference. Time and space did not seem to be a factor anymore as he continued to search, but nothing seemed any more or less significant than anything else. Sorcia counseled him that it would take some time, but still he could not help the feeling of disappointment. Not so much because he could not see or feel magic, but because it was a possible avenue to his identity. He realized at this point that he was thinking again and according to Sorcia that would be counterproductive to his goal. He opened his eyes to see that his companion had not only moved but set up an area for them to eat. He quickly looked at the sky and noticed that quite a bit of time had passed.

"About time you came back," stated Sorcia, "I told you to not be distracted by the outside world and that is exactly what you did and you did it well. I believe you easily attained the state we were looking for, but I am guessing by your lack of enthusiasm that you were unable to see the magic. That is all right; I was prepared to spend all day teaching you just how to get to this stage. Come on," she beckoned as she led him over to where she prepared a simple meal. "I think we should eat and then jump back into it. We have all day today, but not so with our future sessions, which means that we need to make the best of the time we have."

Perata thought it was a good idea to take a break; he certainly was hungry so he sat down next to Sorcia. He noticed that she was staring at him and decided to ask, "What are you looking at?"

Sorcia smiled and replied, "You look a lot like an elf, a really big elf. It is a little strange, yet fascinating at the same time."

Perata let out a quick laugh and responded, "I do not know if I should be flattered or insulted because I have no idea what an elf looks like."

"Well, an elf looks like you," shot back Sorcia, "only not so rough looking; they are more feminine, more graceful." She then quickly added in overly deferential tone, "but you are definitely graceful in your own way."

Sorcia expecting a laugh or at least a smile noticed that Perata was not paying attention to her but was looking toward the trail. He never removed his gaze from the forest and quietly whispered, "There is someone in the forest and they are coming this way."

Sorcia followed his gaze and saw nothing at first and then there it was a slight movement in the distance. She then recognized the tunic of the city guard or more appropriately the tunic of

Gryffyn the weapon's master. Sorcia let out a sigh, "I should have known."

They both stood up and waited for the man to approach. Perata could tell instantly that this man was very capable. He was much shorter than Perata but his shoulders were wider. Even though he looked like a bull he made very little noise walking through the forest. The old soldier looked around the picnic area and Perata could tell he took in every little detail of what he saw. He waved as he saw them stand and announced in a booming voice, "I thought I would find you here, hope you don't mind the interruption."

Perata could feel the man gauging him with his eyes as he walked up. He seemed satisfied with what he saw and said, "So, you must be Perata, I have heard quite a bit about you. I apologize for not making time to meet you before now but I have been extremely busy." He extended his hand in greeting, "I am Gryffyn Holleran, weapon's master to the Countess Aliondrae."

Perata shook the man's hand, "I am pleased to meet you, for the time being I am called Perata, I wish I could be more forthcoming but I am having difficulties with my memories."

Gryffyn nodded, "So I have been told, which," he paused to look at Sorcia, "is why I came looking for you. The Countess would like me to get you out onto the training ground and go through some exercises. She thinks that you may have been a soldier due to your bearing; I am inclined to agree with her. You have the look of a military man."

Sorcia could hold her tongue no longer, "I can't believe that my mother sent you to look after me, she still treats me like a little girl."

Gryffyn gave the young woman a disapproving look and said, "Sorcia, I took it upon myself to find you. I am sorry if seeing me is such a horrible thing."

The mood lightened instantly and Sorcia laughed, "You are a lousy liar and it is never horrible to see you."

The weapon's master laughed as well then continued, "well either way let's get back to the castle while there is still daylight," he then looked at Perata, "and maybe we can get a few drills in on the training yard and see if something clicks."

Both Perata and Sorcia realized the last remark was not up for debate and started to gather their things. As they rode back to the city Perata listened as Gryffyn recited some of military history of Arxsolum and found that he was extremely interested.

Chapter Six:
Weapon's Training

Perata woke early, excited about the new day for the first time since being in Arxsolum. He felt the stiffness in his muscles from the previous night's drilling he did with Gryffyn. It was a feeling that he recognized, not so much remembered, but it was definitely a feeling of which he was accustom. Due to this their training session itself was successful, not in the fact that he was previously trained with a sword but it was the feeling of soreness and the consequences of pushing his body to the limit that was familiar. Perata may not have been a swordsman, but so far it was the only thing that stirred any sort of feeling inside of him and he was anxious to capture those feelings again. The fact that he was a very quick study and that he enjoyed the competition also contributed to his excitement. He knew that regardless his profession in his previous life he was going to learn the sword in this one. He finished his morning routine and raced down to the training yard without breakfast not wanting to be late.

The sun had yet to crest the horizon and Perata was the first one there. He allowed the crisp morning air into his lungs with large deliberate breaths. He was not sure what to expect of the day's lessons, but he did not want to be winded as quickly as the day before. He began doing the simple stretches that the weapon's master had shown him and let the soreness engulf him, it made him feel alive; a feeling he had not had in some time.

Footsteps echoed behind him; he turned thinking it would be Gryffyn, but the outline of the approaching man did not have the same gate as the old weapon's master yet it was familiar. It only took Perata a moment to realize that the shadow was the young stoic Jaxen. It seemed he would not be training alone, which suited him just fine.

"Hello there," announced the young man, "I was told we would have you joining us today. It will be good to have someone to exercise with instead of just Gryffyn, but just so you know," he ventured in a joking manner, "I am better at the sword than I am at kings."

Perata laughed, "Point taken, and as it turns out I am not overly proficient at the sword so you should have a chance."

It was Jaxen's turn to laugh, "That is not what I heard, Gryffyn thinks you have quite a bit of promise. Said you were a natural, for whatever that means."

"I am not sure what he means either, speaking of which where is he?"

Jaxen began his stretches as well and glanced over his shoulder toward the kitchens, "Gryffyn loves two things in this world, swordplay and eating. Right now the latter is winning out. He likes to get food first thing when he wakes just in case, says it is a habit from his campaigning days. If you ask me I just think he enjoys harassing the kitchen staff."

As if speaking his name conjured the old man, Gryffyn could be seen leaving the armory and heading toward them bellowing in a booming voice that only a commander of men could muster, "Aha, you are both here and ready to go. I like to see that."

He patted his stomach as if he were full, "I hope you were able to get some breakfast because you are going to need your energy. It is going to be a long day."

The two students looked at each other but said nothing. Gryffyn unfurled the large bundle he had been holding and toward Perata he motioned, "I did what I could to find you armor that would fit and I also found you a heavier sword."

He handed the weapon to Perata, "it is nothing special, but with your size and strength a larger weapon would be more practical. This is what you will be using as we go through the forms, however, since you are still new to this," he nodded back in the direction of Jaxen to make sure he heard, "you both will use the wooden training swords to spar." As an afterthought he turned and added with an evil grin, "You will understand why soon enough."

Perata was a little leery about the last statement, but since he did not know what was to happen he just nodded his head in agreement, an acknowledging gesture that Gryffyn took as if he expected it.

The old man then turned his hard stare on Jaxen to see if he had anything to say on the subject but since he seemed satisfied as well, Gryffyn continued speaking, "We begin with the basics to warm up. Perata, for the time being leave the sparring sword here and work with the real one. Just pay attention and try not to hurt yourself. The balance will be a bit different from what we used yesterday but you will be accustomed soon enough. In fact from now on I want you to be carrying this on your hip at all times. The more familiar you become with a weapon the better."

Gryffyn began the class by instructing his students the proper way in which to sheath and un-sheath a sword. Perata was fascinated by the intricacies of the different techniques of how to draw a weapon, as well as the multitude of ways to hold them. He paid close attention listening to Gryffyn speak about how each grip is different from the other and in what situations each should be employed. Perata noticed that even though Jaxen must have learned these things long ago he did not complain in the slightest; he went through the movements just as Perata did; concentrating on his form and technique. Perata knew the boy must be well disciplined and it was demonstrated in the fluidity of his movements.

"All right," yelled Gryffyn after some time, "it is time to move on to a bit of sparring. Jaxen, for his benefit just stay with the initial form Perata is learning. When he is ready then your improvisation will help his, but first and foremost he needs to know the basics." He switched his attention to Perata, "you just went through many different stances, and I want you to choose the one that is most natural to you. Once you decide upon one you will need to stick with it. Consistency is how you build a foundation, once you become more experienced you can experiment with different styles; understand?"

Perata voiced his agreement even though he knew it was not really a question and went into a stance that placed his left foot in front of his right. His right hand took the top portion of the pommel and he kept his elbow up.

Gryffyn adjusted Perata's stance slightly and then warned, "This may hurt a bit, but I will not allow Jaxen to alter his training. If it becomes too much for you then we will go back to individual practice. I believe you will gain more by having an opponent and seeing what you face." He slid his own sword in one quick motion and wheeled it in a carefree manner as if it were just another part of his body. "You will start. This is what I want you to do and how to do it."

Gryffyn demonstrated the movements and then watched as Perata mimicked them. "Good, now at full speed attempt to strike Jaxen."

The first series of movements incorporated a three-attack combo that Jaxen easily defended. "Again," barked the weapon's master. After some time Perata's muscles were aching from the awkward movements but he felt he was making progress as his speed began increasing. When the positions were reversed Perata had a difficult time getting his position correct and continued to take several blows. He always managed to block the first blow and most times the second but the third always struck home. Even though the swords were wooden and he was wearing padding there were already several welts and bruises. After the last blow Perata realized how Jaxen seemed to move so fast. His attacks were not three different moves but one continuous move. He figured if it worked on offense then he could do likewise on defense.

Gryffyn stepped between them noticing Perata's distant look, "Do you need a break? I realize this training can be a bit difficult; most times students are placed in similar skill sets with the idea of progressing at the same level. I can arrange to have a different training partner who is not as advanced as the boy if you so wish."

Perata could hear a slight bit of teasing in the weapon's master's voice, knowing it was meant to motivate him. "I believe I am getting the idea of it," replied Perata. "Let us continue."

Gryffyn expressed his amusement by saying, "how does that sound to you boy, is it acceptable to you if you keep using this man as a pin cushion?"

Jaxen did not seem worried either way; he had taken his lumps from Gryffyn for several years before he was able to spar with any sort of proficiency. He was actually surprised that Perata could even get a sword on his second stroke. It took him weeks before he could block a combo and he was a bit surprised that Gryffyn would start a beginner out at that level. Then again, Jaxen was not one to question his teacher's methods; Gryffyn was not the weapon's master out of luck, he was the best swordsman Jaxen had ever seen. Odds were that he probably knew what he was doing so he just took up his position and waited for Perata to do the same.

When Perata was ready Jaxen launched his attack and as with the previous trials his first swing was blocked, as was the second. He transitioned to the final swing and to his amazement this too was stopped. He did not let his amazement unsettle him and returned to his position immediately, since he did not hit his opponent this time Perata was already waiting for the next series. He went again with the same results; Perata blocked all three and returned to position. This continued for several more sequences until the weapon's master halted them.

"Well done, well done indeed," applauded Gryffyn, "you may just have the makings of a swordsman yet. Now we go into something a little more difficult. Since you both seem to have the form down, I want you to go from defense to offense in one series. Meaning that the second you finish defending you move right into attack. This will continue until someone is too bloody to continue or I get bored. Perata you are defending first. These drills are to get you out of the habit of either being on solely offense or solely defense. Consistency is the foundation, everything evolves from that."

The two combatants took their stances and began. Perata blocked Jaxen's advance then launched his attacks. He did not try to break the movement into three separate moves but emulated Jaxen with great results. He was not able to hit the young man but his attacks were much quicker than the first round. His sword whistled through the air as he found that the previous movement allowed his momentum to keep his speed with much less effort then using the distinct movements. He was also able to set his feet to develop more power and allow him to quickly ready himself for Jaxen's attacks.

They continued their lesson well into the afternoon; all three men were in high spirits when they were interrupted by a couple of servants who brought them out some lunch.

Gryffyn appraised his new student, "well you may not have the skill yet but you definitely have ability. I am thinking that perhaps you may have some weapon experience; we just need to find out which. Although I cannot understand for the life of me why you have not learned the sword, you unquestionably have the makings. Anyway, we will eat a light meal, give you two time to rest and then on to the bow and then the spear, maybe even try some other weapons to find out a little more about you. "

Perata was indeed dead tired; but he was not about to let his weakness show in front of his training partner so he just sat down and started eating. Before he could finish his first bite Jaxen who had been staring at him stated, "Now I know what Gryffyn means by you being a natural. There is no way I could have done what you did on my first day of training, nobody I know could do it. I am excited to see what else you can do, not to mention a little nervous by how good you could be."

"Well, in all fairness," replied Perata, "this is actually my second training session."

Jaxen almost choked on his food he laughed so hard, "of course, well then, that would make more sense. Most people could do that on their second day of training."

Perata also smiled and finished his meal, he reflected on what the old man had said earlier, if he truly was that gifted then why would he not have trained with the sword? He definitely enjoyed it. Before he could come up with an answer Gryffyn was ordering them on their feet. "Let me tell you boys something, you would not be able to stop and eat during the middle of a real battle. I must be getting soft in my old age, but I'll be damned if I let you sit around daydreaming. Let's go, daylight is burning."

The three made their way over to the archery range where Gryffyn grabbed one of the bows and deftly strung it. "This is known as a long bow," he handed it to Perata, "does it seem familiar?"

Perata examined it and its function seemed obvious but there was nothing to indicate he had used one before.

Gryffyn took his silence as a no and strung a secondary bow while Jaxen did the same. "The long bow is used by men on foot; its accuracy and range are unmatched." He then fit an arrow and fired at a target down range. "A good archer can get more than a dozen shots off in less than a minute and perhaps a few less well aimed ones. You boys choose a target and let's see what you can do."

Perata fired a few shots while Gryffyn gave him pointers. It took several tries before he could hit the target. Once he found his distance he started bringing his arrows closer to the center but he did not have the skill of Jaxen. Archery seemed fairly boring compared to swordplay.

As if reading his mind, Gryffyn directed them further down range where there were similar weapons only much shorter and something that almost looked familiar to Perata. While Gryffyn picked up one of the shorter bows Perata studied the other weapons. "All though the long bow has the best range and accuracy, it is more than a bit cumbersome on horseback. These smaller bows compensate for the amount of room a horseman has and when utilized properly are quite efficient. Since we are not on horseback I do not want to spend too much time with these. The weapon you're holding is known as a crossbow," he hesitated slightly, "you have that look on your face, you have seen these before?"

Perata lifted his gaze from the crossbow to the other two, "it seems somewhat familiar, but I really cannot tell."

"Well, let's get you shooting and then we see just how familiar you are with it." Gryffyn choose one for himself and loaded a bolt, while Perata duplicated the procedure with his own. The weapons master then hoisted the crossbow to his shoulder and fired toward the target striking near the center.

Perata put the stock of his weapon into his shoulder and noticed it seemed completely natural. He lined up his sights and released the trigger in between his breathes. His bolt flew true and hit almost dead center.

Both Jaxen and Gryffyn were grinning, "Let's see if you can do that again," prodded the young man, whose shot was just a tad outside of his.

Perata reloaded his weapon and took aim again. He let his bone structure carry the weight of the weapon so that it did not waver and then slowly squeezed back the trigger in the span between his breaths. This time his bolt was dead center.

"Well, I'll be damned," swore Gryffyn, "unless you just got real lucky I would say that you know what you are doing. Keep shooting and let us see which one it is."

Perata continued to consistently strike the center of the target often times destroying the bolts that were already there. It was obvious to all of them that he could definitely fire a crossbow and fire it well. But even with the feeling of being natural nothing else stirred aside from that.

"I think we have seen enough. Did that bring back any memories or feelings?" questioned Gryffyn hopefully.

"It seems right enough like I have done this before, but still nothing more than the initial feeling of familiarity. I was hoping for a release of something, but such was not the case." He noticed the looks on the faces of the two men that we fast becoming his friends and added, "However, it is most assuredly more than previous."

"Well, in that case, maybe we should continue with our investigation into your skills." Gryffyn disappeared for a few moments and came back with several long sticks with metal points on the end. He tossed one each to his students and set the rest on the ground. The three of them spent the next half hour sparring with the spears and another half hour throwing them. Again Perata was a quick study but it was clear he was not proficient with them. He felt a little disappointed after the crossbow but he also noticed some of the advantages and disadvantages that a spear would have against a sword. The length alone would keep a swordsman at bay unless he was able to get inside then the spear wielder would have some problems. Perata realized that it would all be dependant on the skill of the users.

Gryffyn looked up at the location of the sun and halted the training, "we only have a short amount of time left for today, we could continue with the spear or try something different. Master Perata, just so you are aware I try and familiarize my men with all types of weapons including your hands, just in case. There is no way we can go through all of them today, but I think we can at least visit one more before ending today. Which do you prefer?"

Perata quickly stated his thoughts voicing his desire to try another weapon. Jaxen agreed as well, he liked mixing up his training as much as possible to alleviate any boredom.

Gryffyn acquiesced "Let us head back to the sparring ground and if my hunch is correct then you should be good with this next weapon."

Upon arrival the weapon's master went to the armory and returned with a couple of knives. He grabbed one and passed it to Perata, "A person trained with a crossbow would definitely know how to handle a knife...in case the enemy came too close. The knife or dagger is the most obvious choice, without carrying the burden of a sword. That space would be reserved for the bolts. Of course it is not an easy thing to fight off an enemy with a crossbow, so room would be made to carry the dagger, just in case."

Perata examined his blade and knew without a doubt the balance of the knife. He spun it in hand and as his hand closed on the handle a smile came to his face. This too was familiar.

Chapter Seven:
Of Gods and Men

After their grueling work out, both combatants were famished and went straight away to the kitchens to get some food. In between bites Jaxen grabbed Perata's attention "When we are finished eating, if you are up for it, Sorcia and I have lessons with Master Discere. "

Jaxen noticed the odd look on Perata's face and explained, "He talks mainly about history, or politics, or even the history of politics. Don't worry, he is rarely boring and if we can get him off on a tangent he tells of some of the adventures he has had. The man has seen a lot in his lifetime."

Perata had a piece of bread in his mouth so he just nodded his head. He could use a little time to rest his weary muscles.

"Good," replied Jaxen as he slurped down some soup, "You have some time to get cleaned up...lessons don't start until after sundown. I can come and get you or you can just meet us in the library; it is on the second floor, east wing."

"I can find it; I need to familiarize myself with my surroundings eventually."

Jaxen agreed as he shoved the rest of his food in his mouth, "well," he said between swallows, "I am going to try to catch a quick nap, I don't remember working out that hard in quite some time."

Perata watched him walk away, knowing exactly the feeling he was talking about. A nap would be great about now, but first he needed to get cleaned up, his clothes were soaked with sweat and some of his own blood. He slowly stood, every part of his body hurting, and made his way to his quarters.

Upon arrival his bath was already drawn and the water was hot. He felt a slight bit of guilt for all the preferential treatment; others were serving him as if he were somebody important. He realized that he had no other place to go, but felt that he needed to contribute, somehow earn his keep. Several times he offered to help, but each time was adamantly refused. Arguing that point with the Countess was a losing battle, she told him in no uncertain terms that he was their responsibility and therefore he would be treated like a guest. As he sank into the tub Perata decided he would find a way to pay back their hospitality. If they wanted to invite him to the library for whatever reason then he was not about to be rude and refuse, no matter how tired he may be. He studied the areas in which Jaxen had landed the majority of his blows and was surprised to find very little bruising, much less than he would have imagined. Without much more thought, he slipped on the clean clothes that were laid out and buckled on his sword as Gryffyn had commanded. Properly groomed; he headed out the door to find the library, which turned out to be a surprisingly simple task.

It was not just located in the east wing of the second floor; it was the east wing of the second floor. He had been amazed at many things since finding himself in this place, but the library topped them all. It would take days just to count the books that lined the shelves and a person could lose themselves in the amount of artwork that was arrayed seemingly everywhere. The tapestries that hung on the walls were bold in color contrasting the earthy tones of the books and they all were meticulously kept. A wave from Sorcia from the far end of the room caught his attention. Making a mental note to make sure he spent some time here when he had the chance, he took the closest chair and made himself comfortable. They were arranged in a circle so that everyone sitting would face each other. Jaxen barely opened his eyes as Perata sat but he managed a quick head nod. It was good to see that the day's training was difficult for both of them.

Master Discere entered from a small door near the fireplace and quickly took his seat. Directing his words toward Perata he offered a greeting, "Excellent, I am glad to see you joining us today Master Perata; I truly hope you find it worth your time." Then with a grand sweep of his arms he went on, "Today, due to recent events, I thought we would talk about the Gods or at least one of them."

Both Sorcia and Jaxen became alert immediately, but it was Sorcia who spoke first, "You are never in the mood to talk about the Gods. You always put it off by telling us you need more information."

Discere quieted her with the raise of his hand, "you can learn a lot more by listening than talking." The old wizard gave her his fatherly look; then took a seat himself. "The question of whether or not the Gods exist or existed has been debated in the council of wizards for many years. I, for one, think that is the wrong question…the real question is, what makes a God? Throughout history there have been stories of kings so powerful they were treated as such but time has proved they were mere mortals. How do we know this, simple, because they are dead…a god would be immortal. Does this mean that being immortal is tantamount to being a god? Well, it is definitely a good start. There have been undocumented accounts of wizards who have found ways in which to cheat death, at least for a while, and some members in the council have lived nearly two lifetimes. Does this make them immortal, does this make them gods; that is dependent on the definition? As far as we know none of the wizards from the time of the war are still alive. Much of their work and knowledge were destroyed with them. Even though magical ability is decidedly hereditary fewer and fewer people are being born with the ability to control magic and those who can do not hold a candle to the power of many of our ancestors. We even have an advantage, after the War, wizards began consolidating their learning and passing it on to others. Even with our combined learning there is far more we do not know such as how the ancients lived as long as they did."

Discere took a small break from his lecture to take a sip of his wine noting as he did that he had his listener's full attention. "I am sure you have heard the histories of how the Western Army was actually led by one known as Caellestus, and he of course was considered to be a God by his followers. It was said that when any of his armies won battles and there were prisoners still alive, he offered to spare their life in exchange for their souls. Those that did not accept were killed instantly. Standard practice in war I assume, you would keep alive those who would swear fealty and kill those who do not, but surprisingly during the war the majority did not. Man may be quick to do things in which to save their lives, but it seems not at the expense of their eternal life. I cannot imagine what those prisoners saw or heard to make them believe that Caellestus could actually own their eternal soul; perhaps it was just the fear of the possibility or maybe, just maybe it was something more.

Discere stopped talking, as he took another sip of his drink his thoughts coming out as words, "I believe it was something more." Hearing himself speak brought him back to his lesson. His students waited quietly for him to continue, talk of gods was always a fascinating subject, not the gods of uneducated men who blamed anything and everything on some deity or another but something far more plausible. If a man like Discere spoke of things then it was worth listening, because he understood far more than most. "As you are aware the war raged on for many years with great losses on both sides, but what you may not know is why the war ended. Not even the council knows for fact what transpired. Oh, of course many have their theories and some are even feasible" he laughed to himself thinking of some of his colleagues, supposedly educated men, "and some a bit preposterous. I am guessing you have heard and may even entertain a few of these. My personal search for answers has led me to a slightly different conclusion than most. I have reason to believe that

Caellestus was in actuality a powerful wizard who had discovered the secret of how to prolong his life. I do not know how but I do know that he was able to share or steal his followers' life forces and strength as his own. It would have to be some sort of bond or connection. Whether this relationship was symbiotic or more one-sided I do not know, but I am guessing the latter. This of course would explain why he wanted the prisoners to offer their souls. It would seem that the more people he had behind him the more powerful he would be. This also follows what is known about the War's course. Once he started winning battles his armies seemed to be backed by more and more powerful magic. The momentum was clearly on the side of the West and it was obvious to most that the invasion would be successful. The turning point was when our ancestors were able to close the Southern Pass. Not only was it a strategic move in order to allow all of our troops to rally in one spot but it also trapped and killed a vast amount of the invading army. At the time it seemed like a logical strategy to set up camp within the pass itself. They amassed their troops in an area where they could launch their attacks but also defend against the Army of Arxsolum. Looking back it would appear to be a miscalculation I am assuming the idea of the mountain coming down on them was beyond their imagination or perhaps their arrogance clouded their thinking. Whatever the reason, it was a crushing blow, no pun intended. As powerful as Caellestus was I doubt he was able to be in two places at once. If he had been in the south I believe he was powerful enough that he could have been able to prevent the avalanche and easily have overrun Arxsolum. As luck would have it Stamwin launched a desperation counter offensive at the same time; both sides took massive losses. By all accounts the East was failing, but somehow the momentum shifted. I am of the opinion that with the loss of so many followers that a little bit of Caellestus died as well. I can only imagine that a loss like that in a single blow did far more damage to his strength than the East could have imagined. As his strength suffered so did his armies. Once Keydon's forces joined with Stamwin's they began to route the invaders. It was shortly after that the West stopped fighting altogether and the war ended abruptly. The East did not care why the invasion stopped but only that it did. Of course Stamwin takes all the credit for the victory, but if you ask me the Southern Pass was the key. As far as I can figure my theory has no holes." The old wizard stopped to gauge his listener's reaction, this was the first time he had shared it with anyone and was anxious to see what they thought.

Sorcia as always was the first to speak, "How long have you believed this?"

Discere was ready for this question and had his response at hand, "For quite some time but I was not ready to share it until I did more research. I feel very confident that I am closer to the truth than any of the others."

This time it was Jaxen who questioned, "What makes you so certain, it seems to me that your evidence is all circumstantial. Don't get me wrong I think it is definitely feasible, but I have heard other theories that fit just as well. In all our history books on strategy it is said that although closing of the pass was a great move, Stamwin was repelling the invaders before Keydon's troops arrived."

Discere looked back at him and did not hesitate, "Of course, but does your military history explain how he was able to repel the invaders. Do they give any specific change in strategy as to how he altered the course of the War?"

"In truth all I can recall is that it was the counter offensive that shifted the momentum, granted nothing specific. I will admit that the tide did shift about the same time as the closing of the pass, but that could be completely coincidental."

"It could be that the timing of the two incidents is merely happenstance, but I have other reasons to believe this, evidence that as you say is not so circumspect. I am quite the collector of antiquities and one such possession is a portion of a journal from a wizard five hundred years dead. Since it contained no spells and was badly damaged, not to mention written in code, the council did not think much of it, nor did I, at first. I came across it one day and out of curiosity began to decode what I could. That was the better part of decade past. The more I worked on it the more I became intrigued. Long story short, I finished the translation of all legible parts. I will give you a summary of the text. The document is a note from the wizard; I could not glean his name, anyway he was searching for a way to heal his deceased wife, to bring her back to life. Turns out that he may have discovered something useful, but he needed to verify with experimentation. The note that I have is instruction for his apprentice to find people willing to help in exchange for money and power. He made it perfectly clear to only find people that were willing."

Sorcia still looked dubious, "that really doesn't tell us a lot. I gather that you are thinking that this wizard was in fact Caellestus and that what he discovered was how to prolong life or in this case cheat death?"

Jaxen chimed in, "She is right, and it still sounds circumstantial to me."

Discere nodded his head no, "well, I do believe he was referring to stealing people's life force but I do not believe this wizard was Caellestus," he paused a moment but had a smile on his face as the smoke from his ever present pipe floated lazily around, "I know this because the note was to his apprentice, and his name was Caellestus."

No one in the room spoke, if their mentor's theory was correct, then he had just proven the debate that Caellestus was not a god, but a wizard; albeit a very ancient and powerful wizard.

Jaxen was not swayed so easily, "So you found a document that has the name of a wizard some 500 years ago, this does not prove they are one in the same. Is it not possible he was named after the God?"

"Ask yourself this, would you tempt the wrath of a god by naming your child after him, naming a mortal child as if he was equal to that of a god or is it more likely that they are one in the same?"

Sorcia was shaking her head, "if what you believe is true then it would dispute those who believe in gods because Caellestus was their biggest argument. They had proof he existed and you don't disagree, in fact you say he existed but that he was only a man. I admit it could dissuade many from believing him a god."

Perata then broke his silence, "that is not necessarily correct; it goes back to what Master Discere said earlier. Everything depends on what your definition of a god is. It sounds to me that this person was able to live centuries, control vast amounts of power and influence thousands upon thousands of men. Maybe that is what makes a god a god?"

The old wizard laughed, "You are exactly correct Master Perata, we should probably decide on the criteria of what makes a god before we decide who is and who is not."

"I must be missing something," interjected Jaxen, "If your theory is correct and this guy could steal people's so-called life, then why did he just not take everyone's and gain enough power to swing the tide of the war?"

"That my young Jaxen is an excellent question," replied Discere, "I think the answer lies in the fact that a person's life-force or soul cannot be stolen only given. That would explain why his prisoners were given a choice either to join him or die."

"That is awfully convenient;" scoffed Jaxen, "so that aside, in your opinion did Caellestus die during the war or if not, where is he now?"

Discere's look became a bit grim, "Unfortunately I do not know. It is possible that he survived the war; there are no accounts of him being found or captured. Maybe he went into hiding to regain his strength."

"Well if that were that case," offered Sorcia, "would we not have heard something, anything? I mean it has been a couple hundred years since the war, you would think that would be enough time to regain his strength."

"I thought about that and what occurred to me is that the amount of time from the note, rough estimate, to when the war started was a couple of centuries. What this tells me is that it takes time, but then again if you don't die then time is on your side. As frightening as it is, the possibility exists that he is still living. There are temples dedicated to him throughout the known world."

Jaxen retorted with a playfully mocking tone, "There are also alleged temples to many different gods throughout the dominions. In Reynil I hear there is temple dedicated to the sea, its followers believe it to be a god, does this temple prove that the sea is actually a god? We both know that is not the case."

Discere enjoyed conversation with his students; they were not easily convinced one way or the other and were sharp enough to draw conclusions on their own. The addition of Perata was also a pleasant surprise because he had no past bias to influence his thoughts. Their discussion continued on for quite some time ranging over different possibilities with no real answers being found, only more questions for the individuals to ponder as they headed off to sleep.

Chapter Eight:
Liquid Sword

Perata laid awake thinking about the last couple of weeks. His days were fairly routine; weapon's training in the morning and discussion in the library at night. Sometimes Gryffyn would join them and even Aliondrae made an appearance from time to time. The lessons helped him create a picture of where he was; perhaps it did not answer where he was from but it was a start. He was learning everything about Silexunatra yet none of it sounded even slightly familiar. All he was finding on his search for answers was more questions.

His mind bounced from topic to topic and he had yet to fall asleep but then again he did not sleep much any night. His thoughts wandered to Sorcia; she was excited about the upcoming weekend, of course, she was excited about every weekend. It was their free time, hers and Jaxen's, no lessons, no expectations. They were able to do as they wanted. Perata enjoyed their company so he readily agreed to do whatever they had planned. His guess was that she probably wanted to go into the forest again, although not for another lesson in magic. It was quickly apparent he did not have the gift. A vague disappointed to be sure but at least he knew another detail about his past; he was no wizard.

He sat up in his bed hating the fact that he could not remember; it was a void within him that could not be filled. Patient as he was, frustration was inevitable when he found only a few things familiar, nothing more. Looking out the window he could tell dawn was coming, which meant it was time to meet Gryffyn and Jaxen for their daily training. He did not mind; in fact he was relieved to get moving. Swordplay might not tell him who he was but it was by far his favorite pastime. It was a respite from his constant search, a moment to refocus his energies on only the necessary task at hand, which for the most part was keeping up with Jaxen. It was clear that there was a lot more to learn but he was quickly closing the gap between himself and the young warrior. He shook his head as it still perplexed him that he did not already know the sword. He was built for it, his athletic ability and strength mixed with his patience and planning made him an excellent candidate. The fact of the matter was that the only weapons that he seemed to be previously educated with were the crossbow and the knife. He did not particularly like the crossbow; it was too slow and too cumbersome. Knives and daggers were a different story; they were closer to swordplay. He could quickly determine the balance of the weapon and calculate distance accurately, which made him deadly when throwing. He was capable of hitting his target on every single throw from any distance with any knife. The only person who was better was Sorcia, who was exceptionally good with a dagger. She did not bother to take into account the distance, rotation, or any of the numerous factors needed to be able to throw a knife accurately; she did it by instinct and she was flawless.

As far as combat with a knife went the aspects came very naturally to him and after a few training sessions he was already perfecting his technique. He even demonstrated moves that the weapon's master had only seen once at a conference in Reynil, but he had never had a chance to learn. Perata thought about this as he made his way down to the training yard, why would he know how to use a knife and not a sword. He definitely preferred the sword; it just did not make sense. His thoughts were interrupted when he saw a figure down on the training yard.

"About time," greeted Gryffyn jokingly, this was the first time he had ever arrived before Perata, "I was thinking that we would start with the basic sword drills and then I would like to show you a new technique…something a little different…it's called deyecuisinawel in Elven…loosely translated it is known as 'liquid sword.' A method very few people know about much less have the ability to learn." He paused for the briefest of moments before he went on excitedly, "I really think that Jaxen is ready for it, I have been working with him and shaping his movements for close to twelve years. He has advanced far beyond his age, and ever since you have been his training partner, well… he has never been better." Appraising Perata with a look that bordered between expectation and nervousness he continued, "Plus I really think your style would be well suited for this type of training. Normally I would not even show it to a student unless they were already experts; in fact I have only taught it to one other person. But, I have been getting Jaxen ready since he could hold a sword, and you," he looked at his pupil with approval, "well…you are probably the most gifted student I have ever seen." He heard Jaxen entering the yard and quickly reiterated his plan for the day; Perata could almost feel the eagerness exuding from his words.

Jaxen, on the other hand, showed only a modicum of excitement at the statement, of course he never really showed much emotion; that was just his nature. In truth, he felt that he had been ready to progress to the next step long ago; at least he used to think that. Recently he had realized that there might be more to training than he previously thought. Either way he would do as he was instructed and he would do it to the best of his ability.

Jaxen began stretching, he had always heard bits and pieces about this mythical next level from Gryffyn and even his father, but the majority of what he remembered being told was that he was not ready. Now, this morning he is being told he is, but in all honesty he could not imagine there being much more he could be doing. He was pushing himself harder than ever before; every day he was sore and exhausted. His new partner was taking him to his limits and his skill was increasing rapidly; he progressed further in under a month than he had in most years. He had to; Perata, who was showing signs of becoming an unparalleled swordsman had attacks that seemed to come out of thin air and you had to be an expert just to keep him at bay. Only Jaxen's experience kept him ahead and that margin was quickly narrowing.

What amazed him most about the strange man is what he could do with the little knowledge he possessed. Jaxen's moves were textbook perfect, but Perata just seemed to flow as if the sword was part of him, and he could attack from every angle imaginable. He improvised his moves to a degree that made the young man have to react as effectively. Jaxen's learning had advanced exponentially since Perata's arrival. It was not that Gryffyn was teaching him poorly before; in fact he was an exceptional teacher and an even better swordsman. Jaxen had never met a man that could beat Gryffyn with a sword. It was just that Perata's techniques and tactics brought a whole new element to the training. An element that excited and thrilled their teacher to such a degree that he was willing to step up to more advanced learning; training that most people in the world rarely see.

Gryffyn started out the session with the exact same speech he gave at every session. "There are many different styles and techniques that have been taught throughout history, many that you will learn, some you will use, some you will forget, but the most important is the most indispensable. Everything that you learn is built upon the basics. If they are not done correctly, everything else that sits upon that foundation will not be worth a damn. Now, I know what you are thinking, that once you have achieved a certain level, the basics should just be there. You should not have to practice them; they should be second nature. Well, I am here to tell you that the majority of swordfights between so called 'experts' are over in less than thirty seconds, which means someone is dead or mortally wounded quickly. Why is this?" Neither Jaxen nor Perata answered because they knew it was rhetorical. "It is because a combatant forgot the basics."

Gryffyn stared at his two students as if trying to drill this information into their heads with his eyes. He always gave this speech the same way before they began a lesson. He believed that it was the best way to drive home the fact that even the things that seemed to be the simplest needed to be done correctly and done every time. "We start with unsheathing the sword."

Gryffyn could not impress upon his students enough that many fights could be ended with this simple movement. He spent countless training sessions harping on the fact that the speed and power generated by a person who correctly pulls his sword is enough to cut a man in half. If the movement is done properly they could win the fight before their opponent even had his weapon half way out. In addition, the proper technique puts the person instantly at guard, which is very helpful when your opponent is already armed.

They practiced using both hands and from several different positions, such as standing, crouching, sitting, and even being on the ground. Neither Jaxen nor Perata complained about this, which Gryffyn liked. Some of the other soldiers he had trained, including the Countess's husband, thought these useless drills and a waste of time. The weapon's master knew that Edward would have replaced him with someone more to his liking, except that Aliondrae forbid it. Gryffyn and her first husband were the best of friends and it was he who gave him this post. Nothing would make Aliondrae countermand that assignment. If Edward only knew the actual extent of Gryffyn's knowledge, he would feel foolish for wanting such a thing. The dislike was not one-sided; he detested the Count as much as Edward hated the Weapon's Master.

Gryffyn returned his attention to his students. Now was not the time to think of such things, things he could not change but on those he could, such as his student's skill.

After some time of working unsheathing their swords, stance changing, and proper hand positioning, Gryffyn decided that they were warmed up enough to begin. He called his two students to the side of the yard and told them to get comfortable. "First, I just want you to watch the entire form and then we will go over each step independently. Do not worry if you cannot catch how the movements work, it is very complex, in fact much of it varies upon situation and the opponents reaction…just watch so you can get a feel for what I am looking for."

Then he began. The method was familiar to Jaxen, who realized that all of his exercises from simple wrist movements to his leg movements were just building his muscles for this kind of transition. It was definitely an offensive or aggressive style, but then again, Jaxen could not see any openings for a counter-attack. Every movement led directly into another attack. Even when Gryffyn moved backwards he was still attacking. The form itself incorporated every aspect of the sword from pommel to tip. When the movement brought the combat close, the pommel, the hand-guard, even the wielder's elbows became weapons. When it seemed that an opponent would have slid past the damage radius, he would still be vulnerable to what could only be called the turning movement, which incorporated its own kind of attack. The turn allowed the combatant to come from high, low, left, right, or any combination and led right into another series of attacks. The attack sequence was uninterrupted.

Both Jaxen and Perata realized that even though many of these strikes were from a short distance they still contained power, as if there was a force inside of the weapon's master that he released at the exact moment of the strike. It seemed strange that they would contain so much power when it appeared as though he was not straining his muscles. The old weapon's master was definitely a strong individual, but at his age he should not have been able to produce that kind of power, or at least not maintain that kind of intensity for such a long period. Both of the students could see that there were two main keys to this form, being able to set up the next attack with the previous and then being able to do so with authority.

They looked at each other, both knowing that this was not a technique taught to ordinary soldiers. Jaxen, who felt he knew quite a bit about swordplay, had admitted he had never seen the like.

The entire presentation took about fifteen minutes. Jaxen could not believe the number of attacks that were contained in such a small amount of time, but it was far more than he could possibly achieve with his current knowledge. He shook his head in disbelief, fifteen minutes ago he considered himself a master, now he realized he was a mere fledgling, a novice.

When Gryffyn finished the two students just looked at him in awe. They had both known he was dangerous with a sword, but what they just witnessed was far beyond their expectations. If possible, they respected the man even more.

The entire morning was spent learning the first movements of this strange form. All the while Gryffyn explained that the power of the strikes came from within and would only be effective when the body and mind were one. He called it the balance. The term brought back memories of Jaxen's earliest lessons, when he was forced to learn movements that other students were not. He had asked his father why he alone had to do them, but the only response was 'so that he could find the balance.' He did not know what that meant and since neither his teacher nor his father wanted to elaborate he had pretty much forgotten about it, until now.

Even with his advantage of years of training he and Perata were roughly at the same level. Perata seemed able to find the balance much more effectively. The only thing that kept the two even was that Jaxen's muscles were already oriented to moving from one stance to another. All he had to do now was add the power. Perata on the other hand seemed to be able to direct power into all his strikes and it would only be a matter of time before he improved his transitions.

Gryffyn was very pleased with the level at which his two students were grasping the form. He had always known that one day Jaxen would be ready, but until recently that day seemed a distant dream. Now he had two students who were performing far beyond his expectancy. There were very few actual sword-masters in the world today, perhaps less than a handful. There were just not that many students who were capable of such a high level, it took years upon years of training, discipline, and innate ability. Even if the student had the potential, the odds of finding a proper teacher would be rare.

There were plenty of expert swordsmen out there, whose skills were exceedingly brilliant, but to those who knew, these experts were nothing when compared to a true master. The differences between the two were slight but at that level it was more than enough. The expert would probably be able to fend off the attacks for some time, and possibly even mark his opponent, but eventually he would not be able to keep up the pace or the vigilance. The master attacked continually, but in actuality, used very little energy. The power or the balance is not just muscular in nature, which means the majority of his muscles are relaxed during the movement. This would allow him to maintain pace much longer than a swordsman who is stronger or has more endurance. Even if the expert is faster, the uninterrupted attacks of this form allows for short, quick movements, which will neutralize their opponent's speed. Also the master's technique is not just offense or defense; it is both at the same time. His opponent may have excellent attack routines and impeccable defensive capabilities, but his defense is vulnerable while he is attacking, and his offense is lacking while in defensive posture. The true master, on the other hand, knows no difference between offense and defense; it is one thing to him.

Gryffyn shook his head in disbelief as he thought to himself, "Two potential masters in the same place at the same time, what does it mean?" His thoughts strayed to Jaxen's father, while he was lying on his deathbed; he made a request, his last request, "To teach his son the sword." Of course Gryffyn would, he owed his friend that much.

The problem was that desire alone does not guarantee success. The prospect had to have the ability and a willingness to work for it. Luckily, Jaxen was naturally disciplined and would do what needed to be done, the first time and every time. Gryffyn remembered hoping that would be enough. After watching Jaxen in training for the last month he witnessed something happen.

Jaxen always did what he did because it was expected of him, but lately it seemed that he wanted to get better for himself. He wanted to learn, which was the last and most important ingredient needed to make a true swordsman. Gryffyn now realized that he would finally be able to fulfill his friend's wish.

He would also be able to give Jaxen his father's sword, one of the finest swords that had ever been forged. It was crafted by the elves who first developed the system. The sword itself was rumored to be forged with ancient magic, because no fire could ever burn hot enough to temper the strange metal. It seemed whatever magic was used to forge such a weapon was lost during the War of the Dominions. Whether those few who had the ability were killed before they could pass down the knowledge or if the knowledge was contained in written form that it was destroyed when the nation burned is just as likely but either way it is not a sword that money can buy, only upon earning the title would it be granted. Very few in the world existed, much less outside of the Elven nation. Jaxen's father's sword was given to him from Caoudrol, the King of the elves. It was almost identical to that of Gryffyn's, although the weapon's master's was given to him from his teacher, a human named Gardon. He disappeared after teaching Gryffyn, always saying that he no longer had need of such a weapon but that he could not just abandon it, so he sought out a proper student. The sword was much more than an weapon, it was an insignia and for those who understood it was an indicator that the man holding it was dangerous.

Gryffyn always believed that Jaxen would be his last student and that he would earn his father's sword, which saddened him a little. He had always wished he could pass on his own sword as well. He was very pleased at this moment, not only was he able to fulfill his friend's dying wish, but now, he would be able to do just that, to pass his sword to his newest student, and by far his most talented. It seemed as if the sun was shining down on him; nothing could spoil his mood.

Chapter Nine:
Only Time Knows

The sun was blazing and the day was growing warm; Aliondrae moved to the window in the hope of catching an afternoon breeze. Her gaze quickly found a familiar pair on the training grounds. From her vantage point she could see Jaxen and their new guest sparring in a fashion that took her by surprise. She had always known that her son was a hard worker but even she was amazed at the pace in which the two men were exchanging blows. Knowing quite a bit about swordplay herself, it was easy to realize that both these combatants were exceptional. Gryffyn's good mood of late was starting to make more sense. He had always wanted Jaxen to become as skilled as her late husband and spent many years and even more hard work developing that skill. She caught herself smiling as she remembered him, but it was not his face she was seeing. It occurred to her that she was staring at the strange man with no identity. She could not take her eyes off of him. Admitting to herself that he was a physically attractive man did not explain the feelings she was experiencing, something more appealed to her. She shrugged off her thoughts and decided she would blame the heat and nothing more. The man was not even that handsome, a bit too rough looking, but his confident demeanor that never seemed rattled was definitely something she was not used to. She had seen her share of vain men, her current husband for one, but this man was not vain he was just capable. Even in his present predicament, being in a strange land with no clue as to where or even who he was he still was unnerved. She would be going crazy if roles were reversed, yet he took it in stride. She heard the door open and turned to see Discere walk into the room.

The old mage noticed her flushed complexion and her vantage point; taking in the situation at a glance, he smiled, "They are progressing well; Gryffyn has been raving about them for some time now." Discere understood what it meant to have a gifted student; he was convinced that Sorcia could become one of the most extraordinary wizards of her time. She was truly talented but did not have half of the discipline that her brother had. Of course, that is not something that he could teach, she would need to find her own reason to advance. He could only guide her best he could.

"Yes they are doing well, extremely well, it seems that our guest is a good influence on my son," She laughed, "I have never seem him actually enjoy himself as much as he has been lately." She turned back in time to see the two combatants paying attention to Gryffyn's instruction. "Now if he could just get my daughter to become a little more focused then I would be impressed."

Discere smiled upon hearing his thoughts echoed by Aliondrae's words but changed the subject, he actually came to see her for a reason. "Have you any word from Edward," asked Discere.

Aliondrae noticed the inflection he put on her husband's name. The old wizard had never judged her for her decision to marry Edward for he understood the reasons behind it, but neither did he acknowledge him as ruler of Arxsolum. "No, not of late, I am guessing that he is doing what he can to gain favor with the king... If I can say one thing about him...he is ambitious," she then added as if trying to convince herself, "which is good for Arxsolum."

Master Discere held his initial response in check and instead answered with, "My contacts up there have informed me that very little action has taken place. It seems that the enemy will not leave the protection of the Elven forest and Tallox does not wish to enter. Neither force wants to engage the other unless it is on their terms."

Aliondrae, being royal born, was schooled in military strategy. She gave Discere a questioning look, "That should not surprise you, first rule of warfare."

"You are exactly right, but not the first rule of an invasion. The way I understand it is that the West initiated the war by attacking the Elves and now they are content to just stay there. That makes no sense. They are allowing us time to build up our defenses. I have to question their motives."

Aliondrae had yet to give the build up much thought since she never really considered it an invasion. She was a bit shocked when Edward wanted to take the army north, but really saw no reason not to. This was the first time that Discere even brought up the topic since the forces marched out months ago. The fact that the wizard seemed concerned was enough get her attention, "Do we even know if a force is gathering to invade, perhaps they just had a dispute with the elves? Honestly, is it really our battle?"

Discere made a grim face as he pondered, "We have always had an unwritten alliance with the elves for as long as I can remember. Perhaps not an alliance but definitely an understanding, they left us alone and we left them alone. I cannot imagine them instigating any sort of trouble with those outside their borders. They do not much like being outside their forest. This leads me to believe that the aggressors are those that now occupy their land. Based upon their actions what evidence is there that they will not invade us in time? It also alarms me that they were able to invade Evanidus successfully. I have known quite a few elves and they are formidable; within their woods even more so. That being said I do believe it is our battle. That is of course if you are speaking in terms of the East, but you are most likely speaking in terms of Arxsolum."

"When do I ever speak from any other point of view?"

"In that case maybe the conflict to the north will not affect us, let us hope that is the case," he turned his gaze out the window again at Perata and then questionably noted , "but, you did not oppose when Edward wished to join Tallox?"

Aliondrae caught the wizard's inference, "make no mistake, I do not want my husband or any men from Arxsolum to be put in harm's way. Truth be told I wish they would not have gone, but maybe it is a good thing to garner a little favor from Reynil. At that time I did not really believe there would be any bloodshed; I thought it more political nonsense than anything else. After what you just told me, well, maybe I am right since no one is invading into our territory. In fact, I would like to know where my cousin got his information about an invasion anyway. He might be the King but I never considered him overly bright."

"I can answer part of that for you. It turns out that Caoudrol himself requested his assistance; and from what I know about the Elven Leader that could not have been an easy decision. I can only assume that his people's forced departure from their beloved nation outweighed his disdain of the human race. With nowhere to go Caoudrol must have been desperate and desperate people will do extreme things."

Aliondrae looked astonished, "I guess I never realized it was that serious. The elves are truly displaced from their homeland? I really need to pay more attention to things going on in the world. I just cannot imagine an entire nation of elves…" she never finished her statement. "You have an absolutely valid point, what type of force could chase them from their homeland? I understand their numbers are not what they once were, but still, you would think they would have more success in their own land."

"That is the mystery, elves typically do not like to share information with races; it is their culture. Due to this, very little information has been made public aside from the fact that an invading force caught them off guard and they suffered heavy causalities. I believe their forces still hold ground within the forest, but the majority of the nation is in possession of the invaders. I for one am more than a little concerned that elves were taken by surprise and taken so quickly."

Aliondrae studied the old wizard carefully, she knew that even located this far south that he always knew what was going on with the rest of Silexunatra. He was better informed than the king himself and if he did not know what was going on then no one did. "Well, I guess it was prudent to send our army then, they will be more useful up there than here…but I am sure I can count on you to keep me informed?"

"Of course, if I hear any news I will deliver it myself." The two resumed watching the combatants spar.

"So what do you think of our guest, any progress on his identity?

"Another mystery, he says that his memory has yet to come back and I am inclined to believe he is earnest. A most remarkable man, that one; I am not just talking about how quickly he picked up the sword either. As you know he has been joining the twin's lessons in the evening and I would bet he could recite each one. It is as if losing his memory has allowed him room to learn. I also know that he does not sleep much."

The countess had a quizzical look on her face, "how do you know he doesn't sleep much? Are you keeping tabs on him and is there a trust issue I should be aware of?"

Discere realized how his words sounded, "No, no not at all, in fact I like having him here; he is quite interesting. Hence the reason I know he has not been sleeping, because I have been awake trying to figure him out and noticed he too has not been able to sleep. He has been in the library late every night. I am sure he too is trying to find some answers. His resistance to magic is unheard of… let me put it this way, all of Silexunatra is linked; wizards are able to see the connections and manipulate them to a degree. Perata just does not seem to belong; he is somehow disconnected from everything, which is why our magic does not affect him." Discere put his hands together, "I do not think we are going to find the answers to his identity here or in the library. Whoever he is and wherever he came from I can assure you it was a great distance. I did not tell you or anyone for that matter, but the night of the storm, the night before he came to be with us, I felt something, I cannot explain it because I do not fully understand it. As best I can describe it…well, it was like a rift or a rendering. I believe our guest came through that rift but I do not know from where or even when. I doubt he even meant too." The wizard looked old, but his eyes were sharp, "Silexunatra brought him here, for what reason I do not know." He stopped talking knowing what he just said sound incredible; very few understood the world like he did. "Before you say anything let me try and explain a little more. We are all part of this world, as I said earlier we are all linked. Silexunatra allows things to happen that keeps the balance…keeps itself healthy. Strange events have been developing in the recent years; things I have noticed that I believe are responses by Silexunatra to maintain balance or in some way providing the tools to restore balance."

Countess Aliondrae did not say a word; she did not know what to say. The person she considered the sanest was speaking like a mad man. She knew that he was well beyond his years but never had he given the slightest inkling that his mind was going. She did not want to hurt his feelings and he seemed so sincere, "what type of events are you talking about; I have not noticed anything out of place."

Discere heard and understood the placating tone that was used, "I am not looking for your sympathy and I am not insane. Since you are not a wizard it is difficult for you to see the world especially when you're not looking. I have devoted my life to the study and observation of our world. When something happens I feel it. Did you ever wonder why I decided to leave the council and come here to Arxsolum sixteen years ago?" He did not wait for an answer, "I came because of one of those events I was speaking…I came because of Sorcia. When she was born, I felt it, most wizards felt it but few knew what it was. She is not just gifted in magic; she has the most innate ability that has not been seen in this world since before the War…I came here to make sure that she was properly trained."

Aliondrae paled, everything still sounded like nonsense. She had always figured that he came to Arxsolum because he was getting older and wanted a slower life. She just considered herself lucky that such an accomplished wizard would be able to guide her children, the timing never really seemed that unusual, "What does Sorcia have to do with any of this? I really don't understand."

"I know, but you must believe me when I say that Sorcia's ability is far from normal. The storm that preceded Perata's arrival was far from normal. The elves being forced from their ancestral homeland is far from normal. These events along with many others that I have noted are all leading up …" he trailed off.

Aliondrae could see on his face that he was not going offer any more information freely, "leading up to what? Tell me why you are so afraid."

"Caellestus," he said quietly then continued in a louder voice, "I believe that Caellestus is behind the invasion in the North. I believe it is he who is upsetting the natural balance with his dark arts and I believe Perata and Sorcia are Silexunatra's way of restoring it."

Aliondrae was even more shocked than earlier, "A god has returned to Silexunatra and my daughter and a man who does not even know his own name are what? Are they going to battle a god? Are you listening to what you are saying, it is nonsense"

"He is not a god…he is a wizard. Granted he is a very old and powerful wizard who has knowledge far greater than all the council combined, but he is still just a man."

Aliondrae gave him a look that let him know that bit of information did not make her feel better, so he continued, "I cannot predict the future, I can only interpret events that have happened so far and attempt to see what may happen. I do not know what roles Sorcia and Perata will play in the upcoming battle or if there will even be a battle beyond Evanidus. But I know that if something more does occur that those two along with many others will be needed."

The Countess placed her head in her hands; the affairs of state have always been a heavy burden. Sometimes she wished she could just be ignorant of all matters and live her life in bliss. No longer did she think the wizard was going mad, she realized now that he was worried. He was a very educated individual and if he had something to say then she was going to listen. She was taught from an early age that although it was wise to learn from experience, it was even better to learn from other's experience. "What do you advise then, do we confront Perata, do we send him north to Edward? What do you suggest?"

"I do not know, like I said I do not know the future. He was sent here, I think this is where he should be. For now all we can do is help him; continue his training and wait. The same goes for Sorcia, I will continue her education and guidance the best I can. I was not sure I wanted to let you know all of this but it is for the best. We need to watch for signs," he looked out the window again at the stranger who was now working forms with his sword, "Silexunatra has provided us the tools we just need to figure out how to use them. I will leave you to your thoughts; I am sure you have many questions but now is not the time. I need to continue my research and I will let you know what I discover." Without another word he headed out the door.

Aliondrae did indeed have a lot of questions but they were far too disorganized to present any of them. Her thoughts jumped to her daughter, she was aware that Sorcia was gifted but to hear it said that she could be the most powerful wizard of her time was definitely overwhelming, she was just a little girl. The Countess had to be honest with herself, Sorcia was never really a little girl, she was quite precocious from day one and now headstrong as a young adult. Aliondrae forced herself to stop worrying, if she was indeed as adept at Discere believes then she will be just fine. Her gaze wandered to Perata who was finishing up with Jaxen. Her son had definitely taken a liking to this man as did Gryffyn and she had no reason not to believe Discere. Maybe he was sent for a reason.

Chapter Ten:
Imminent Peril

The keep's great hall was filled to capacity for the New Year's festival. Scores of tables were abundantly laden with food and drink. Minstrels played an assortment of instruments while the audience clapped and danced to their tunes. Perata took it all in while he was seated at the head table along with Gryffyn and the twins. It was Aliondrae's table but she was out greeting her people, doing her best to spend time with everyone equally. 'A difficult task,' thought Perata to himself a smile barely touching his lips. He was not enjoying himself, he was too anxious to enjoy himself. He was starting to remember some of his dreams but they made absolutely no sense at all. There was nothing in Arxsolum that even remotely matched the images that he could recall. These were the first dreams he had been able to remember since arriving in the keep but he was not even sure if what he was seeing was reality or jus the nature of dreams. The mere thought of them gave him a headache because even though he felt he understood them while asleep, that understanding vanished upon waking. He was hoping that with this new information Discere would be able to assist him in organizing his thoughts, yet the wizard was nowhere to be found, in fact he had been gone for two days which was beginning to pique Perata's curiosity. He was not one to question the coming and going of the wizard, but a disappearance of this length could mean something or perhaps it was the fact he wanted to speak with him that made the duration seem longer. He was anxious to pass on the information while the dream details were still fresh in his mind. He had already written down all that he could recall but in case the mage asked him a question he would rather the images still be clear in case he missed something in his writing. He cast a quick glance around the hall on the chance that the wizard would just appear, but such was not his luck. He gauged his comrade's feelings toward the absence of Discere and no one else seemed worried the mage had disappeared without so much a word. Sorcia was actually elated to have some time from her studies and was in no hurry for her teacher to return. As amusing as Perata found that to be it still did not lighten his mood. As much as he enjoyed his time in Arxsolum it was time to find some answers and these dreams could be something.

The sound of laughter turned his attention back to the table; he caught the tail end of a conversation between Jaxen and Gryffyn. The Weapon's master was finishing a joke about a talking horse but Perata missed the beginning so the humor was lost on him.

Noticing Perata did not laugh Sorcia stated, "You seem distant tonight Master Perata, this is a celebration…the last night of the past and the beginning of the future, when the sun dawns so does a new year." She tried as hard as she could but was not able to keep a straight face. "I know…I know, I would rather be somewhere else as well. My mother insists that we be here, for what reason I do not know, something about giving back to the community. It is all nonsense you know; the New Year's festival. I do not believe there is a difference between this night and any other."

Sorcia raised her wine goblet to her lips and took a large drink while her other hand gestured at a servant for another. "Master Discere explained it to us when we were young, he said that the council of wizards in their infinite wisdom created the calendar and arbitrarily picked what day would be the end of the year: which happened to be this day. There is nothing special about it, had things gone differently then maybe our New Year's festival could have fallen during the decline of the winter or perhaps even the height of the summer. This day does not coincide with the farmer's planting cycle or the seasons or anything that would make any sense. Still, people treat it as some great magical day where they can somehow create a better life for themselves." She graciously accepted another glass from the servant, "I can tell you it is not a magical day, my guess is that the day they decided to make a calendar was the day they decided should mark the first day. I personally don't care what day they use since it is merely a method to record the passage of time, but I am amazed at the superstitious nature of our people. Many of them have these traditions, these rituals that they believe will somehow affect the next year; this festival being one of them."

Perata listened to her ramble knowing that it was mainly the wine talking and interjected, "I see no harm in celebrating when they reach a goal such as the end of another year."

Sorcia reached out and squeezed Perata's hand, "that is exactly what it is supposed to be a celebration but look around you. These people are not celebrating like they would the anniversary of birth, they are not joyous…they are frightened, they are tense. Somehow, somewhere they have developed these traditions to counter that fear, some of which are extremely taxing on an individual. They do these things because they wish to ensure they have a successful year. Oh, I have argued with more than one person about not sacrificing their best livestock to Silexunatra or throwing their gold and silver into the river. I may be young, but I know with no uncertainty that Silexunatra does not care whether or not someone kills an animal in her name or if gold is thrown back into the ground. I also know that it will have no effect on whatever happens the next year. In fact, doing so may adversely affect them. When they are sitting there hungry because they have no meat or no money they begin to think that maybe they did not give a large enough sacrifice and then will give more the next year. Worse yet, if they have a good year, well guess what, they still give a larger sacrifice so that they can have an even better year. Do you see the ignorance in that? I just wish I could get them to understand that what will happen will happen regardless of how many animals they kill or how much money they try to give. They would be much better off if they just kept their animals and their money for when the year is bad." Sorcia stopped to take a breath realizing that she was off on a tangent, "I did not mean to go on a tirade like that, but the point I am trying to make is that perhaps if the people are that daft then maybe they should suffer."

Perata looked at the young women, highly intelligent, well-grounded and yet so naïve at the same time. He had to admit that he liked her passion though, as misguided as it was at the moment. "You need to understand that if you were not born who you were then you might be one of those people. They are simple; they do not have the benefit of education or money like you do, they do not have the gift of magic. Perhaps that sacrifice that you speak gives them at least an illusion of control over their lives. You are right that fiscally it is not prudent, but you do not take into account how it helps them psychologically." He pointed out towards the assembly of townspeople. "Take a look at their faces; I do not see fear, they do not look tense, they are happy, more importantly they are hopeful. It does not matter what happened last year because now they have a clean slate. They get to start over and maybe that illusion of control will give them the boost they need to make a better life for themselves; a self-fulfilling prophecy if you will. You, well you are lucky; you have not had to suffer, so you probably never needed to start over."

Sorcia did not hang her head even though she felt Perata admonished her, "You sound like my mother. It is our duty to help the less fortunate, we need to help them understand, blah, blah." She shook her head, "It's not important, I just thought you would understand."

Perata sensed her disappointment, "Sorcia, I am not telling you what they do is right or wrong. I for one would not do those things, seems like a waste to me, but I am not them. You say that you know in no uncertain terms that what they do is wrong, yet you cannot convince them. That tells me that they feel strongly about what they do. If their actions, these rituals of theirs, affect you so much then you must find a way to reach them. However, if what they do does not truly affect you, then let them do as they please, you are not personally invested in their lives." Perata made a sweeping gesture of the hall, "Each person must walk their own path; you cannot walk it for them. You can guide them, give them the benefit of your education like Discere does for you or you can let them find their own way. People have their own reasons for doing things, reasons you may not know or understand. You and your brother did not have to help me when you found me and your mother did not need to allow me to stay here, Gryffyn did not need to take it upon himself to instruct me, but you each did what you did. For what reasons, I do not know, I can surmise but I do not know? I can also guarantee that some of those peasants would consider some of the things you do foolish and a waste of time. The point is that every person is different and you cannot nor would you want to make everyone like you. You do not need to agree with what people do, you can try to understand it from their point of view or you can try to let them understand it from yours, but in the end people will do what people will do." Perata took a sip of his own wine, "I think you are just upset because you are more like your mother than you want to be, you do not want to see these people suffer you just do not know how to change them."

Stunned, Sorcia did not know what to say. This was more like the man she had come to know, he was insightful and he saw the world from a much different angle than others. He personally did not care whether the peasants were ignorant, sacrificed livestock or threw away their money; he did what he did for his own reasons just as others did what they did for theirs. She thought about his words questioning whether or not she truly cared for the people of Arxsolum but before she could come to a conclusion she noticed Perata was getting up from the table, his attention was drawn across the room. She followed his gaze and saw that Master Discere had just entered and he looked haggard, his robes were tattered and his hair was wild.

Sorcia had only been a little curious about his whereabouts but now she was concerned over her teacher's well being. Without thinking she also got up from the table and made her way through the crowd in his direction arriving on the heels of Perata but neither approached because of the tone of his voice. He sounded tired and was imploring Aliondrae, "we must speak in private; this is a matter of the outmost importance, but it is not for prying ears."

The Countess sighed, "Is this not something that can wait until after the festivities?"

"No, I believe it is something you will wish to know immediately and then you can decide for yourself how important it is."

Jaxen and Gryffyn both arrived to greet the old wizard and to find out his news. They noticed, as did Perata and Sorcia did moments earlier the strain on the old man's face so neither said a word. Aliondrae was aware of everyone's desire for news so she broke the silence, "let's all take a walk outside so that we can speak in private."

The rumble of what could only be consider thunder frightened the Countess more than it should have; her reaction was based more upon the way Master Discere just stared in the direction from which it came. He had a gaunt look about him and had not said a word since the hall. She could tell that he was doing everything he could just to continue walking. They, which happened to include Sorcia, Jaxen, Perata and Gryffyn, found themselves along the ramparts of the castle wall, "Well," said Aliondrae expectantly; "It is just us now, please, what is so important? Why all the drama?"

Master Discere stopped, yet continued to stare toward the Mountains. In a portentous voice he said very slowly, "Two days ago I received an old friend who I had not seen in many years, he brought with him some strange tidings. Even though he was not one to embellish I needed to verify what I was hoping was just his imagination. I…" He paused, as if not saying the words could make them untrue. He knew that was ridiculous and went on, "It seems, however, that what he claims is true." He took Aliondrae's hands in his own, "My lady… someone is working day and night to reopen the pass." He looked from the Countess to her children, watching the growing look of concern and confusion on their faces. He reluctantly continued, "I do not believe their intentions are noble, they have several wizards and an army larger than any seen since the Great War; Arxsolum is in their path."

The Countess scanned the horizon, automatically fixing her gaze on where the pass was located letting the information sink in before reacting irrationally. She and the mage had been speaking of war recently but she was not prepared to have an army at her gates. The silence was chilling, his words sat heavily on her shoulders as she pondered the idea that her army was many leagues away and without her army Arxsolum was vulnerable. If Discere was right then a decision would have to be made that would affect the lives of everyone in her city and it was her responsibility to make it. How could she decide the fate of others?

In an attempt to understand the unfolding events, Sorcia asked even though she already knew that it would go unanswered, "Is this for real? Is war truly here?"

Aliondrae turned toward the old wizard, trying her best to keep her regal bearing and asked, "Do we have enough time to get word to Edward? Will our army have time to get back?"

"Realistically," answered Discere, "I do not believe so. Even if word reached him this instant, they are at least three months marching away, not to mention the fact that they may already be engaged in battle." He noticed the look on her face and added, "But rest assured, I will send word by the fastest means possible and I will send it tonight."

"Three months. That's a long time," whispered the Countess. The burden of the news was physically visible on her face. "How long until this army can get through the pass?"

Master Discere took a deep breath, "Well, by my calculations the invaders could possibly get through the mountains in two months, but then such things are highly unpredictable, it could take more, it could take less."

Perata, who was quietly studying Aliondrae, turned his gaze to Discere, "How much do you know about those who approach? I cannot imagine that Arxsolum would have enemies."

"Well, it seems that the origin of the army is unknown. I do know that a man named Stragess leads them, and he seems more than proficient. I contacted the council of wizards and they have told me that he has already taken several cities in the Western realm and has left few survivors. Most that do survive have become slaves and it is those unfortunates that are doing much of the dangerous work." Discere looked like he was in thought, then continued, "The council believes this man is interested in glory and is trying to take advantage of the chaos that has gripped the West, but I am of the opinion that he answers to a higher calling."

Jaxen seemed confused, "Higher calling, some king, empire, what?"

"No my son, no king or land. I believe that Caellestus has returned and Stragess answers to him."

Jaxen and Sorcia were utterly blown away by what they were hearing. They had been recently discussing Caellestus, but neither one actually believed that he was still alive. It seems that with one statement their lives were thrown into turmoil.

Sorcia asked the question that was on everyone's mind, "If our army does not get back in time then what happens to us?"

It was Discere who was the first to respond, "Well, without our army, there is not much we can do. We should gather our people and seek refuge in Reynil. We have enough time to allow our people to gather what they can carry and get them moving. Most of them do not have horses but I if we pull together everyone should be safe." Even as Discere spoke these words he could already see the objections written on the faces of those around him.

"Hold on, you want us to run, I do not think so, I am not going anywhere, if we have time to get people out then we have time to prepare our defenses." Jaxen looked to Gryffyn for support, the old man was nodding his head in agreement, and in an indomitable voice stated, "this is my home and I if I choose to leave, you can be damn sure that it will not be because I was forced. I don't care if it is a wizard or a God, or a whole burning army. If they want this city they will have to go through me."

"Jaxen…" beseeched Aliondrae, "you are young and do not know of what you speak. Your heart is in the right place, but without our army we will not stand a chance."

Sorcia quickly backed up her brother, "No mother, Jaxen is right; you did not raise us to tuck our tails and run like some whipped puppy. I am staying also."

Aliondrae knew that this was not the time to argue with her children, "Gryffyn, you know war, what do you think? Can we hold them off till our army arrives?"

"My lady, many of the towns near here do not have more than a local militia, and they are poorly trained at best. I believe the best course of action is to evacuate those we can. It will be a death sentence for anyone still here when that army arrives but I will most assuredly be one of them."

The Countess did not like what she was hearing, she believed as they did but he said it himself that it would be a death sentence. She raised her head high as though making a decision, "There is no time to waste. We must inform the people at once and let them decide. I will not order anyone to do anything against their will but I will strongly recommend evacuation."

Gryffyn gave the exhausted wizard a quick glance, "Jaxen and I will make the arrangements, and you my old friend get some rest. My lady, I will send word when all is ready." He then gave her a fatherly hug, "I do not envy your position and what you must now do."

Chapter Eleven:
Command Decision

Aliondrae went straight away to her chambers to prepare for the announcement; she knew that whatever she said need to be stated in the appropriate manner. She tried jotting down a few notes but nothing sounded right. Never before did she have trouble speaking in front of an audience, as it was part of her daily life, but this time was different, what should she say? Her words were about to change the lives of many people and not for the better. The knock on the door startled her, it seemed only moments had passed and she wished for more time. Without a clue as how to proceed, she donned her most regal face and headed for the great hall.

Due to the festival the great hall was already filled to capacity, now it seemed ready to burst. Rumors had started to fly the moment that Aliondrae left the celebration and Gryffyn's announcement that Countess would be sharing important news seemed to confirm them. Some people hoped it was about their husbands and sons who made up Arxsolum's army coming home. Others spread tales of the Southern Dominion's army being destroyed and that invaders were entering the forest of Nemorosus. The Countess had yet to hear these rumors personally but she was aware of how people could react. The best way to inform the city of this dire news without causing widespread panic was perhaps to outline possible choices before giving the people the whole truth. As she stood upon the dais looking over her people she realized that they deserved nothing less than the truth. Raising her arms to silence the noise and with a quick look over to Discere who refused to rest, she began to speak. A simple spell by the wizard caused her voice, though not much more than a whisper, to be heard clearly by everyone in the room. The quiet of her voice and the manner in which she spoke had a profound effect. All present understood instantly that it was not news of their loved ones coming home, something was wrong.

"People of Arxsolum, thank you for attending this evening, I wish I did not need to interrupt your celebration, but what I must tell you tonight is urgent. First, I must ask you to please withhold all comments, questions and outbursts until I am finished speaking and then we will all decide on an appropriate course of action, together."

The Countess looked around the meeting hall seeing the effect that her words had upon her people, she searched for the courage to tell them that their lives would forever be changed. Taking a deep breath, she somehow found the strength to continue, "The rumors of an army amassing in the west are true. As you know, our army has left to join the forces of Reynil in the hopes that these forces never reach Arxsolum's borders."

The people in the hall were completely silent, most had already guessed this much and many thought it had nothing to do with them. Aliondrae went on, "What you do not know is that a second army has been formed near the lower cities of the Western Dominion. This army has already taken a few cities that we know of and the men from these cities were forced to join this army or were killed. The surviving women and children who they have kept as slave labor are used as leverage to keep the men in line. I cannot begin to explain the total disregard for human life that this force has already demonstrated; it appears that they will cross any line to achieve their goal."

The confusion on her people's faces was evident. Why should they care what happens to cities in the Western Realm, especially in the lower cities, they were considered the enemy. In their belief, an enemy of an enemy is a friend.

"What you must understand is that this army's origin, both armies in fact, are unknown to us. What we do know is that they have swept the Western Dominion with very little resistance and we have reason to believe that they will not stop until they have conquered us all."

"Begging your pardon, My Lady," shouted an old shopkeeper, "but if the armies of the Southern Dominion already know all this and are prepared to meet them," he paused, trying not to look unsympathetic to families whose husbands and sons made up the army, "what can we do about it? If the war actually reaches us, well then there is not much we could do about it."

The Countess closed her eyes and took a deep breath, "this second army, the one in the lower regions…we have information that they have been working for the last couple of months to re-open the Southern pass." She turned her gaze directly toward the shopkeeper, "which means that the war has already reached us."

The shock of what she last said stunned the crowd, and the following silence was almost deafening. After what seemed an eternity to the Countess, chaos broke out. People began shouting and crying. Many were in shocked disbelief, but they responded to the confusion around them. It would be only moments before it turned to panic.

"Please, please," pleaded the Countess, "We must handle this in an orderly fashion." This was her worst fear; she knew that something had to be done and done quickly. She turned to Master Discere, who was being supported by the stout Gryffyn, "You two, do you have any ideas? We must do something before people get hurt."

Master Discere took only a second "I will do what I can my lady." With that he raised his hand and chanted a few words. There was a flash and a startling "boom." The noise was sharp and was much louder than that of the yelling townspeople.

The effect was immediate; everyone stopped and looked toward the noise. The Countess took advantage of the moment, "Listen to me, we must decide a course of action. Our army may not be able to make it back in time for our defense. That means that until they do, we are on our own."

The confusion started again immediately. "We must flee!" shouted someone from the crowd.

"I can't leave my home," returned another. The exchange of yelling continued for several minutes, everyone voicing his or her opinions. The only thing that people agreed upon was that it would be certain death to resist. Some focused on where to go and what to take. Others just wanted to surrender, fearful of leaving their homes. "Our army is not here, if we just let them pass they will leave us alone." Several people cried in agreement to these remarks. "We can buy them off, give them whatever they want."

At this, Perata stepped up to the dais and asked in a quiet voice, "Do you believe an invading army will just let you be?" Master Discere's spell was still on the dais, so everyone heard his words. It may have been the question itself or perhaps the way in which Perata asked it, but whatever it was it silenced the confusion once again. "I do not remember many things, but I guarantee that no general will just let you be. It would not be a strategically practical move to leave potential enemy on his flank. At best, he will kill you mercifully. But then again, based on his previous moves it would be more likely that he would draft, by what means necessary, any able bodied man in this city. He could also keep his troops motivated by rewarding them with the women and more than likely turn the elderly and children into slaves. He will then take this city and use it as a launching point for the rest of his invasion so that he can do the same thing to each and every city that is in his path. Whatever his course of action I can promise you he will not leave you be. You can flee or you can fight, but surrendering should not be an option."

The people of Arxsolum listened to Perata, most only knowing that he was from a distant land and a guest of the Countess, but the conviction of his words gave him an authority at this moment. "I have walked these walls and seen the landscape," he paused driving his words home, "They were created with one purpose in mind, that purpose is war. This keep, this city, was built to be able to withstand an onslaught from an invading army for a sustained period of time. "

"What do you care, this isn't your home, you aren't one of us!" cried someone from the crowd.

Perata looked directly into the eyes of the person who spoke, making him look away. "You are right, Direga," using the name of the wainwright who had spoken, "I am not one of you and this is not my home. Truth be told, I do not even know where my home is."

The fact that he had known the man's name surprised many of the onlookers, including Direga himself. When he spoke again they listened a little more closely. "What I do know is that this is the home of people who saved my life, they took me in without any idea of who I was. They have given food and shelter and made me their guest." Again he paused, "This is their home, and they will not run and they will not surrender. I will be damned before I let them stand alone."

The barkeeper from the Sterling Dragon spoke up, "Those are brave words sir, but we are not warriors, we are shopkeepers and farmers. You can not be asking us to fight a trained army; we would lose more than our homes."

Perata was un-phased by the question; he turned his unblinking eyes up the barkeep, "Daron, I once overheard you tell a customer that the most dangerous person in the world was the man who had nothing to lose. I should have corrected you then, for you see, a person with nothing to lose may be quick to start a fight but the man with everything to lose is far more dangerous once the fight has begun. The person with nothing to lose has nothing to fight for, no reason to endeavor. You, Daron, you and those that call this place home will have to fight for your very existence."

Every ear in the room was listening to his words, including the Countess; his certainty was overwhelming. "Listen to me, all of you," he continued, "We do not have to defeat this army; we only have to hold them off long enough for your soldiers to return."

"Master Perata, that is an interesting story, but we still know nothing of war…" Daron was cut off by a look from Perata.

"War can be taught, I can teach you, but be aware that it is a hard lesson. The way I see it you have three choices, you must decide what is more costly. You can surrender and give up your freedom, you can run and give up who you are, or you can fight and perhaps give up your life. Personally…I will take my chances fighting, because there is a difference between being alive and living. The choice is yours." Before anyone could answer, Perata walked from the dais and left the chamber.

After he left the hall Perata walked through the city for hours. He had no idea why he decided to speak up at the meeting, these were not his people and it was time for him to be moving anyway, but he did speak up and for reasons that he did not know. His thoughts went back to his earlier conversation with Sorcia, maybe he did care a little what happened to these people, like Sorcia, but did he care enough to find a way to reach them or should he have left them to their own course. The only solace he found was in the fact that he did owe his life to the twins and they did not want to flee. He would feel the same way if positions were reversed and maybe this was a way he could pay them back. He could help them; a plan began formulating the moment he heard the wizard's words, but it would not succeed without some help.

He was surprised why he believed this so strongly, his own past remained a mystery, but he could clearly see what steps were necessary to defend this city. Whatever it was that he did in his former life it had something to do with warfare. Ever since the first day he saw Arxsolum, he had been noticing its strengths and weaknesses. He imagined how he would attack this city and how he would take it. He recalled the landscape and the underground water supplies, they were not coincidence; the builders of this city were genius.

His thoughts centered on who he may have been; perhaps a general or maybe just an overanxious soldier. Not all the pieces fit though, such as not previously trained with more weapons. It seemed obvious that any good soldier would be proficient with anything that could be used in his profession. Aside from that it made perfect sense, well that and his second realization; beyond a shadow of a doubt he knew he could kill a man and feel absolutely no remorse. 'How very appropriate for a soldier,' he thought to himself, 'If not a soldier, then I missed my calling, because I would be very able in such a profession.'

His thoughts were interrupted when he spotted one of the city guards heading his direction, "Master Perata, we have been looking everywhere for you. The Countess requests an audience as soon as you are able."

With a slight smile for the guard's coincidental wording Perata replied, "I guess I am 'able' now. Please, lead the way."

Following the guard into the castle, he noticed along the way that many of the townspeople were still in attendance and were staring at him apprehensively. After making a mental note of it, he knocked on Aliondrae's door.

"Come in," came the reply.

As Perata walked in, he was only slightly surprised to see the number of people in the room. Master Discere, Jaxen, Sorcia, the old weapon's master, several key shop owners and some seasoned guards rounded out the group. They quickly offered him a seat, and the group, out of respect, waited for Aliondrae to begin.

"Master Perata, we were all impressed and moved by your words earlier today." She looked around the group and in doing so created a sense of unity. "What we would like to know is if you truly believe them?" Before he answered, she continued on, "Because... well...since you have come to stay with us, you have shown remarkable talents in many things. You have excelled in every task that you have undertaken, from swordplay to numbers. In fact, Master Discere believes that you maybe the most intelligent person he has ever known, and that gives you tremendous clout. So, Master Perata, can we do this? Can we hold out until our army returns?"

The entire group was looking at Perata, who in turn looked each of them in the eyes, gauging their sincerity. "My lady," He said softly, "I meant what I said earlier. This place was designed to withstand a siege and designed well. It is strategically located and soundly built. It can withstand projectiles and fire. It can hold massive amounts of provisions. It has an underground water supply that will sustain the inhabitants for quite some time. Even if these invaders know that your army is gone, they will not know your strength. If they see that the walls are manned and that the keep is ready, they will not know from where this new army came. This will give you the advantage, for you will know their numbers, their strengths, and their weaknesses. But," he made a point to look at everyone in the room, "before you make a decision, you must take into consideration that your army may not return in time or not at all, if that happens, then you and your new army, will be in for quite a struggle."

Aliondrae gave a nervous smile that held no humor, "Master Perata, I believe that you know of what you speak, except that if you are serious in helping us, then it is not my new army, it is your army. If you accept this charge we will pay you any amount you ask, in fact," she motioned to several people in the room, "many of the major business leaders are here to discuss your fee."

Perata did not smile, "I do not want your gold. The price of which I speak is not measurable in coins, and it is not to me who you shall pay." He could see the confusion in the group. "If you are going to do this, you have to do it all the way or it will not be successful. There is no backing out once you have started, and if you decide to stay, then you stay until it is over. I will ask things of you and your people that may conflict with your morals, with your ethics. I will ask you to maim, to kill, and worse."

Perata took in everyone's manner in one glance. "And if you want me to lead, then everyone, including yourself your highness, will follow my orders without hesitation or argument, whether you agree with them or not. These are my conditions and there is no compromise."

Aliondrae looked around the room and noted as each person nodded in agreement. "These people you see before you are the community leaders and they are the voices of the people. We accept your conditions and we will follow your orders, Commander Perata."

Perata showed no emotion to this comment; his mind was already planning the first couple of steps. He said flatly, "Master Discere believes that we have approximately two months to prepare. That means, for the next two months we will get this city and the surrounding area ready for war."

Chapter Twelve: Preparations

Perata reviewed his list of things to do, slightly discouraged that his best hunters were also some of his best workers. Unfortunately he had to prioritize his tasks and hunters were what he needed now. They were sent far into Nemorosus to catch all the game that the forest held, or at least as much as they could. Once accomplished, they were to flush any remaining game as far from Arxsolum as possible. If Arxsolum's army did not return and this happened to turn into a waiting game, then Perata was damn sure he would have all the food. He would do whatever necessary to make sure that the natural resources would only serve his people and not the invaders. If they wanted food then they would have to bring it with them, which would probably go quickly.

His thoughts switched to that of Sorcia, he was anxious to hear word from her. It was her task to round up a handful of people who had special skills and he was not convinced that she understood what type of people he was looking for. At that moment there was a knock on the door; hopefully it was what he was waiting for.

"Enter," he shouted as he stood up to greet his prospects, hoping they fit the desired profile. What he was about to ask of these people would most likely lead to their deaths so he was not expecting many to jump at the offer. The majority of people left in Arxsolum were not even real soldiers, just ordinary people who were being sucked into an extraordinary situation. As he looked at those that filed into his room, his concerns were lifted. He could see from their eyes that killing was not foreign to them, well some anyway. The others looked as though they were young soldiers, woodsmen, and even thieves, but they did have potential. Sorcia's resourcefulness surprised him. She not only understood what type of person he was looking for, but it seemed she knew where to find them. Not to mention the fact that she was able to get them to come with her. These people did not look like they would be persuaded easily.

His gaze wandered over some of the less dangerous individuals. A preliminary assessment indicated that some would not make it and others would not be willing to undertake such an assignment, this was to be expected. The training he had planned for this crew would weed out the weak and bring out the potential in the strong.

Before Sorcia could begin with the introductions Perata said to them, "I know that you are all a bit confused as to why you were summoned here. I had asked Sorcia to find people who had…," he hesitated looking for the proper phrasing, "let us say special abilities. I need people who know how to hide, people who know how to take care of themselves, people who can be devious, who can be deadly. I need people who think on their feet." He took a breath, "What I have planned for you is completely voluntary, because it is highly dangerous, in fact it could be considered suicide, even more so than not leaving with the evacuated. Aside from that point, I do not want you to take this lightly, if you decide you are in, well then you are in until it is finished. It must to be that way, because we, as well as every single person held up in this keep will depend on you. Their lives, their family's lives will be in your hands." Perata paused so he could gauge the reactions from the small group. What he saw was promising. It seemed that even though some of these people could care less about many things, they cared about Arxsolum, and he was counting on that fact. It was their territory and they would kill to defend it.

Perata looked for the easiest way to describe what it was he wanted of them, "Basically, I want you to spy on the enemy. I want to know what their uniforms look like. I want to know how their food and water are kept. I want to know their names.

I want to know when they sleep and when they urinate. I want to know everything. But, and this is the hard part, to get this information, you will have to get very close to them, be part of them. This means that there is a high probability that you may get caught. If you get caught, well... then you are on your own, no one will be able to save you."

He let the information sink in. Satisfied that he made his point he continued, "Aside from gathering information you will be asked to do others things once the campaign starts; very bad things, such as using poison, slitting throats and anything else your imagination can think of. You will not be inside the protection of these walls when the attack begins and will need to find ways in which to avoid dying."

A small woman spoke up, she seemed somewhat hesitant "You want us to poison their food, wouldn't that make us just like them?"

Perata looked at her and instantly realized that even though she was slight, there was an anger inside her that was being closely guarded. He was not quite clear why this woman was with this particular group but if she were going to make it, then she would need to unleash that anger, "What is your name?"

"Lexis," she answered.

Perata walked up to her and said in a cold, cruel voice, "Lexis, would you ever go to their cities and try to take them over? Would you enslave their children? Would you rape their women? Would you destroy anything and everything they hold dear?" He never raised his voice, but his tone was building. "Because that, Lexis, is what they will do. You are nothing like them. Even if you hate them with blinding rage, you did not instigate this war, and unless you do that, you will never be like them. Remember, they are coming to kill you, Lexis, and everything you know." He faced the rest of the group, "They are coming for all of us. So you can forget anything you have heard about what is moral or immoral. This is war. There are no rules; there is only the victorious and the defeated. So, if you would like to live, then you will do what is necessary. But like I said, this is purely voluntary," he directed this last remark at Lexis, "So if you do not think you will be capable of such things, then you should leave now."

Lexis responded more defiantly, "I would like to stay, if that is all right, I…I know that you are right, I…it's just that I was caught off guard, that's all. I would like… I mean I can do this. I have lived in the shadow of the mountains all my life and know them well. I can help."

"All right," he said, the conviction of her voice confirming his previous thoughts, to the rest of the group he posed the same question, "Is there anyone who would like to leave at this time?"

One man grunted something about not worth dying for and went to the door; he was followed by a few more. Perata was not overly concerned about this because he could tell by looking at them that they were not the men he needed. He evaluated the remaining individuals in the room. Perhaps the thought of someone, some army, invading their homes, hurting their friends, and killing their family, was enough incentive to stay because that was the type of person he needed. Those that remained were enough to work with even if he lost a few more along the way. It was definitely a start.

Time was their worst enemy at the moment so Perata began to detail their objectives. First and foremost, he needed information. They only way they would stand a chance was if they knew the enemy inside and out. He rattled of some examples of the desired information such as troop strength, speed of movement, and descriptions of their leaders.

"You get the point, I will provide each of you with a more detailed list of information that I would like, but also report other information you come across as well. In addition I want you to brainstorm possible systems of communication; any ways that you would be able to send and receive information effectively. The quicker I can receive the information the better decisions I will make."

Sorcia who had stayed in the room stepped up, "I can use my magic to speak with Master Discere…I don't think the distance will be too great and it is instantaneous."

Some of the others in the room looked at her in a new light but no one said anything. Perata noticed the glances and remembered that most people distrusted magic and it occurred to him that could be something he could use to his advantage later. His mind quickly ran through the some of the feats that he had seen Sorcia accomplish with her magic and realized that would be a great asset to his little group, but he was not completely sure that she would not be more useful inside the castle. Besides he wondered if the Countess knew that her daughter wanted to volunteer for a mission like this; that could prove to be a problem. Perata did not say anything either way, it was not his place to tell her she could not use her skills to help defend her homeland, plus this could solve the problem of who their leader would be. She was capable; he just hoped she was mature enough to handle it; only one way to find out. He turned his attention back to the group. "That is a definite possibility, but come up with a back up or two to be safe. As I said you will not be in the castle when the fighting starts, meaning that you will all be given a crash course on how to live, hide and kill in the mountains, because they are to become your new home." For this he needed to enlist the help of the weapon's master, he would have a few tricks, but for the most part they would depend on each other to share their knowledge. They would also need plenty of provisions that could be stored in hiding places because in all likelihood, they would be outside the city for quite some time.

"One of the most difficult things that you will need to do is to not engage the enemy until the battle has begun, information is the main objective, at least at first. For example, if we know what their uniforms look like, we will make you duplicates so that you can get close. Close enough, in fact, that during the confusion of the first wave, you should be able to plant the poisoned food and water in their stores, ideally with no one being the wiser. You may come to a time when your emotions will have you wanting to do things that could jeopardize your mission. You must control yourself, you will need discipline and I promise your time for revenge will come."

As Perata continued on with more details about what he expected, the group was quickly realizing that what he wanted them to do was much different then traditional warfare. This was not two armies facing each other on an open battlefield; this was something much less honorable, but he had told them to forget everything they thought they knew of battle, because war has no rules. When finished, he informed his agents that their training would start at sunset and that they should meet at the castle gates. He quickly noted the marks he scrawled on his to do list and wished that he had more time, figuring that he would teach them as much as he could in a month. The other month would be used to learn the mountains and their secrets, to make hiding places and plan escape routes. "Just so you know you will find the training very intense." He then added with a side note, "It needs to be."

At that moment there was another knock on the door, Perata took this as a cue and ordered, "You are dismissed, remember training begins at sunset. We will go over more of the details then." He opened the door to allow the band out and to admit his next guests.

Master Discere entered the room followed by several others, a motley looking crew to be sure. But then again, he was looking for their knowledge and not their physical attributes. It was the wizard who spoke first, "Master Perata, may I introduce to you the cities apothecaries, physicians, and," He paused not knowing how to refer to a couple of the more despicable characters that were in his attendance, "and others. These people are the most knowledgeable in the subject of what you have requested and the delivery of such. I myself am also familiar with and have in my possession; other, let us say more interesting types of potions." He added the last with almost a smile, the idea of using them on another human was against his beliefs, but at the same time to be able to see the effects was enticing indeed.

Perata went right to the point, "You can all guess why I have gathered you here, it is simple; I...that is the army will need as much poison as you can acquire. We will take anything and everything that will in one form or another incapacitate or kill another person. We will also need to know how each type is to be delivered... whether it needs to be ingested or if can just touch the individual, does it need to get under the skin, things like that. Then we must make a plan as to how to achieve said delivery. So, lets start with you, Lineaus, what do you have or can you make that fits the description of what I am looking for and how much?"

Lineaus paled at the question and replied with effort "I am a healer, I really don't have anything that fits your description, and truth be told I'm not sure I would give it to you if I had it." He looked defiantly into Perata's eyes, but what he saw were not the eyes of a madman, but of a person who was determined. This brought him to the realization that there would be much more death and suffering of his people if he did not help. "Well, I guess I do have something. It, well...it is not much, it really only makes a person violently ill, but it is enough to keep them out of battle. I'm afraid I don't have anything that will kill or injure.

Perata listened without judging the physician; he knew that the man dedicated his life to saving others, not harming them. He was glad to hear at least that he had something and replied to Lineaus, "Actually, severe illness is perfect, because if a person dies it eliminates only one person from the battlefield, but if a person gets ill, well... then it eliminates them and anyone who has to take care of them, it also means that they still need to be fed, not to mention the effect it will have on moral." He paused and looked toward the apothecaries, "But we will still need something with a little more kick. I am sure that you gentleman must have something, something perhaps to rid the city of pests?"

The head apothecary said "Well, yes we could gather up quite a bit of deadly poisons but they would need be ingested to work, I don't know if you can force them to eat it, but you can have all we store. I believe that the type of poison that can be used on projectile weapons and the like may be far more difficult to come by because," he looked at the two unsavory individuals in the room, "it would be considered illegal here in the Southern Dominion."

Everyone turned to look at the two men, including an expectant Perata. One of the men started "Yes those types of poisons, the kind you would put on the tip of a dagger for example, are illegal. As a matter of fact, my associate and I are individuals who are concerned about this type of contraband and have been securing all of it we could find away from those who would use it in an unethical manner." He did not care that nobody believed him, and went on, "of course, I think we would be able to part with these materials for such a worthy cause, of course for lets say, a small handling fee."

At this request, Perata slowly walked up to the man until they were face to face. He did not say anything for several seconds, the mixture of Perata's size, his silence and his strange looks made the man extremely nervous. Then without warning Perata smiled a frighteningly cold smile and spoke in a whisper that only the man could hear. His face drained of color and he nodded in agreement; he had dealt with some incredibly dangerous men in his business, but never before had he been as afraid as he was at this moment.

His partner, although not knowing what was said in the exchange, quickly jumped in, "Of course, there is no need for a charge; we will give you our entire supply. Most of it will attack an individual's nervous system, which will paralyze the individual and cause death within minutes. I must admit that we don't have that much, but a little is very effective." He could still see his friend was shaken up so he continued. "The best way to administer this poison is to coat the tip of a blade or an arrow. If it gets under the skin, then it is almost certain death."

Perata seemed very pleased to hear the last. Then he said more to himself than anyone in the room, "Then we will do just that. Coat all the arrows that we will be using in the first wave of the attack. That way we will have the most targets so as to cause the most damage. Hopefully the effect will go beyond the first wave and make them think that all of our missiles are fashioned in a similar manner. At least it will give them pause and let them realize our resolve." Perata snapped out of his thought process. "All right, what I need you to do is gather as much of your material as possible and we will ration it accordingly. Your point of contact for this will be Master Discere," He looked at the master wizard and spoke to him, "I know I am asking you to do many things, but this is very delicate operation and I believe that you have the qualifications as well as a good grasp as to what I want accomplished. Can you handle it?"

The wizard did have a good grasp on the scope of the situation, due to understanding the nature of the invaders and agreed that it should be him in charge of this aspect of the defense. "Yes," he said to Perata and then to the others, "please bring what you have to my laboratory and we will go from there, also I want you working night and day acquiring more."

Once they had all left his room, Perata turned his attention to the things that still had to be accomplished. The list seemed endless; he knew he had to take care of the important things first, but they all seemed important. The next step was to check with the engineers to see how their projects were doing and then inspect the landscape excavations. His thoughts wandered to his hunters, hoping they were having success. "I need more people, more time and more people!" The few smithies not north with the army were attempting to arm a city. The fletchers were working day and night making as many arrows as possible. He even had the remaining children learning how to put the feathers on the shafts to bolster production. The women were doing the work of men. Nobody was allowed to slack. It seemed he had everyone doing something, whether it was feeding the workers or working themselves. He still had to make time to train these people adequately, not only with projectile weapons but in close combat as well. It was not his intention to create expert soldiers, but he had to teach them enough not to kill themselves or each other. His head was aching from the stress; he was having his doubts that these people could hold off a trained army. "Stop it!" he swore aloud as he slammed down his fist. He could not allow negative thoughts to enter his way of thinking. He would just have to keep looking for anything that would give them even the slightest advantage. It was getting later, he still needed to eat then begin training his band of spies.

Chapter Thirteen:
Shades of Information

As the sun dipped below the horizon, Perata took a quick note of the group that he termed his shade unit. He had already met Sorcia and Lexis, but now it was time to meet the rest of the recruits. His eyes fell upon a wiry looking man who looked as though he belonged in big city and was seemingly out of place in the countryside.

"You there" motioning to the man, "what is your name, and what are your skills?" Including the rest of the group he stated, "And please do not refrain from telling me anything due to any sort of legality issues. We have far more important things to consider; besides, if any of you make it out of this alive, Arxsolum will owe you a debt of gratitude far greater than any indiscretions that may have happened in the past."

The man's movement lent a certain confidence to his voice and Perata knew this man could handle himself. "My name is Phillos; I have a gift for making people, well… let's say … disappear, completely." He said the last not intending to brag or intimidate only to inform.

Perata had no doubt that this Phillos was every bit as gifted as he said, but still had his reservations about his ability to fit into a mountain landscape, which would definitely be needed for this assignment. "Phillos, that is an excellent skill to have and exactly what I am looking for, but do you believe that you will be able to hide from an entire army?"

He looked Perata in the eyes and as a wisp of a smile danced across his lips, "I can hide in plain sight, when I need too."

Perata shook his head at those words starting to believe that the man could do just that. He then turned his attention to the fourth member of the unit, who seemed to have a soft look to him. "And you sir, what is your name and what are your skills?"

The man took off his cap with a flourish declared, "Well, commander I answer to the name Tonagal … and I am a man who can acquire things."

Curious, Perata asked, "Acquire things, what do you acquire, exactly?"

Without missing a beat the eccentric thief replied, "Anything that I need, exactly. You name it and I'll get it."

At this Perata had his doubts, but the man seemed eager enough. The fifth recruit was a giant of a man who looked like he had been in more bar room brawls than an entire army. If he was half as tough as he looked he would do well, "You," pointing at the giant, "same question."

The man's answer came in a surprisingly soft voice when he replied, "Marhran."

After a couple of seconds Perata, expecting more of an answer prompted him, "And what of your skills, Marhran?"

The man again answered in a soft but defiant voice, "Sir, I really don't have any skills like the others, I just don't want this city to be invaded. I will do whatever it is you ask of me to prevent that."

Perata nodded his head to the large man, "you will get your chance." He then turned his attention to the next person in the group, which he thought was an unusual looking person. He knew from conversations with Sorcia that this man was a dwarf. He also thought he remembered discussing the fact that dwarves like the mountains; this one certainly looked like he lived in a cave. Either way he was sure the man knew how to survive outside of a city.

The dwarf, noticing Perata look at him choose to speak, "I be Rammel, I've been trapping game in those mountains for years; it be my home. I know every tree, trail, and rock that runs through her. I know her strengths, her weaknesses, her beauty and her evil. That be my skill."

"Your knowledge of the mountains is going to come in very useful. In fact so far all of your skills are going to come in useful, once you can learn to function as a team."

He meant what he said, they could be shaped into what he was looking for but that meant he would need total commitment. As he had no time to waste, it concerned him that he could not test their resolve right then and there.

"I want you to know that if you choose to undertake this course of action, it could more than likely lead to your death. No one will think any less of you if you choose to leave." Perata waited for any sort of response other than silence. "What I need you to understand is that while the others are at least partially protected by the city's walls, you will be out there alone with the enemy. To stay alive you will have to be like ghosts and like shadows. You will need to be able to hide, run, and kill all the while surviving on nothing but your own wits and the trust of your fellow members."

No one in the group said a word so Perata continued on, "All right, first thing that you need to know is that information is king. I need to be aware of every little detail that is going on with the enemy, leave nothing out. You will need to learn tricks, games, songs, whatever it is you have to do in order to remember everything that you have seen." Perata looked at each of them in turn and added, "You would be surprised at how much actually happens in any given instance. You will need practice so your first assignment is to break up into two groups and go into the Kicking mule. Bring back as much information as you can about the place and the people in it; that simple. Any questions?"

The group looked around in disbelief, and Sorcia was the first to ask. "All we have to do is go to the Kicking mule and bring back information?"

Perata looked right at her and said, "That is it; report what you find to me at sunup tomorrow. Oh by the way" he added, "try to be discreet, because when it happens for real, you will not want to be noticed." He then walked away thinking to himself that this group has a lot of potential, the problem lies in the fact that they all prefer to work alone and that they have survived by not trusting anyone else. Now the only way they will survive is if they can function as a unit.

Sorcia stood there in bewilderment, expecting more. To herself more than anyone else she asked, "What is the point of that?"

It was Tonagal who answered, "The point my young friend is to see if we can actually acquire this information, which he believes, and I agree, is fundamental to our success. May I suggest that we separate and see how well we do, I know that I could use a drink?"

Sorcia agreed and joined the group of Marhran and Rammel, somewhat excited to speak to the dwarf. "I guess I can think of worse things that we could be doing."

The two groups entered the Kicking mule approximately the same time. Phillos looked at Sorcia's group and in a hollow voice said, "A giant, a dwarf, and a princess, now that is discreet." He then headed toward the opposite end of the room. Sorcia wanting to respond realized that they probably were a strange looking group. She then thought of something her father told her as a child, 'If you try to fit in you're going to look as though you're trying to fit in, be yourself and people will assume you fit in.' Instead of shooting back a remark at the gruff man, she just ordered her companions a round of drinks and turned to the others to discuss their assignment. "O.k. what do we see here? What information does our commander consider important?"

Surprisingly it was Marhran who answered first, "Well, he said that all information should be reported and that he would decide what is useful and what is not."

Rammel grunted in agreement and while turning to look around stated, "All right then we just pay attention to everything."

The tavern itself was fairly empty; all of the work that Perata was having the townspeople do was taking its toll physically. The majority of people were home sleeping at this hour, resting up for the next day's chores.

Phillos took this chance to voice his opinion to Lexis and Tonagal, "Well, I believe that our esteemed commander believes that we all have a respect for and a knack of acquiring information, but I think he is looking for something more. I don't know about you two, but this is not quite the type of training I had in mind."

The thief nodded in agreement and said, "That may well be true, but I have been watching this Perata and I have a feeling that he knows what he is doing, so I propose that we just go with it and see what happens."

Lexis feeling a little intimidated and alone in her present company just nodded in agreement. Phillos noticing her discomfort felt a rare pang of sympathy. A man in his business did not have much use for emotions but something about her. Maybe she reminded him of his childhood when he was alone and scared, or maybe it was her determination but whatever it was he decided then and there to take her under his wing and show her how not to be afraid. To her he said, "Don't you worry about a thing, we'll take care of you." She gave him a slight smile knowing that she probably should not trust a man who killed people for money, but something about the way he said it rang with truth. She decided that if she ever wanted to be able to take care of herself then she needed to become more like him.

As the night progressed very few patrons walked into the bar and very little if anything was happening. The two groups of information hunters looked around and attempted to point out details that may be useful. Tonagal and Phillos happened to be pretty good at it, noticing things about the patrons that neither Sorcia nor Marhran would even think to note. One person in particular was sitting at the bar, acting intoxicated but none of the group happened to see him order a drink. It was Tonagal who finally noticed that he was pouring something out of a flask into his cup.

As the tavern keeper was getting ready to turn in and both groups felt that they had been there long enough the door opened and Perata walked in. The members all eyed him expectantly but all he did was receive a package from the bartender. He then turned and walked out of the tavern.

"What in the abyss was that all about?" Sorcia said to no one in particular. "This is ridiculous, I'm leaving." She looked at her companions, "I think we are done for the night."

The members of the group readily agreed that it was time to go, but they knew that they were supposed to report their findings to Perata before sunup and nobody knew what it was he wanted. The two groups decided to get together and compare notes. Finding that their information was similar they decided to relax. The flamboyant thief spoke up, "as luck would have it, I have come across some pretty interesting bottles of wine recently. Would anyone care to sample a bit with me since going to bed at this hour and then getting up at dawn seems to be more trouble than it would be worth?"

Everyone in the group agreed that it would be a waste to sleep now when they would have to rise in a couple of hours anyway and took Tonagal up on his offer.

Sunup came pretty quickly and all of the companions were ready for some sleep. They just wanted to get their silly report over with so they could go to their beds. Without waiting long both Perata and Gryffyn could be seen walking up to them.

Before anyone could say anything, Perata started out "Good morning everyone, I hope you are ready because it is going to be a long day."

The unit looked at each other and then Sorcia said. "We didn't get any sleep last night because we were out doing what you told us to do. Now we're tired and would like to go to bed."

Perata looked at the group and said "I'll tell you what, I will ask you three questions on information regarding that tavern, if you get them all right, I will allow you to go and get some sleep. If you get it wrong, well, then it is time to work. What say you?"

She looked around at the rest of the group hoping for any type of support, but before anyone could say anything, Perata said, "Before you answer that, I will give you one last chance to walk away, no questions, no regrets, no problem. Like I told you before this is entirely voluntary, but once you commit then you commit all the way."

Perata waited for anyone to resign, "You need to understand that if you do not walk away now that there will be no other opportunity to quit, this is your last chance. If you have any doubts whatsoever, I suggest you just head on home now because if you have any chance of surviving then you need to be very disciplined, which means that all of you will have to follow orders without hesitation. In addition, if you accept now and choose to later refuse, you will ruin the entire team, and I cannot allow that. I only want people who will do whatever it takes to complete the mission. What you need to know is that if you accept, and then disobey an order, I will kill you." He made sure everyone present understood him and then asked, "Now, do you really want to be in on this assignment?"

Nobody moved, they might be miserable but this was nobody's first sleepless night. None of them would be the first to desert their mission while others stayed. Perata then said to them, "I hope I made that as clear as possible because now you are all property of Arxsolum and any actions that undermine the defense of this city or its inhabitants will be punished accordingly. Do you all understand?"

The members all agreed and Perata went on, "Let us get down to business; we have a lot of work to do."

Tonagal in his ever congenial manner spoke up, "with all due respect Commander, I still want to be a team player but, the princess is right, none of us had any sleep last night and we would probably be more efficient if we started training later tonight." He looked around at the group. "I am guessing that most of this type of work is to be done during the night anyway so why not get acclimated now and train at night."

Perata laughed and replied, "I will tell you what, I will give you the same opportunity that I offered earlier, if you think you can correctly answer my questions I will let you and your group go get some sleep. However, if you get my questions wrong, then you will have to practice your information gathering tactics again tonight, after a long day of training." Perata eyes held no sympathy for the group. "Do you want to take that risk?"

Sorcia, Marhran and Lexis all seemed a little nervous but both Phillos and Tonagal were confident that they could answer his questions and said almost as one to ask away.

Perata seemed to like their enthusiasm and quickly said, "What color tunic was the bartender wearing last night?"

Phillos did not even give anyone else a chance to answer before he smugly replied, "Daron Linkstron, owner and proprietor of the Kicking Mule was wearing a green tunic with a small stain, most likely gravy, on the bottom left hand corner." He felt very confident of his answer and was sure he would be able to answer the other two.

Perata listened to the answer and was impressed by the attention to detail and returned "Excellent, now let's get a little more difficult. Question two, there was a man sitting near the end of the bar, was he right or left handed?"

The members of the unit started talking among themselves, Sorcia arguing that it was an unfair question that they would have no way of knowing, but Tonagal silenced them and turned toward Perata. "The man at the bar was right handed. Both his flask and his dagger were set up for a right hand reach."

Again Perata was pleased to hear the answer. "Final question, when I walked into the tavern, I was holding something in my hand. What was it?"

At this the group started arguing again because nobody looked at his hand when he walked in. Lexis and Marhran thought maybe he could have been holding a coin to pay for the package he picked up, but Sorcia thought he was trying to be tricky and the true answer was nothing. Neither the thief nor the assassin could recall seeing anything. Perata waiting for an answer spoke up, "I am not kidding about having a long day ahead of us so if you could go ahead and give me an answer we can get about our business."

Since the group could not recall seeing anything in his hand, Sorcia decided to answer, "You were not holding anything in your hand when you walked into the tavern."

"That answer is incorrect, I was indeed holding something and you should have noticed what it was. Anyway, now that we have that settled, we can finally get started."

Sorcia asked in an exasperated voice, "Well, what were you holding? You can't just say it was something and not tell us what it was."

Perata replied in his usual voice, "This is not a game, Sorcia, when I tell you that you need to start noticing every small detail if you want to survive this war then you better start doing just that. So, you will just have to try again. As for today we are going to start with some simple diversion tactics." He looked directly at the robust Tonagal and added, "However, since we could all use a little physical conditioning we are going to make a trip into the mountains. Rammel, lead the way."

Tonagal in a half-hearted attempt to delay hard work questioned "What about breakfast, we need to keep up our strength if you plan on working us hard?"

Perata was glad he asked and let the entire group know, "Actually, from this moment on you will need to be prepared. I can promise that those coming through this pass are not going to let you be just because you have not had breakfast. As for today we will be learning how to catch our food. I am sure Rammel has some tricks up his sleeve."

The rest of the morning was spent making their way deep into the mountains, further than most of them had ever been before. They set their camp near a pond that Rammel suggested, while Perata made sure that each member of the group was actively paying attention to where they were going. Repeatedly he expressed the fact that knowing the ins and outs of this terrain would be their biggest advantage. "It is important that no matter where you are you have more than one escape route planned out. After we eat we are going to decide where this invading army is going to come through. Then we are going plan everything off of that." He looked over at Rammel, "You are the expert, how do you think they will make their way through?"

Rammel, who appeared crazy anyway started to laugh, which made the rest of the group a little nervous. "If I be a betting man, I would guess that they would follow the actual trail of the old pass due to the fact that it is the only possible way to bring any supplies with them and there really be no other established trails" He then added, "but there's nothing to stop any advanced patrols who may have some aptitude from traveling like we be now."

Chapter Fourteen:
Flag of War

Perata shut his eyes for only a second knowing that any longer and he would be sound asleep. The last month had gone by like a blur, yet each day seemed to bring more and more work. He had to admit that the town was pulling together nicely. His hunters were having great success in the northern parts of the forest, gathering large amounts of game. The southern part was being cleared quickly, after much debate. No one, including Perata wanted to see such a beautiful thing like the forest destroyed. If they make it through this war it will take along time before Nemorosus would return to its former majesty. Perata knew that many people were just beginning to realize the cost of this war. He understood their loss; most of his limited memories took place in that very forest. He had so few that he cherished them, but this was a necessary part of his plan. His engineers were building war engines that would launch boulders and spears at the invading army. In order to build these engines as well as furnish the projectiles it was going to take a lot of wood. As with most of the strange things he was having done to the kingdom the point was two fold. Perata knew that if he did not destroy the forest then the enemy would. They would be able to feed and shelter their army as well as build siege engines of their own. Clearing away the pass would allow passage of the army, but they would be expecting to utilize the resources on this side of the pass for completion of their attack. Perata laughed to himself, "It will be a nasty little surprise for when they get here." His odd behavior was tell-tale sign that he needed some sleep, but a light knock on his door meant his nap would have to wait. "Come in, Aliondrae, its open."

The Countess walked in, looking as tired as he felt. She had been a great help in getting everything accomplished, and she did so without complaint. Perata could see why her people loved her and he realized that he was doing this for her as much as for the twins; this family had taken him in as one of their own and he would not forget that.

"You always seem to know when it's me or perhaps you scowl so much that I am the only one who will disturb you in your room. In either case I just wanted to see how things were coming." She took a seat opposite of Perata who seemed as serious as always and in an effort to lighten the mood she said, "I realize I don't have the vision of a military genius, but as I look around, this place looks like it is already been through a war, and it seems we lost."

Perata gave a little laugh, enjoying the moment, knowing that the sound of merriment would be a very rare occasion in this city for a long time to come. "Well, truth be told, things are actually right on schedule. I was just going over our wares, and we have enough food and water stored to hold out for at least two months after the siege begins." He did not mention that it would probably be longer due to the amount of people he expected to die during the actual engagement. "Also your people are working hard clearing the forest; I figure it will take a couple of weeks more and we can leave off. Our supply of weapons is still an issue, as is training but Gryffyn is confident that he can get them ready."

Perata's mind wandered again to the training of his army. Both Gryffyn and Jaxen have been teaching everyone strong enough to wield a bow how to shoot one. Those not strong enough are being trained as runners to supply arrows whenever and wherever they are needed. The tactics are pretty straight forward, using guide markers and placing people consistently in the same spots has yielded fairly good results. The guide posts, mainly naturally occurring markers in the land, allowed the men and women on the wall to know about where their arrows will land. Everyday the townspeople practice their shooting noting where their arrows can reach and where they cannot. Every night, the younger children pick up the arrows that can be used for next days practice, unfortunately many of the arrows become damaged, but it is a necessary loss. All the fletchers in town have been assigned extra hands to help them and the production has never been higher, but still they were far short of the amount that Perata wanted. It is the hope that the sheer number of arrows will make up for any lack of skill, but how long would the supply last, that was the lingering question.

Gryffyn constantly reminded him that he had never before been in a battle with out a trained army consisting of skilled archers and backed by a strong infantry. He was worried about when the enemy breached a section and they both knew it would happen eventually. Since they would not have many real soldiers they would have teach the townspeople enough to do some damage or at least give them the confidence to stand their ground. With only an a few hours a day of close combat training for two months they would not be able to stand toe to toe with the invaders, but hopefully with the defensive advantage they would be able to keep them at bay. The longer they could keep them off the walls the greater their chances. Even the children were practicing tactics on how to repel ladders and climbing ropes.

Aliondrae noticed the far away look on Perata's face and realized that he was thinking about his preparations again, a constant habit lately. She reached out and touched his hand gently, "Perata, I do not mean to interrupt you, I know that you have many things to do," she paused for a moment and gave him a very serious look. When she began again she was shaking slightly as if not sure she could bring herself to speak, "I know that you have Jaxen training every day on how to command the defense of this city, and although I think it is too much stress for such a young man, even for him, I understand the need." Her eyes met his, "What I do not understand is what is happening with my daughter. I haven't seen or talked to her in weeks, and when I saw her last, she looked like a ghost. I need to know, as a mother, what is her part in all of this."

Perata did not lower his gaze, even though he had been dreading this moment ever since the day Sorcia volunteered to become a shade. He took a deep breath and told her straight, "Your daughter is part, well actually the leader of a group of men and women who are gathering information on our enemy. They have been in the mountains for the last couple of weeks, setting up provisions and hiding places for…"

Aliondrae did not allow him to finish, "provisions, why would they need provisions stored in the mountains?"

He could tell by the look on her face that she already knew the answer, but he felt he needed to tell her and that she needed to hear it. With as much compassion as he could muster, he replied, "Aliondrae, Sorcia and the members of her unit will not be within the walls of the city when the attack begins, nor will they attempt to reach the city. Their mission, the second part of their mission is to wreak as much havoc upon the enemy as possible and disrupt any communication and unity that they may have. What this entails is…"

Aliondrae suddenly stood up stopping Perata before he could say more, she had already guessed as much but it did not hit her until he actually said it. She attempted to use her most regal voice, but instead it came out barely audible "No, no I forbid it. Sorcia is just a girl, she is not a warrior. She is not meant for this."

Perata had a speech planned out for when this argument took place but for whatever reason he could not recall a single word. "Countess, Sorcia is far more than an average girl. You know that. She rivals Discere in the strength of her magic and has as much heart as anyone I have ever encountered. She was made to undertake this sort of assignment. We need her and her skills out there if we are going to have any chance of pulling this off."

At those last words, Aliondrae broke down and sank into Perata's arms, "I am a terrible mother; I can't even protect my own daughter, much less an entire city. I cannot do this anymore; I've made a terrible mistake." She stood up like she was going to go somewhere, "there is still time to evacuate everyone and get them to safety. I will not be responsible for making people stay, it is too dangerous."

Perata held Aliondrae and softly answered, "Everyone that is here is here of their own free will. Yes, they are scared but, you, you Countess, give them the strength to stay. It is all right to be afraid, but you must be willing to face your fears. These people, your people, see you as their leader, not me, not your husband, but you. You need to be strong; you need to be a leader."

Aliondrae took a moment to compose herself, relying on her years of court manners. Surprisingly she was not ashamed of breaking down in front of this man even though she had never showed weakness to anyone before, not even when her first husband died. She was not ashamed because she knew in her heart that this man was far stronger than any other person she had ever met. In truth, it was actually him that was going to give her strength to continue. "I am not a leader, you are the leader, the city appointed you the commander of our forces, it is in you they trust. You are far better equipped to lead than me, you are more intelligent and more experienced. Even Master Discere or Gryffyn for that matter would be better suited for this; they are both smarter than I."

Perata took a moment to let her calm down and then replied, "The true measure of a leader is not intelligence, but how well he or she can utilize the intelligence of those who follow. Make no mistake, you are the leader of these people and there is no one better suited for the position."

Aliondrae let the words sink in, for some reason or another she believed what he said. She was the leader of these people and she knew she would have to shoulder the burden. Once she felt she was ready, she pulled away from him and in an effort to change the subject asked, "How is Master Discere holding up, you know he is older than he looks."

Perata smiled and said, "Yeah, but he is also tougher than he looks and somehow I think he likes the challenge of it. He seems to like to solve problems."

The court mage had been spending day and night finding ways to counter any magic that the war wizards would bring and in doing so experimenting with ways in which he could be more formidable. It was as if the old wizard never slept, he cast his magic until he was physically exhausted then spent his remaining time in study until he was mentally exhausted. He and perhaps he alone fully grasped the repercussions of losing this city; it meant losing the war and possibly more.

"Speaking of Discere, I was talking to him earlier about Arxsolum's war history and how they had such an edge when it came to battles. It seems that the Army of Arxsolum believed that they could not be beaten and I want to know what gave them that confidence, because we could use it now. He mentioned something that caught my interest. He said that when Arxsolum was at war they actually had a special flag that they would fly over the walls; a flag that has never known defeat. Do you know this story?"

"Of course, everyone in Arxsolum knows that," replied the Countess. "The actual flag itself is a pretty gruesome looking thing. It appears all black, but it is said that in every battle that a different symbol has appeared on it, depending on who was commanding the forces. Master Discere believes that it has some ancient enchantment on it that captures the essence of those who fly it and displays their spirit. I don't know about that, that is his expertise, but I am guessing that those are just embellished stories told to increase the value of the tale. I know when I was a child and I looked at it, it was just black, blacker than night, terrifying, but nothing more."

"Are you saying that you have seen this flag?" asked Perata his hope rising for an idea that had been going through his mind. "Do you think you could possible have it duplicated?"

"Duplicate it?" returned Aliondrae, "Why would you want to duplicate it?"

Perata wanted to explain why he did not want to use the city's normal flag without offending the leader of that city. "Well, I am guessing that General Stragess knows that your army is up north, so if we flew those standards it would not really give him any pause. But, if we flew a flag, let's say a flag that would give the people of Arxsolum a sense of confidence and unity, and could also make Stragess wonder what army was defending the walls, well; I say it would help immensely. Sometimes morale is the only difference between winning and losing a battle."

Aliondrae laughed, "I appreciate the lesson on morale, but what I meant is that I still have the actual flag. It is stored in the treasure room and has been there for the last two centuries."

Perata felt a tingle go down his spine, that was a good omen, a good omen indeed, and he began to think how he could utilize this to his full advantage. He looked up at Aliondrae who happened to be staring back at him, realizing that it was probably the old mage's intention all along. "That Discere is a crafty individual, isn't he?" They exchanged smiles both heading for the door at the same time, "so shall we go have a look?"

Their walk down to the treasure room seemed to both of them something more than a task that needed to be done, it might have had something to do with Aliondrae's breakdown, or perhaps they were relying on each other's strength. Whatever it was, a bond was forming between the two of them, a bond of mutual respect and maybe something beyond that.

Perata had been in this city for nearly half a year now and he had known a couple of women. His light coloring and his unusual accent seemed to appeal to the local women, not to mention the fact that he was a guest of royalty. He had always tried to be discreet about his undertakings but he had a feeling that Aliondrae knew everything that took place in and around her castle. He started wondering if perhaps she was the reason that he stayed so long. The desire to find his past was something that was with him everyday he woke up yet he stayed. The only thing that he knew for sure is that he was not going to find the answers here. He had spent countless hours with Discere and Sorcia attempting to magically explain his condition, but to no avail. The fact that magic did not affect him as it did others was also very intriguing. The only two people that seemed amazed by it were Discere and himself. The former, however, never liked to speculate until he had a firm grasp of what it was. Perata on the other hand did not even have a clue as to how to proceed in that area. His failed attempts at using magic ended with only frustration and offered no clue as to his condition. There had to be something that would give them a direction for him to begin his search. One thing that he noticed but never mentioned was that in the many months that he had been in Arxsolum, he never had to shave or cut his hair. He did not remember much, but something like that was a little bizarre. So many different things were going through his mind that the insanity of the impending battle was the only thing that kept him sane. He knew that he would eventually have to deal with his identity. 'Well,' he thought to himself as his hand accidentally brushed the Countess's, 'no matter the outcome of this battle, I will need to leave this city.'

Aliondrae who had her own demons was also in a peculiar predicament. Her city, along with its people, was facing almost certain destruction. Her children were out doing who knows what and her husband was thousands of leagues away. The only thing that she could think about was the man that walked next to her. She realized that her little visits with him were becoming more and more frequent while the reasons behind those visits were becoming less important. She knew it was wrong, but there was just something about this man that made sense to her, but she could not put her finger on it. He was definitely confident and fearless, but it was more than that. Whatever it was, it was the reason she put the future of her city into the hands of a stranger, a man who seemed to come out of nowhere and did not belong anywhere. At least she was justified in her decision by Discere, who felt he was sent here for this very reason. As she stole another glance at this amazing man she thought to herself, 'I may be dead in a month.' She pushed the thoughts out of her head as the came upon the treasure room.

Perata was not quite sure what to expect of a room named the Treasure room, but what he saw was definitely beyond his imagining. The room was more of a vault and contained the combined wealth of Arxsolum in gold, silver and jewels, as well as quite a few non-treasure items such as the flag and some other artifacts that were more than likely worth a fortune. The flag itself was encased in a glass box and looked like a simple piece of material, but it was still in excellent condition. As the two unfolded it he realized it was much larger than expected and it was strangely ominous like Aliondrae described. As Perata stared at it wondering if it would have the desired effect upon the enemy he noticed Aliondrae shudder and drop her end of the flag. "Are you all right?" he inquired.

Aliondrae steadied herself, "yes, of course, I just thought for a second I saw...something. I think the lack of sleep is finally catching up with me."

Perata was intrigued; maybe the flag did have some ancient enchantment upon it. He looked back at the flag to see if he could see anything but there was nothing. Perata had seen enough magic to know that just because he did not see anything did not mean something was not there. He became curious, "what did you see exactly?"

Aliondrae still seemed a little pale but her voice was strong, "honestly I don't think I saw anything much less be able to explain it. Let's just consider it nerves." She smiled at him, "fair enough?"

"Fair enough," he replied even though he had the strange feeling she was not telling him everything. He believed that if just seeing this flag had elicited that sort of reaction out of the Countess then perhaps it was what they were looking for. "Let's fold this up; the more I think about the more I think this is exactly what Arxsolum needs."

Chapter Fifteen:
Fool of the Alliance

The oversized tent was filled with various levels of command including the General of the Eastern Alliance as well as the leader of the Elvin Nation. The threat of invasion from an unknown and perhaps a very formidable enemy was enough to bring together the majority of cities of the Southern Dominion and what was left of the Elven Nation. Help had also been solicited from the Northern Dominion, but as of yet none was forthcoming. The King of Reynil self-titled himself General of the Eastern Alliance and took command of everything. Many of the other more skilled commanders were not happy with his decision, but as he was King they would do as ordered. Tallox's plan centered around confronting the enemy on open ground before they were able to gain a foothold in the East, similar to the defensive posture assumed during the War of the Dominions.

They were there to discuss possible battle plans, but as usual Tallox was not ready, in fact he was busy conversing with one of his aids about what he wanted for dinner. The patience of those in the tent was being tried as they waited for an essential report to be read which was waiting on Tallox. When the King was properly situated he turned his attention to a young corporal who stood anxiously in front of the group. He gave the corporal a brief head nod that let him know that he was ready to listen.

The man started, "my Lords," he paused to wipe the nervous sweat from his face not wanting to report the bad news, "it seems they have disappeared once again. Our scouts cannot tell how many or to where they have gone."

General Tallox looked at the Corporal like he had expected this news. "Yes, yes, somehow you have misplaced an entire army." He stood up looking down at the man. "Is that what you expect us to believe, that you have no idea where they are?"

The Corporal stammered, "Sir, it is, my, our…belief that they have either withdrew beyond the edge of the Elven Forest or are somehow hidden deep within it. We have sent scouts out but all of their reports are negative, there is no trace of them aside from the few earlier skirmishes." He was regretting having volunteered to deliver this news after his friend had suddenly fallen ill. He made a mental note that he would visit that friend, and was going to make him wish he were truly ill, that is, if he made it out of this tent alive.

Tallox spoke again while returning to his seat, this time using a much softer voice, a tone that made the Corporal very uneasy, "tell me soldier, do you think that they have just given up and gone home? Is it your belief that they saw the might of our forces and ran for fear of their lives?"

"No, sir," replied the corporal quickly regretting his answer the second he said it. "Well, I mean it is possible, sir. Our forces are far superior and it would be a wise move on their part. But, I do not believe our enemy is that crafty and they will probably try to confront us." The Corporal took a deep breath, feeling pretty good with how he covered his answer.

With a smugness that could only be associated with the overly privileged, King Tallox spoke down to the young Corporal, "This enemy of ours is craftier than you think soldier, and far craftier than you, which is why you stand there and I sit here. Now, you are dismissed, and if you value your life, bring back something that we do not already know."

Without looking back the young man snapped a quick salute and ran out of the tent as fast as his feet would take him, cursing his sick friend the entire way.

"I will be amazed if we can win a battle with these incompetent soldiers," snapped Tallox knowing that it would belittle whoever the leader of that man's unit was. According to his uniform he belonged to the city of Barawal, but it did not really matter to him. He considered them all idiots and scoffed to himself about the training and discipline of some of the soldiers.

In an effort to get matters moving another member of the council spoke up directing his question at Caoudrol the Elven leader, "what of the Elven scouts, they know this wood like no others, only elves can hide from elves in their own forest? What news do you have?"

Everyone, including General Tallox looked at the Elven King because that was a very good question. The Elf, knowing that the time had come, stood up and slowly stated, "I have seen many things in my lifetime. I have witnessed things that would destroy a lesser man, and what I am about to say is by far the worst thing I could imagine. Old loyalties are gone, what we as a people once held sacred is no more." Deliberately he bowed his head in contemplation.

Tallox, becoming very impatient with his slow words, cleared his throat. Such was the nature of Elves. They saw time differently than did the humans, which the King believed was the reason their race was diminishing.

Caoudrol noted the prompt, hating the fact that he had to rely on the help of these humans. They were such an irrational race and never fully understanding of their events, but as it were, he needed them. "You are right; it would take an elf to escape detection of our sentries." He lifted his head; his one hundred and seventy years of age were showing more of late. "We, the people of Evanidus have come to the notion that among our enemy there are other Elves."

The room broke out into a flurry of conversation at that remark, but Caoudrol lifted his hands to silence the outburst. "You must understand that whoever these other elves, these dark elves, they are not considered part of our nation." He paused to let his words sink in and then continued. "What this means to us is that we are dealing with an unknown entity. There may be hundreds or even thousands of these skilled warriors mixed in with the humans that we have seen."

At that Tallox stopped him, "Caoudrol, please do not embellish your words, I would find it difficult to believe that your nation, which is somewhere near three thousand elves would not be aware of another group numbering close to the same. I think it would be more likely that perhaps some of your guard have probably been bribed or even working as spies for the enemy."

The leader of the Elves became livid with anger; questioning loyalty was probably the worst insult that could be given. He knew, however, that he would have to conceal his anger for a while longer if he was going to save his land. "My lord, it would be highly unlikely that one of my people would join with them. It should be noted that in the War of the Dominions many of our histories were lost yet my personal historians have found some information that very few know. Centuries prior to the War an unknown tribe came to our nation seeking to unite our common race, unfortunately the information on the events since then, such as who they were or where they had come from is not known. In truth very little evidence of their existence remains. What is known for sure is that when the War ended, there was no common record, written or spoken of this tribe anywhere, which I find very strange. My chancellors have speculated that this tribe, these dark elves were not welcomed back into our forest, for what reason we may never know. I believe they do exist and it could only be these who have penetrated our defenses so quickly."

Tallox laughed out loud and with very little respect for the leader of the Elves and responded, "Do not flatter yourself Elf, you were taken so quickly because you and your chancellors probably deliberated on whether or not to defend yourselves."

Some of the other council members joined in his laughter, most of them never really knowing anything at all about elves, but the few that did know were not laughing. Elves were not a race to be taken lightly; their wizards commanded ancient magic's and their swordsmen were unmatched.

Again, Caoudrol had to restrain himself, he wanted to pull his sword and teach this insolent human a lesson in respect, but that would not save his home. The nation had not yet recovered from the losses suffered during the War and this second invasion could be their undoing. He would do what was necessary for his people including placating the humans a while longer. Caoudrol proudly met the gaze of Tallox and said, "If you will excuse me, I have other things that need attending."

Tallox replied, "Just go Elf, find out who your spies are. Do not worry about the battle; we will fight it for you." To the others in the room he said, "Now let's get down to business."

The Alliance had been enduring a difficult time in the North. They had set up camp just outside the Eastern front of Evanidus because Tallox felt the forest would not allow for the invading army to attack in a controlled force. He ordered his men to build fortifications for when the invaders came through but the problem remained that the enemy would not engage. Any attacks that did come were only small skirmishes, but never in the same area twice. It was obvious to many that they were stalling, but the reason was unknown. Some believed that they were trying to pull the army into the forest to gain the advantage, which they thought might actually be better than waiting. Others in the council believed that the forest was actually giving the enemy too much coverage and materials. No matter what the council suggested it was Tallox who made the decision and he felt that since the Elves owned the forest, and were supposedly so formidable within, that it was up to them to eventually flush the enemy out. The invaders would either retreat or advance and if it was the latter then his troops would destroy them on an open battlefield. Many of the council disagreed with Tallox, but fear held their tongues. All but Count Edward, who believed these people, were mostly fools and the King more a fool than most. If it were up to Edward, Tallox would not be on this battlefield, much less the throne. "General," suggested Count Edward, "I understand that we have an excellent defensive position here, but it does us no good to just sit. I think it is exactly what they want us to do; we are playing right into their plan. They are waiting until the second half of their forces comes up through the pass at Arxsolum, which will put us in a vice that we can not possibly win."

The consistently arrogant King looked at Count Edward. "My dear Count, I appreciate the support of you and your troops in this engagement, however, you sir, are not schooled in the art of war like I am." Tallox did not mention that this would be his first real battle, but his military advisors assured him that he had a natural talent for strategy. "What it is they want, my dear sir, is for us to believe this ridiculous rumor of them spending untold sums of manpower to tunnel through a mountain that no one has been through for hundreds of years. Then they will want us to divide our forces to go defend this hoax. While half of our forces are off chasing rumors and stories, the other half will be engaged by the entire force of the Western Dominion." He slammed his goblet down on the table with enough force to spill it contents. "And I sir, will not be caught off guard by such an amateurish ploy. We will maintain our position of strength and when they come at us," he laughed, "they will know defeat."

Count Edward had heard this speech before and knew it was no use arguing, in fact the logic actually made sense, if the rumors were false. It was the sort of misdirection he might use, although he did not believe it was amateurish. The only thing that bothered him was that his information came from a man who was seldom wrong. He was not overly fond of Master Discere, but he respected him and his ability to know things. The day he saw him walking toward him about a month ago telling him of an army opening the pass, well, he believed him. What was maddening was that if the rumors were true then that second army would sweep across the land with absolutely no resistance and Tallox and his fool Alliance would still be sitting in front of this damned forest.

His city and his fortune would be wiped out and he would be hard pressed to regain either. His thoughts went to his wife, 'If Discere said the same thing to her then she should be half way to

Reynil by now with every townsperson in tow, probably leaving anything of real value behind.' He believed that his wife cared far too much for those peasants and was beginning to regret leaving the city in her hands, for in his mind it was his city.

"Damn fool" he growled to himself, "your arrogance will lose this entire kingdom." He considered the last part over in his head 'could lose this entire kingdom. Hmm, now that is something to think about.'

Edward was a very shrewd man. He had started out with nothing but the clothes on his back, but he did have a knack for business, and before long he attained everything he had put his sights on, including the Countess of Arxsolum. He remembered the day he first saw her; they were all at a dinner, a dinner that was meant to be his finest hour. Edward and his partners were trying to buy a large portion of land that belonged to the city. This was the deal that would make him rich enough to retire. Things were going well until the Count's wife entered the room and actually had the audacity to interfere with the deal. Aliondrae persuaded her husband not to sell the land because she thought it was beautiful and did not want it ruined. Edward had invested a lot of time and money in this deal and because of a few words by a woman he had lost both, along with his partners trust. He was nearly killed that day, both physically and financially. As he laid in the gutter that his partners left him in he vowed two things, first he would get even with the Count for pulling from the deal and second he would get that land. He succeeded at both. Edward smiled at the thought 'What would happen if Aliondrae ever knew the truth?' He caught himself beginning to laugh and quickly stifled it as Tallox was finally finishing up his rhetoric.

"My personal scouts have reported to me that the supplies are running short in the Western army which means they will need to attack soon with their only option to meet us here. If they wish to sustain any sort of threat to this land they will need to quickly overcome our forces and take the entire Southern Dominion in one decisive move. If they can accomplish that it would be difficult for us to push them out. That is why we are here, it is why we are fortifying this area, this is where the war will be fought and won. In order for them to accomplish their strategy, they will need to utilize their entire force like a battering ram, and it may be large enough to do so. I, however had the foresight to set our battlements close enough to the forest so that they will not have time to regroup or reorganize, yet far enough away so that they can not use the forest for cover. This, gentlemen, is why they have concocted the story of another front. They see that they have been out maneuvered and they are becoming desperate. I have them caught between the proverbial rock and a hard place." He looked at the members of the council and with the authority only a king could muster he issued, "So we will wait here until I deem otherwise. Now, leave me."

The council members exited the tent, many unhappy with what they had heard, the king's mind was set and no one had the power to change it. Edward believed the meeting was to discuss possible actions, but it turned out to be a waste of time, the same old story, sit and wait. They had been encamped in this location for months and nothing was getting accomplished. He could not believe what Tallox said about them running out of supplies. They held the whole damn forest and an open supple chain to the West, there was no way they were running out of supplies. By the time he reached his tent he was about to explode. The only reason he kept his controlled exterior was that one of his own scouts had returned.

"Sir," the scout saluted, "I have news of Arxsolum," he waited as Edward directed him inside the tent and then continued, "it seems that the evacuation has yet to start, and by these accounts never fully will."

Edward looked at his most trusted lieutenant, he knew his information was as reliable as could be in this situation, but he was still angry about the war council and let some of it out on him. "How confident are you of this? Would you be willing to bet your life on it?"

The scout paled at the question, knowing that he was deadly serious, "sir, please understand that this information had to travel many days and that during those days it would be impossible for me to know of any change."

Edward stopped him, "Just answer the question, are you confident about your report?"

"Yes sir" responded the scout, "there has been no evacuation that I am aware."

Edward dismissed his scout believing that a man should be confident whenever he said something, unlike that fool corporal from Barawal; Tallox had him crapping in his pants. The report did surprise him though, 'what does that mean? Did Discere not give her the same message or does she plan on surrendering?' The latter part made his skin crawl because he knew an invading army would not be kind. It galled him that someone else would take advantage of what he owned, which in this case was Aliondrae. It was not much her well being he was concerned with, but more so his reputation.

This latest news did serve to support a plan that had been running through his mind as of late. Even if the pass was not truly being reopened he could still use it to his advantage. When a confrontation did take place both forces would be weak from the exchange and the winner no matter who it was would be easy pickings for fresh troops. He needed to be the one with fresh troops. 'King Edward' he thought to himself, 'such a nice ring to it, but how do I keep my troops fresh without alerting Tallox?"

Without ever sitting down; he turned around and headed back to Tallox's tent. "My lord General," he said in his sincerest voice, "You have their strategy completely figured out. I was thinking though, that if we could somehow fool them into thinking we fell for their second front hoax. Maybe we could pull some of our troops back, making it look like they're heading south, but in actuality have them waiting to come back. This might cause the West to be overconfident and attack."

Tallox was silent for a moment, "it is funny that you mention that Count Edward, I was just about to send for Commander Draxton to have his troops do exactly that. But, since I have you here now, I think that it would be easier to just have your troops execute this move. Besides Draxton is completely unreliable and may give away our entire strategy."

Edward just smiled as he listened to Tallox go into details of how to execute their new plan, but Edward only half listened because he had a plan of his own.

Chapter Sixteen:
Information is King

Perata's shade unit had been reporting enemy activity regularly for a month and they gauged that the invaders would clear enough of the pass to get small patrols through within the week. Once that happened it was fairly easy terrain the rest of the way to the city. One main thing that their reports noted was that the workers were mainly slave labor, presumably captured men and women from the cities that they have taken so far. This meant that their troops would be well rested but it also meant that there were a large number of individuals that could possibly be used as allies. Phillos concentrated his looking glass on General Stragess, he saw a much larger man heading to meet him; a routine that these two did quite a bit. The assassin believed that they went to this remote area to talk in private because it would be difficult for anyone to overhear them without being seen first. Unfortunately for Phillos that is exactly what he wanted to do. His belief was that if the information was not even shared with their troops then it must be something very interesting. The problem still existed that it was difficult to tell what was transpiring between the two from such a distance. He promptly motioned toward Lexis, "track down Sorcia and bring her back here as quickly as possible."

Lexis ran off without a word, she had a good idea what Phillos wanted to do. She had been spending the majority of her time with him and was beginning to understand his thinking process. Basically he wanted to know what those two individuals were talking about, and that meant that he either needed to get closer or he needed a wizard. In this case getting closer was not really an option. Lexis flew through the mountain landscape barely making a sound, after the last month and a half her body had become lithe and strong.   She loved the way the wind shot past her as she ran. Her confidence was growing daily, not just from training but because she was part of an elite team.   A team comprised of very capable people who believed that she too was capable.   Two months ago she did not feel she would make it much longer without her husband and now she could not imagine herself being that timid woman.   She spotted the rock that hid their hiding place and slid through the entrance.   During her approach she had kept one eye closed so that when she entered the darkness she would be able to see, a trick that Phillos had taught her.   She quickly found Sorcia and explained the situation.

Sorcia did not like the idea of using magic that close to the enemy camp for fear of being detected, but the reward might be worth the risk.   She also reassured herself with the fact that most of the wizards were busy helping clear the pass and that her magic would easily go undetected amidst that racket.

They reached the assassin's vantage point and surveyed the situation below.   She saw the two individuals and estimated the distance.   She knew this would be a tricky spell, one that she had not used since she was young and never from such a distance. "Only one way to find out," she said to no one in particular.   Her eyes closed and she quickly found the magic.

Both Phillos and Lexis felt an eerie chill then heard a strange humming noise.   Their vision started to blur as if they were traveling at an incredible rate of speed.   The noise became more and more focused until finally becoming audible and at nearly the same moment their vision cleared.   The two men appeared to be only feet away yet they seemed to take no notice of the spectators who decided to drop in on their conversation.

"Well said Lockstan," the small man complimented his second in command, "but what are your thoughts on our progress?"

"Sir," replied the tall captain, "If the weather holds we will have opened a lane large enough to allow the men and horses through by week end. It will take a couple weeks more to get the supply wagons through."

The General was pleased with the progress, knowing that once he got through these wretched mountains he would be able to impose his will with very little opposition to stand in his way. It drove him insane that this small realm contained so much fertile land while so many people on the western side were starving. He began formulating this plan when he first learned how the West had lost the War of the Dominions. He knew that the pure audacity of going through this pass would be the key to his success. No one would believe that it was possible, much less try something like this, but Stragess had worked his way through the ranks by thinking outside the box. He studied the composition of the collapse and noticed that the main area of the pass was still there, only blocked. He concluded that with his wizards and some forced labor; he would be able to create a lane large enough for his army to go through. He also knew that the fools on the other side would, of course, think that the main invasion would come from the north. They in turn would do the same thing their ancestors did and consolidate their forces. He and he alone believed such a simple plan would work so well. It also helped that even if word got out no one would believe it until it was too late.

He was brought back to reality by Lockstan's voice, "Of course, we could just forego the majority of the supplies and take the city on the first day. That is if they don't just open the gates and let us in."

Stragess was not sure if he liked the man called Lockstan. He was a good captain, if not a bit too young and far too aggressive. The son of a rich man who felt he had to find something more to life, more than just money. He was searching for something and that search led him to the Army. His station in life afforded him the opportunity to enter the military as an officer and he had risen quickly due to his strength and intelligence. He worked as hard as any of his men and when dealing out discipline, he was harsh but fair, which made him popular with his men. The only weakness that Stragess could pinpoint was that the young man had never really met adversity. Everything that he attempted, he achieved without too much effort and he always expected to win. Stragess believed that the man was very gifted and he conceded that he might even be a little jealous of him and his fast ascension through the ranks. He would never admit that or let it interfere with the matters at hand. He personally had to bite and claw for everything he now had where as this boy had everything given to him. The one thing he did not have was experience, real experience. The boy had never been in a real war and had never truly been tested. The true measure of a man is not how smart, how big, how strong, how rich a person is but in essence, how that man reacts at the edge. Some men will hold, some men will break but every man who finds the edge will find their true selves. Lockstan had yet to come close to his edge and until then would never be great.

The young Captain caught the strange way in which his General looked at him and quickly added, "I will make sure that the supplies get through as fast as possible." Lockstan did not mind taking orders but always felt he would do a better job. He accepted that Stragess was an able enough General and a fair strategist, but he was far from the genius he had heard him to be. He put far too much faith in his plans and his God. The entire invasion was based upon this one idea to come through a pass that had been closed long before his time. Yet he was the innovator that not only created two armies, but also calculated the opposition's plan and had contingencies for it. If they stayed planted in front of the Elven forest they would be cut to pieces from behind. He also had a knack of being able to enlist all sorts of help from other races that typically would not talk to humans much less join with them no matter the promise of spoils. He questioned the General on how he was able to do such things but Stragess only answered that it was his God that converted the other races and gave him these strategies. Lockstan did not have much use for Gods but he feared them and the influence they had upon men. Stragess did explain that men would more freely give their lives for a cause if they believed the cause was bigger than themselves.

Lockstan realized that the General was waiting for him to continue, "Our most recent reports show that the mountains are not yielding much lumber and the game seems scarce."

The General seemed mildly surprised at this report, "Interesting...how scarce?"

"Well sir," replied the young Captain, "the hunting parties have not seen any sort of game in the last month; at least none to speak of. Granted no one has ventured very far into the mountains due to the difficult terrain. Still we would expect to see more than this. It should also be noted that our stores are full enough to last until we get through."

Stragess clasped his hand behind his back, a habit he had when he was thinking, "You are most certainly right, this time of year even this high in the Mountains there should be animals everywhere, even if it were only small animals; which means that there is a reason behind why they are all gone." He looked at his Captain, not because he wanted him to answer, but more to make a point. "One possible reason, and the most obvious one is the amount of noise those blasted wizards make when they decide to clear some rubble. I would not be surprised if all of Silexunatra could hear us coming." He gave a slight chuckle as he thought of the power his war wizards were capable of delivering, "I guess that is the price we must pay for quick work. Anyway...it is highly possible that is the reason for the scarcity of game. Too bad really, I was hoping that we could refresh our stores before we go through. We will be camped here for so long that I am afraid we will use up all the immediate resources."

"I understand," replied Lockstan who always tried to pick up as much military strategy he could, "never go into a battle unprepared. We don't even know what the terrain looks like on the other side or if there will be hunting available, for all we know it could be a giant desert. Should I order a rationing of supplies?"

General Stragess shook his head no and replied, "I visited the other side of these mountains as a child. The entire region is covered with forest as far as the eye can see. Even after all these years it should contain all the food and resources we will need if our supplies run low. There are even some areas to fish if we are so inclined." He laughed again barely hiding his excitement for his long awaited return, "besides…as you said earlier it would be surprising if they don't surrender immediately, in which case we can take what we need from them." He stopped laughing as his analytical side took over. "Then again, all of this is a little disconcerting … because if I knew I was going to be invaded I would hunt up everything in sight and then do my best to flush the rest as far away as humanly possible. Now the question is, do they know we are coming or is it just a case of so much activity that animals are afraid to come out. Send a scouting party as far through the mountains as possible and have them report what they find. I need to know if the city known as Arxsolum is aware we are coming, or if the not so delicate method of our wizards is scaring the animals away. Although, in truth, I do not think it will make much of a difference one way or the other."

"I will lead them myself," answered Lockstan in his usual self-assured way as he began to walk away.

He was quickly stopped by Stragess' voice over his shoulder, "No, not you." He seemed almost amused at the Captain, "just send the usual scouts."

Lockstan was slightly disappointed but he knew his place and replied, "Yes sir." He quickly started off to alert his scouts heading to the place he knew they would be.

The image of both Stragess and Lockstan became blurry and again the loud buzzing noise seemed to permeate the area. In an instant, time and space seemed to snap back to normalcy. Phillos looked around and it was as if he just awoke from a dream. The first thing he saw was Sorcia looking as if she would pass out any second. He reached out to support her knowing that working magic could take its toll.

Sorcia never liked to show weakness to anyone, but her close quarters and intense training had brought these strangers closer together than family. They had all been pushed to their breaking points somewhere along the training and what they learned was that they could depend on one another. Perata maintained that a team that worked together properly could be much more than the sum of the individuals involved. Sorcia began to laugh at the thought of him, for a man that did not know much he knew quite a bit. She looked up and saw the concerned faces of her two friends. She could only imagine what they were thinking, probably thought her mind snapped from the strain. "I am all right; I just need a few seconds to regain myself." She took a deep breath and went on to explain. "Although the spell was not an overly difficult one the distance made it seem like I was trying to balance on water while juggling stones over my head. So you can imagine that it was not that easy. I will admit that I am rather surprised it worked so well." She meant the last, in the past it was only sound that seemed to be altered, but this time vision was also changed. Her ability was definitely increasing.

"It did work well and now we know that they are sending scouts into our mountains, which means we have time to prepare," answered Phillos.

Lexis thought about it a second, "wouldn't it be better just to stay out of their sight and let them go by so that they don't know we are here. It will be fairly obvious that we are preparing for them if we intercept their scouts."

It was Sorcia who answered, "One of the reasons that Perata was adamant about destroying so much of the forest was so that these invaders would not be able to gather food and materials. If they know that these things are not available then they will forage for more food and supplies on their side."

Lexis nodded in agreement, "That makes sense, but how do we stop them from reporting. Again if we detain them then the General will know something is not right."

Phillos chimed in, "True, he would know something is wrong, but he would not know what. He could not prepare for every contingency that might have befallen his scouts. If they get through then he knows exactly what to prepare for. I am tending to agree with our commander that information is key."

"Then what do you propose we do? Do we just kill them?" asked Lexis in a surprisingly cold voice.

"No," replied Sorcia who was not yet ready to kill someone. She knew when war came to her home that it would eventually come to that but at this point she was not even sure if she was capable of taking another person's life. "We don't need to kill them, in fact we should find out what they know."

Phillos looked hesitant, "you want to take prisoners? I don't think that is a good idea; that is never a good idea. We don't have the manpower to watch over them much less the space. You also have to think about food and water. Prisoners are usually more trouble than they are worth."

Sorcia knew that the assassin had a valid point; however she was not ready to give in just yet. "I tell you what Phillos, we see what they have to say and if they become too much of burden then we do whatever is necessary. Sound fair?"

Two months ago Phillos would never even have listened to the suggestion of a teenage girl, royalty or not. When Perata had named Sorcia the leader of their little unit, Phillos was the first to argue. These last couple of months showed him that Sorcia was not a typical individual; he learned to respect Sorcia's ability and even trust her opinion. She was the leader but always kept in mind the fact that her team had a lot to offer. She asked their opinions and included them in all the decisions. He liked her way of offering compromises to difficult situations yet she was not afraid to stick to her beliefs when she knew she was right. He would defer to her judgment on this because he knew she made a good point. Maybe they could learn something from these scouts, if not then they would do away with them. "Sounds fair."

Sorcia then looked to Lexis, "What about you? We need to do it as a team or not at all."

Lexis smiled, she enjoyed the fact that they asked her thoughts on situations and knew that they actually listened to her opinion. "You guys know I am with you, no matter where it leads."

Without knowing why Phillos also smiled. He took a look at the two women who were standing next to him. He would give his life for either one without a second thought and he knew these two would reciprocate. "All right, now we just need to figure out the best way to capture them."

Chapter Seventeen:
Vanished Innocence

As he walked through the camp looking for his scouts Lockstan noted the differences in the amassed soldiers. He could not believe some of the miscreants that comprised the main portion of the army. Compared to his unit they were pitiful, they were unorganized, undisciplined and unkempt. He would never allow this if these were his men. He truly believed every one of his men was worth at least ten of these and he was probably right. The only thing that kept his disgust in check was the fact that he was privy to the real reason these conscripts were here and it was pretty much the same reason as the slaves. They were all fodder, bodies to be used then thrown away. No matter how well a war is fought there will always be causalities and it might as well be these men that pay the ultimate price. He had questioned the General on why they do not try and make some semblance of a military unit out of them. The answer he got was brief but to the point; he was not going to spend time, effort or gold to train an army that was only loyal to gold. All he had to do was promise them vast amounts of gold from the conquests of this war and they would serve their purpose. When Lockstan first heard the General's deal with the conscripts he thought Stragess was out of his mind, until he realized that dead men do not collect their share. He laughed as he came near the tent where he believed his scouts to be. They were notorious for gambling and this area seemed to offer quite a bit of that. He made a mental to make sure he found some more fitting duties for his men so that they did not become too soft during this idle time or spend too much time with these lowly mercenaries.

He quickly spotted Bothar and Scandren playing dice. "Gentlemen," Lockstan interrupted, "you have an assignment."

Several of the men at the table looked at the individual who spoke as though he had authority. A few actually contemplated making belligerent comments about the use of the term gentlemen and the audacity of anyone who would think a dice game should be interrupted. Their words stayed on their lips upon seeing the size of the man speaking and their prudence was confirmed when two men immediately jumped to attention and simultaneously replied "Yes sir!"

Lockstan was smiling on the inside knowing that his men would follow orders without question, he thought to himself, 'It is too bad none of this other lot understood that.' He quickly moved to the purpose of his visit. "Find Tomas and head into the mountains. I need some information on what is happening on the other side."

The two men did not ask any question or probe for more detail. They knew what their job was and they knew how to do it. After collecting their winnings amidst a chorus of grumblings from the others at the table, they headed out in search of their third companion.

The bear of a man called Bothar quickly rounded up Tomas, and the three-man squad took of in the direction of the pass within minutes of the order. They always kept their supplies within reach and in order for such was their job to be ready at a moments notice.

Lockstan felt a pang of envy watching them leave, he was ready to see the enemy, ready for some action; he was ready for something other than waiting.

The scouts made quick time getting past the slave workers and soon entered into the un-cleared portion of the pass. It was here that they would have to climb and pick any route passable to continue toward the other the side. They were not surprised at the ease of their ascent during the first day because they were all capable and covered quite a bit of ground. As the sun found its way below the horizon the small group made an impromptu camp near the base of a large cliff to protect their backs. Their discipline demanded that they set a watch rotation even though none of them believed they would have any trouble this first night.

Bothar was awakened before the sun rose; it was his good luck to pull the third and final watch. He sat with his back to the fire careful to never look into it for fear of losing his night vision. Even though he did this he relied very little on his sight and more on his hearing when it came to standing watch. He not only listened to the noises he could hear but also the noises that were not there.

Just before dawn he had the sensation that he was being watched but his usual detection senses were not picking anything up. Either he was being overly paranoid or those that watched him were real good. Trusting his instincts he lightly kicked the two long spears that were on each side of his feet. The ends of these spears each touched one of his companions. A hard jolt would awaken them in an instant and have them spring into action, however in this case he just used a light touch. This way they knew to wake but not to alert anyone they were actually up and ready. This method always had a way of turning the advantage of surprise.

What Bothar could not understand is why nothing had happened yet, no attack, not even the sound of a bowstring being pulled taut or the click of a crossbow. He waited patiently straining his hearing to catch anything that would give the watchers away.

The anticipation of the ensuing battle mixed in with his irritation of waiting started to raise his blood pressure but only a little. It took a lot to get Bothar or his companions nervous; they lived very hard lives and were great at adapting to different situations. This seemed to be one of those different situations, what or who was out there seemed a mystery?

He came to the conclusion that it did not really matter because he knew that he and his team were ready and the element of surprise would be theirs. He ran through every possible scenario of attack he felt that could come and plotted his strategy for each.

They might rush in, try to sneak in, possibly use a net or ropes, they might just try to kill him where he sat. He went over and over these different tactics eliminating those that did not fit. He was feeling very confident that these people were more interested in attempting to capture him than kill him, which made him smile because it meant they would not just start firing missiles and they would most likely lessen their blows in order not to kill. He on the other hand had no such plans. Every stroke of his sword was going to kill or incapacitate someone. If by some chance one of his attackers lived then he might question him, but then again he might not. He did not like to take the word of others and his orders were to see what was going on the other side of the pass. Hearing about it from an unproven source was never a wise move.

As the morning sun began breaking over the horizon his apprehensiveness was lessoning and was he was feeling very content. It was as if everything was part of a dream and the feeling continued to grow. It was only then that he realized something was wrong; he was losing his focus. He never lost his focus. His body seemed to become heavier and heavier no matter how he struggled. All he wanted to do was close his eyes and drift off into sleep. He tried to fight it but the feeling had too tight of a grasp on him. With his final coherent thoughts he realized that of all the attacks he imagined, none of them included a wizard.

Sorcia finished her enchantment more drained than she thought she would be. "You were right Phillos, they fought harder than I would have thought possible."

The steel-eyed assassin had been watching these men since yesterday and could tell they were not men to be trifled with. He was beginning to second-guess their decision to try to capture these men and contemplated that it might be best to just kill them now and dispose of the bodies. Sorcia, however, still felt they might have some information that could be useful. The problem arose as just how to capture these men. It was clear to the entire group that these men were far too wily to fall for any traps they could set with limited time and it looked like they would fight to the death.

It was actually Marhran who suggested the plan and everyone, including Phillos thought it was worth a shot. They had a wizard why not take advantage of that; if it did not work then they would go for the kill.

Sorcia had waited for the proper moment to begin her spell slowly making sure that she had a hold on these men before she unleashed her power. She did it this way because although it is difficult spell to fight off especially cast by someone with her power, it could be done if the person knew it early enough.

She realized quickly that even with all their caution and stealth, all three men were awake and ready; this sent a tingle down her spine. If they would have tried physical means to capture them it may have turned ugly.

She then continued her spell even more cautiously, slowly weaving her magic within each person. It was already nearing daybreak before she felt she had them and then she unleashed.

The power washed over the men like an avalanche. They all resisted but none of them stood a chance once they were within her magical grip.

Her thoughts were interrupted by a hand gesture from Tonagal. The group had been practicing an improvised language utilizing only hand movements. It started out fairly simple but had been growing more and more complex as the unit became more adept.

Sorcia threw water on the first of the three men to awaken him completely. All three were segregated so that they could not hear what the other two were saying. It was decided that Sorcia would ask all of the questions while Tonagal and Phillos watched the captive's behavior. The thief had a knack for knowing when someone was lying and Phillos would step in only if needed to ensure they answered in an appropriate manner. Sorcia waited for the man to look her direction and then began with a simple question, "What is your name?" She wanted to try and gain little pieces of information out of each one in an attempt to use against the others.

The man was a bit surprised to see such a young girl and ignored her question completely. He then proceeded to look around to get a clearer picture of his surroundings. Much to his dismay he did not see his companions; in fact he did not see much of anything, just the young woman, a thin man who moved like a snake, and an oddly proportioned man who had the look of a shopkeeper. He was amused that it was the woman who spoke and not the men, although the manner in which she spoke was of one that was accustomed to getting answers. It was a motley group to be together this far into the mountains and it meant only one thing: they were here for a reason and that most likely meant watching for intruders such as he. He realized then that those on the other side of the mountain were well aware of the impending invasion, but if all they could muster for defense were these three then it really did not matter.

Sorcia patiently waited for the man, but when it seems no answer was forthcoming the thin man begun to move in his direction. The woman stopped him with a gesture and then asked again, "What is your name?"

The man began thinking as fast as he could; he had a couple different options. He could lie, say nothing, or play the innocent role but as he looked at the wiry man none seem to bode well. He knew that if he did not come up with an answer, the same answers as his friends' then things were going to get painful. He did not mind pain, but he needed to conserve any strength he had so that he could possibly create a chance to escape. He felt the question was harmless enough to answer truthfully and nothing would be gained by lying so he responded, "Bothar."

Sorcia smiled to herself. She learned along time ago that if you wanted someone to do something that they normally would not do then you needed to have them do small expectable things that seemed harmless at the time. These small concessions would eventually lead to what she wanted.

"Bothar," she continued, "would you like some food or water?"

This question threw him. He wondered why they would offer him anything that would help him. He racked his brain thinking of the down side of taking food or drink. Maybe it was poisoned, but if they wanted him dead they would have had their chance so that seemed unlikely. Of course they might have a drug that would make you want to talk, but again they could have made him swallow that when he was unconscious. He decided the smart thing to do would be to take the food and water and save his strength.

He also believed if he did not answer in a timely manner the offer might be withdrawn so he quickly answered, "Yes, both if possible."

Sorcia motioned for Phillos, who did not seemed too thrilled about this whole line of questioning. She noticed his irritation but let it pass. Her stepfather Edward had actually showed her that by giving something you can create a feeling of obligation. That feeling, no matter how small can be an opening to coerce a person into larger things. Her method was definitely much milder than Phillos's way of questioning, but she believed it would be more effective in the long run. Granted the assassin's way would definitely elicit responses, but she feared tortured people might have a tendency to tell you anything that you want to hear just to end the pain. Then they would have to figure out what was the truth and what was said in the moment of self-preservation. Sorcia understood the threat could be more valuable than actual torture.

Once Bothar had some food, Sorcia continued her questioning. "Your friend told us that you were with an invading army and you three were scouting ahead to find out information about the other side. My question to you is why?"

The information was true, but she inferred it came from his companions. Hopefully it would create a sense of betrayal from his companions.

Bothar did not even bat an eye at the question. He was not surprised at what she knew, and he believed it was possible that she may in fact be guessing. One thing he did know is that his companions did not tell her this. He and his companions had been through much worse and if they talked they did not say anything of use. The young girl's tactics may work on some people but he knew better. In fact, he felt this was in his best interest and if he needed to stall for time all he had to do was start talking but not about anything in particular. Of course he would have to make sure the things he said were vague and did not catch him in a lie, which by the looks of the thin man could mean his death. He was fairly sure that these people knew he was an army scout, playing dumb would probably not advance his cause. He needed to bide his time until there was an opportunity to escape. "I am just following orders," he said fairly pleased with that answer, vague but truthful.

Amazingly enough Sorcia seemed satisfied with that answer as well. She did not really care why; she only wanted to get this guy talking and give him just enough rope to hang himself. She politely said "Thank you Bothar," and turned away. With a quick hand gesture, she and Phillos left to question the others while Tonagal stood guard on Bothar.

As they approached the secluded area it seemed the captive was still sleeping. "Lexis, wake him up," Sorcia ordered as she prepared herself for round two. She looked up at the exact moment that Lexis went to shake him awake and saw that he had somehow freed himself from his ropes. The man grabbed Lexis around the neck with one hand and freed her dagger with the other. In one quick motion it was at her throat.

"I must say that the stay has been fun, but I will be leaving now," he said derisively then mainly to Phillos he cautioned, "Even twitch and I end her." He believed the wiry man to be the greatest threat and he would use Lexis as a shield as long as he could in his effort to escape.

Phillos cursed under his breath, he knew this man would not hesitate in killing Lexis. He would slit her throat and then take his chances with the other two. Phillos looked into Lexis's eyes and could see her frustration; he was slightly surprised to see that she was not frightened, she was angry. Her anger stemmed from being caught so easily and then being used against her friends. He realized quickly that she was contemplating doing something desperate, which would only end badly. He kept his eyes on both individuals afraid to look away from either. Then it happened, he was not completely sure what. No one seemed to be moving, the only difference was the hilt of a dagger caught in the man's eye. The man collapsed releasing a stunned Lexis who also had no idea what had occurred. The assassin turned his head slightly and then it was clear. There stood Sorcia her hand still outstretched from her follow through, a look of horror frozen on her face. The man considered her the lesser threat, a mistake he would only make once.

His attention was brought back to Lexis who was kicking the dead man in an effort to release her anger but it did not seem to satisfy her. She reached down and snatched back her dagger that had been held to her throat. She gave one more kick and headed in the direction of the other captives. Phillos wanted to go after her but he knew he should first say something to Sorcia who still had not moved from her position. The first kill was always the hardest. Several things came to his mind yet nothing seemed appropriate, they both stood there for several moments. In the end he just said, "We need to check on Lexis, she had a look in her eyes."

Sorcia did not answer him; she stood there for a moment more and followed Phillos's lead. They reached the spot where their third captive should have been. It was deserted, no Lexis, no Marhran and no scout. Without exchanging words they continued on to where Bothar was located. When they arrived Lexis had positioned her captive so that he faced Bothar. Marhran stood off to the side with a slightly puzzled look on his face. Lexis with her dagger still drawn placed it on the throat of the unarmed man making sure that Bothar had a clear view. Then without warning she slid her dagger from one end of his ear to the other. Blood sprayed from the slain man's neck covering Lexis in a coat of red. She then turned her sights on Bothar.

The lead scout knew the situation had changed; no longer was it to be a game of question and answer. He cast a glance over to the others in a silent plea for help yet they did nothing to stop her advance. Bothar always believed he would be killed in battle; never in his worst nightmares did he think he would be slaughtered like a helpless lamb. The thought of that raised his ire. He looked at the blood soaked apparition coming toward him and in a last act of defiance spit in her face.

Lexis did not slow her movement even a bit as she ran her dagger to its hilt in the man's chest; never averting her eyes from his as his life drained away. She knew that she did not need to kill either of these men, but when the other scout had a hold of her that old feeling of helplessness came back. She would do everything in her power to prevent that from happening again even if it meant going against the wishes of her team. She turned, ready for her chastisement from the others but when she looked into their eyes there was no judgment.

Sorcia understood why she did what she did. She also knew that it was her decision that put Lexis at risk. Up until today everything still seemed like a game, it was exciting. She did not think her actions would have real consequences. Her head hung down, this was no game and it was not fun.

Chapter Eighteen:
Rammel's Revenge

The flaps of Lockstan's tent flew open and General Stragess entered without warning. He directed his gaze upon the man sitting behind the desk and questioned, "What news from your scouts."

Lockstan was slightly perturbed by the interruption and had it been anyone but his commander he would have had the person's head. As it was he needed to maintain his place, "Sir, the scouts have yet to return and have not sent word."

The General seemed un-phased by his answer but his voice gave a slight indication he did not like the news, "I was afraid of that…this means we will need to start mobilizing the troops and supplies through the pass. Have them ready at first light and push everything through."

Before he could turn and leave, Lockstan quickly commented, "Sir, with all due respect, the excavation is not complete. Without clearing the rest of the debris we stand the chance of rockslides, which as you know could delay us further. I think it would be prudent to secure the pass before we start sending our troops and supplies through."

Stragess eyed the large Captain and answered with a deliberate tone, "I understand your concern, but now is not the time for caution, now is the time for speed." He noted the confusion on the young man's face, "Let me be more clear, your scouts have yet to return, why is that do you think?" Before any answer came, he continued his questions pausing slightly between each, "Are they the type who would just run off or not follow orders? Is it possible they just became lost? Do you think there was a chance that all three were killed by some wild beast?"

Lockstan vehemently defended his men, "Those are three of my best men, loyal to their souls, and there is no way they have become lost or were taken by beasts." He stood wondering where this line of questioning came from and where it was going.

Stragess motioned with his hand for Lockstan to settle down. The General had also known these men and knew his words to be true. "I agree with you completely, which is my point, I am guessing that it is a possibility that your scouts are dead or captured. What this means to me is that the enemy knows we are here, which means surprise is lost." He paused to make sure his Captain was following the logic, "The only way to gain back that surprise is to breach the other side sooner than anticipated. So if the enemy does know we are here and we continue on with our current pace they will have time to flee or worse yet set up an ambush for our forces. I highly doubt the latter but it would not be a bad defensive move to try and hold the pass."

The General loved to lecture about the pros and cons of differing strategies. He would play out different scenarios in his head always trying new tactics. "Let's say for the sake of argument that they did set up an ambush. What is the best way to deal with it?"

Lockstan knew the answer to this, he and Stragess had spent countless nights discussing just such a question. He responded, "Charge it, you charge an ambush and overrun it. You will lose men but much less than if they can sit and pick you off especially if they place the ambush in an area where you are exposed and they are not."

"So based upon that assumption it would be best to have all our forces pushed through as quickly as possible in case they are setting up an ambush. We not only would surprise them but also catch them unprepared."

Lockstan was still unsatisfied but he was also well disciplined and would not question his orders further. Stragess on the other hand sensed the young man's hesitation and continued. "I know what you are thinking, you are thinking that we do not know if there is an ambush waiting for us and should not proceed without further information. In most cases you would be right. However, if there is no such ambush and we force our troops through, what is the worst that could happen?"

Lockstan was grateful of the opportunity to voice his opinion. He thought about the question and then gave what he believed would be the worst possible scenario, "a landslide could bury our supplies under a mountain of rock and the slaves that carried them. We would then have very little resources to continue clearing the path that we already cleared and our invasion would be over before it even began. I truly believe it would be in our best interest to fortify the pass along the way and that way guarantee safe passage of not only troops but also our supplies."

The General laughed, he was impressed with the answer and acknowledged that his second in command had a very valid point. He could change his mind and have the pass fortified before moving. The downside would be that if the enemy knew of them then they would have more time and right now time could be their biggest ally or worst enemy. He felt that he needed to act and act quickly or else suffer far worse than losing some slaves. This was one of those occasion where a commander needed to make a decision not based on facts but feeling. This was a lesson he needed to pass on. "You will learn that in battle it is not always best to play it safe. It is sometimes better to do what the enemy would not think you would do even if you could hurt yourself doing such. This can give you a chance to steal victory from defeat. You take a chance and trust that you are the stronger. It is a risk, but so is war, and sometimes you are wrong." He then smiled, "but the key is that you need to be able to afford the cost of your errors. In our case I believe we can. We have three types of soldiers in our army: the professional, the slave, and the conscript. The first fights because he is loyal to the cause. These are the men you do not want to lose. The second fights out of fear for his life, these you want to keep around for the grunt work. Now the third, the conscript, fights for money. They are greedy, undisciplined and untrustworthy. It is in the best interest of a leader to keep only enough of these types of troops as is necessary for reasons both monetary and for moral. They are nothing and not only do you expect to lose a majority of these men; you need to lose the majority of these men." He gave a slight chuckle, "the funny thing is that when they see their comrades die, they do not care because they think only of their share of the bounty."

Lockstan was not a supporter of mercenaries just for that fact, but he did believe they would be needed when they finally met the armies of the Southern Dominion. "Sir, are you saying that you want us to lose men going through the pass, before we even engage in battle?"

"No," replied Stragess, "but if by chance they are planning an ambush our best chance to gain the advantage is by overrunning it quickly and gaining back the advantage of surprise. If there is no ambush we lose nothing and gain time. The ability to make this decision is based on the fact that the end justifies the means and of course we can afford to lose some men."

The more Lockstan thought about it the more it made sense, but that did not mean he had to like it. First his scouts did not return and now an order to move troops through the pass before it is ready, Lockstan was beginning to get a bad feeling in the pit of his stomach. He reminded himself that he was a soldier first and foremost he would do as he was ordered. In this case it meant preparing the troops for deployment.

The camp was already in full motion by the time the sun broke over the mountains. Lockstan initially had a difficult time getting the conscripts up and moving but after cracking a few skulls he got his point across. Even with his motivational techniques in full swing it was still slow going. The soldiers needed to travel single file in most places and had to scramble in others. The Captain concluded that it was going to be damn near impossible to get any wagons through. He had two choices, he could have each person carry a portion of the supplies or he could wait until the bulk of the army was through and let the clearing continue. He felt the latter was the best move because it would allow the soldier's hands free to fight if need be and it did not countermand his orders.

As the day progressed Lockstan became mildly pleased with the advancement and believed that at this pace they would have the bulk of their army through in two days time. He looked up at the steep mountainsides to gauge the integrity of the walls. For a moment he believed he saw a flash or movement, something high up on the Northern face. He scanned the area carefully with his looking glass but after finding nothing decided it was only his imagination; most likely due to the sun peaking over the mountains and distorting his vision. He was still leery due to his scout's absence, but he could not imagine anyone capable of scaling that far up.

· ·

Rammel stayed crouched motionless behind a large outcropping of rock. He chastised himself for getting careless and dropping one of his chisels. It was his mission to slow down the intruder's excavation and to do that he was going to do some excavating of his own. He came up with his plan soon after he realized someone was making an awful lot of racket on the Western side. Upon further investigation he realized what was happening, someone was clearing the pass. He spent the last decade of his life in these mountains and they had become his sanctuary; he was not going to sit idly by and allow anyone to trespass. Unfortunately there were far too many for him to scare off by himself; he would need help. He decided to go to the only man he ever trusted, which meant a trip to the city of humans because that is where the wizard resided.

Discere was very surprised to see his old friend at the door and even more surprised by his news. They had first met many years ago before the dwarf left his homeland. It was because of the old wizard and the stories he would tell that made Rammel want to see these far off lands with his own eyes. Even though he was one of the most gifted Dwarven masons, he was not content to remain inside his stone creations. The majority of his fellows felt either betrayed or maybe even that he must be mad for leaving. Even without the support of his colleagues he decided that he wanted to see what the world had to offer even if it meant alienating all that he knew. His desire became an obsession and he left to find what was out there.

What he found was that most places were not overly friendly toward his kind and they treated him like a pariah. In the best of cases he was only shunned, but more times than not the humans turned to violence and his distrust grew daily. He soon realized that he would not be welcomed anywhere nor would he go back home. He did the only thing he could of and sought out the wizard who started it all. He found that Arxsolum's inhabitants were not nearly as bad as others places he traveled. Aside from the usual stares and sometimes pointing the people treated him fairly. He decided to make his home nearby. When he became aware of the invaders and what they were attempting he alerted the only person he thought could do anything about it.

At first it seemed to Rammel that the humans would not have the means to stand against these trespassers. He was dejected and began visiting other options until he heard that they were going to fight and that some men were needed in the mountains; he offered instantly. His entire life was spent in and under mountains and he loved to fight, which made him the perfect individual for such an assignment. When their unit was brainstorming possible ways to slow the invader's advancement Rammel offered his suggestion. He could climb with his pickaxe as well as he could walk and could easily reach heights where humans would have difficulty breathing. He believed with the right amount of preparation and strategically placed stress that he could cause quite an avalanche of rock.

Things were coming along nicely and it seemed he would have a nice little surprise ready for when the intruders decided to come through his mountains. That was until they decided to come through today. He was gauging their pace and was impressed by their skill, granted they were nothing compared to Dwarven craftsman but their securing of the pass was structurally sound. That is why he was surprised when they opted to go forward this early, they did not finish shoring up the walls. He was not sure if this would make his job easier or more difficult, but in either case he needed to work fast. He knew that speed was of the essence but at the same time he could not allow himself to drop another tool as he was not yet ready to be seen. "Oh, they will see me soon enough," he laughed in the way that only dwarfs could as he thought of that moment, but now he had to focus.

He peaked his head around the outcropping and watched as the invading army snaked its way through the pass. He was dismayed that they were making such good time. His original plan was to bring down as much of the mountain on top of the first trespassers and slow their progress. Now it looked as though he would be hitting around the middle, which as he thought about it, would be just as effective. Neither side would be able to communicate with the other hopefully creating a little havoc. Unfortunately none of them were bunched together as he had hoped but now was not the time to be picky.

He felt the area that he had been working on for the last month; his practiced touch could tell that it was almost ready, but it needed a little more persuasion. His hand found what he was searching for; it was just the slightest of sensations. No one but a dwarf would have detected it, perhaps it was a dwarf's natural ability or countless years co-existing within the rock, either way he had the ability to manipulate it. Rammel placed one of his chisels in the necessary spot and then let his hammer reign down. The amount of force that he could generate was amazing. Standing only four feet six inches Rammel weighed over two hundred pounds and none of it was fat. His arms were the size of tree trunks and he could crush rocks with his bare hands. He was as tough as the mountain he occupied.

Rammel heard the distinct crack that he was waiting for. One more and it should start a chain reaction that would pick up tremendous speed and force on its way. His hammer rose once again and he mustered all the force he could into his down swing. Another loud crack rewarded his efforts; this one told him it was time to move. He quickly scrambled around to make sure he would not get caught up when it all came crashing down. He reached his spot of safety and listened to the sound of rock slowly sliding on rock. It was only a matter of seconds before gravity would begin to take over. Holding his breath as the rock he unleashed traveled toward a second outcropping. He was confident he loosened enough support that when the first one hit then it too would cascade down the slope picking up speed and more rock until finally crashing to the ground below.

As the third area let loose, he knew that it was a success and was able turned his attention to the tiny images below. He could see that some of them had heard the rumbling and were staring up looking for the source. A few of them realized the impending danger and began to run frantically causing those who did not comprehend what was going to try and flee as well. There was nowhere to escape; the narrow pass and the rough terrain impeded any quick progress forward, while the constant push of soldiers coming from behind blocked their retreat.

Rammel heard a loud crash as the first of his onslaught found its mark. The large dust cloud that seemed to engulf the entire area clouded his vision, but he could definitely make out the screams of those below. Rammel did not relish in killing this way, preferring single combat but he was very proud of the fact that he dealt the trespassers a costly blow. The rockslide would delay their workers another few days and his accuracy caused untold casualties. The exact amount of people who were caught in his trap would be difficult to gauge since they were coming through haphazardly and not all at once, but since they did not shore their dig the avalanche was quite large. Rammel took a last look at the confusion below and saw to his dismay the large captain who nearly spotted him earlier was still alive, "Next time, next time I get ya," the dwarf growled to himself.

Far below Lockstan had his hands full trying to establish order and was barking commands to everyone. First thing he needed to do was find out how many men made it through and how many were trapped. He organized search parties to scour over the accessible area and see if anyone was still alive. He then brought in the wizards and engineers to discuss their options. Their opinions were not helpful and their passage was definitely going to be delayed. He saw Stragess coming toward him and began to get agitated. Had the General listened to him in the first place they would not be in this predicament. He overheard Stragess say something under his breath and it sounded like, "Sometimes you're wrong."

Chapter Nineteen:
Nothing is as it Seems

The smell of burning flesh permeated the air even though the pile of charred remains was over a league away. It took four days to clear enough rock to collect the bodies and another few to dispose of them. It had to be done or else the stench would have been much worse. If he had the option he would have left the bodies buried under the rock, unfortunately Stragess still needed to get the rest of his men through. The slaves were working 24 hours a day and the General no longer cared if they lived or died, their usefulness was about at an end anyway. Against his better judgment he even ordered his soldiers to work, something he did not want to do, but he needed speed. Things were not as they were supposed to be. First his scouts did not return from a fairly routine mission and then the blasted ill-timed rockslide. He did not want to believe the avalanche was anything more than a coincidence, but it was hard not to. Admittedly, it would be an excellent move, something he would do if the roles were reversed. Plenty of casualties along with more time and energy spent, and not to mention the affect it had on moral. Perhaps his opponents were more prepared and more cunning than anticipated. The General of the Western forces stopped when he realized that he was making assumptions and not basing his conclusion on facts. He could actually be giving the Easterners more credit then was truly warranted. The biggest mistake a commander can make is not knowing the enemy and that means overestimating as well as underestimating them. It was his job to get a handle on how the enemy thought and acted. To do so meant he had to make his way to the front of his forces so that he could get a better view of the city that would soon be his; it was imperative to see firsthand what was happening there. He was not surprised to hear the city seemed deserted but was dismayed to hear about the devastation of the beautiful landscape he remembered so well. The advance reports were that everything was wiped out; no trees, no crops, no animals as far as the eye could see. Approaching the city it was apparent that the residents of Arxsolum left nothing behind that could be used and he doubted that anything would be left within the city either. It was at that time that his Captain brought him back to reality by pointing at a few columns of smoke rising from within the cities walls. It seemed that the city was not deserted after all.

"By the looks of things you were right. They knew we were coming and for quite some time it seems…to accomplish all of this." He shook his head in disbelief surveying the damage. "What I don't understand is why anyone would still be here?"

Stragess gave an initial sigh knowing that this confirmed his earlier belief about the craftiness and the resolve of these people. Lockstan had a good point, why would anyone still be here. He racked his brain, trying to put himself in the place of his enemy. What would he do if he learned an overwhelming force was coming to wipe them out and they did not have army to defend them? Coming up with what he believed to be the most logical reason for any stragglers, he shared it a pensive voice. "It is most likely the majority took everything they could carry and left…it is possible a small force stayed behind to hopefully give the people more time to get away. If that is the case they are counting on holding the city as long as possible, most likely using as many stalling techniques as possible. With the amount of time created by their little rock slide trick I would think that the residents are long gone and have probably alerted the cities to the north by now. Their army, I believe, is still many leagues away and they could never reach here in time, but they could still pose a problem if they can set up some defenses at another location. Damn!" He slammed his fist on the pommel of his mount, "now we must act, we need to take this city as quickly as possible. If they are attempting to bolster their defenses anywhere along our path then we need to make sure they do not have time to finish." He looked to the city, "as for those doomed souls who chose to be brave… well, if they do not surrender this instance we will overrun them with pure force and kill whoever remains. Then we will travel north as well." He looked over at Lockstan who just nodded his head in agreement. As he followed his commander toward the gates of the city he began to wonder where the General received his information. Perhaps he did not understand these Easterners as well as he let on.

Lockstan hesitated for a moment as he registered the last bit of the General's statement, he was a bit perplexed as to whether or not he literally meant this instant then said, "Sir are you ordering me to ready the men for attack now? We still have a large contingent coming through the pass and for those who are through they have no way in which to scale the walls, no towers or even ladders. It will take considerable time to station them all around the walls of a city this large"

Stragess said over his shoulder, "what I want you to do is have your Sergeants put their men in position so that those in the city can see our strength and our size, it could be enough to scare these would be heroes into surrendering, maybe we can save some time. If not…then we will set up for a proper attack and overrun them. As a matter of fact call up Morian and as many of her clan that are through the pass. Common people always fear wizards; let us see how they react when a group of war wizards are at their gates."

The large Captain agreed it to be an excellent move, a semi-bluff. If it worked they would not have to waste any time setting camp or preparing for an attack. If it did not work they only lost a few moments. He began ordering all the troops directly in front of the city so that the lines of troops would trail as far as they could see on the tower walls. In a real attack he would have men at every inch of the walls so that the defenders would have to guard every inch, but this was more for show; a show of force.

185

The General waited patiently for Lockstan to carry out his orders pondering the defender's tactics of lying to waste the countryside. He knew from reputation that Aliondrae was cunning, but he was truly surprised that she would go this far. It is something that he would do and he was impressed. After a time his small entourage, consisting of himself, Lockstan, and five war wizards were ready and as they made their way toward city gates he thought to himself, 'it is too bad really…I think I would liked a chance to have met such a woman.'

As he got closer he took a good look at the city. It was definitely well built and built for defense. Taking on this city defended with a well-trained army could be quite a formidable task and would take some time. His philosophy was that a siege was the last resort when taking a city and should only be considered when all other means were exhausted. It was costly and usually the city is destroyed along the way. That would not serve his purpose. He needed to keep his supply route open and having this city would allow just that. His study of the city brought his attention to the walls above the main gate. It was there that he noticed movement. It was not the hectic scrambling that he would have expected but merely two individuals speaking calmly, unfortunately they were too far away for him to hear.

....

Aliondrae looked at Perata and it was clear she was nervous. He understood this but still said, "Listen to me and listen well, it is important, now more than ever that you must not be intimidated, you must be the consummate portrait of strength. This is the first impression this army will see of their enemy and it I want it to be them that is nervous."

Aliondrae took a deep breath, put on her most regal appearance and announced, "I have spent my entire life in the court, and I have spoken to kings and queens. I think I know how to intimidate."

Perata looked out at the approaching group and replied, "That may be true, but remember the only person a king or a queen will ever bow to is a conquering general, so you can not just act superior, you must be superior. Remember this is your land, your city and your people." With that said he motioned to the area that Discere had previously enchanted for this moment, "Do not forget, it is you that must initiate the fight, we have to make an impression of strength.

Aliondrae took one last look at Perata who radiated calm while she felt nothing but fear. Concentrating on his last words, she made her way to base. This was indeed her city and the thought of anyone believing differently began to turn her fear to anger and her anger slowly turned to rage. The Countess then faced her uninvited guests and waited for them to speak.

Stragess was shocked a second time today when he realized that one of the persons on the wall was a woman, a very regal looking woman. He wondered if this could be the same individual of whom he was just thinking. The women did not preclude him from noticing the large man dressed all in black standing behind her. His size and the way the sun was positioned cast a shadow over the woman. Stragess was not sure how these two individuals played into the situation but he would make it a point to find out. During the planning stage of this invasion the General had gathered as much knowledge of all the key individuals of Arxsolum from Count Edward down. It was possible that the woman could indeed be the Countess Aliondrae, but he knew nothing of the man in black. 'Only one way to find out,' he thought and then yelled up, "I am looking for the person in charge to discuss terms of your surrender."

Aliondrae nonchalantly took a sip of her tea and said in icy voice, "I am Aliondrae Desenya, this is my city and you General Stragess...by bringing your little army into my land are committing an act of war. Remove your men from this land and then maybe I will discuss the terms of your surrender. Refuse and each and every one of your soldiers who do not comply will be hunted down and killed." Her words, due to Discere's magic, were clearly heard by not only Stragess and his group but by his entire army. She did not yell or scream, but merely stated those words in a conversational tone, which seemed to add to its credibility.

Stragess, based upon the their actions so far, expected some sort of delaying tactic, but he was slightly irritated at her words, her attitude, and her ability to let his men hear her words. He turned to his mage Morian and demanded, "Use your magic and enhance my voice like she is doing."

Morian consulted with the other mages taking more time then Stragess liked. "Morian," he growled and was rewarded when she responded, "my lord, we don't know how she is doing that. It is clearly some obscure spell but we have never encountered it, nor do we know how to duplicate it."

His irritation was beginning to grow and he returned his attention to figure on the wall and projected his voice in the way only a commander could, "My lady, I am impressed by your facade; unfortunately I am going to have to call your bluff. Regrettably for you, I happen to know your husband and his armies are to the north and that your city is undefended…so lose the theatrics. I am willing to give you a chance to spare anyone from dying today and spare your city as well."

Stragess felt that his offer should have quite an impact, but the woman on the wall did not seem fazed even the slightest. He was not even sure if this was indeed Aliondrae; at this point he would not be surprised if she was a decoy, but decoy or not her attitude was really unsettling the General.

The Countess looked down at Stragess and said with very little emotion. "General, I am not accustomed to repeating myself nor will I make a habit of it. So listen closely, remove your men from my presence and my land immediately, noncompliance will be construed as an act of war and my hand will be forced."

After the sheer annoyance of clearing the pass and the amount of soldiers lost on the way through he was growing weary of this women's blatant disrespect. He tried one last time to make himself clear, "Perhaps you do not understand me, if you try my patience I will destroy this city, If you test my resolve I will destroy your citizens, If you trifle with me I will destroy everything you hold dear, but princess, If you do not say the words I want to hear I will I will make you my personal slave and destroy you ever so slowly. Do not play with me for as I have said before I know that your husband…"

Aliondrae cut him off, "yes, yes, yes, you are right my husband and his army are in the north," she put an inflection on the last part and then paused slightly lowering her voice, "however it is not his army that you should be concerned with for it is not his army that defends these walls and we General Stragess…" She stared directly at him as any trace of civility drained from her face, "are now at war." Her voice turned to a roar, "kill them, kill them all."

Her signal rang throughout the keep, and at that moment hundreds of the city's defenders, who had been hiding behind the wall made their presence known, a large black flag unfurled over a city and Discere launched his disruption spells.

Stragess felt his mind race as he realized his position and screamed to his mages, "Shields, shields damn you." He saw the hesitation and confusion on his wizard's faces when they did not do as ordered. Realizing that something was wrong he ducked low on his mount and began a frantic retreat. He felt the shadow first as the shear number of missiles aimed at him blocked out the sunlight and then watched in horror as he saw several of his wizards fall. He knew that their shields should have stopped the majority of arrows, but something was hindering their magic. It was a true demonstration of power by Morian that any of the arrows were blocked at all and pure luck that both Lockstan and Stragess were not killed instantly. He felt a sting in his leg and knew that he was hit the same moment his mount pitched forward sending him flying. He hit the ground rolling and continued his mad dash to safety.

Lockstan faired slightly better primarily because every archer on wall seemed to be targeting the General and his wizards. He could not believe it, officers and wizards targeted as if they were nothing more than common dregs, it went against the rules of war. He looked back and saw that the wizards that were supposed to keep the General safe all lay dead, including Morian. With a growl he vowed to himself, "these people are savages and need to be destroyed."

In all the confusion he barely noticed that many of the less disciplined Sergeants signaled their men to attack. He watched helplessly as a large force of the army surged forward like men possessed. It was only a small consolation to note that his personal units stayed in their ranks and that they would stay until ordered differently. It all happened in an instant; those advancing men were doomed. "You fools," Lockstan screamed, realizing that Arxsolum must have been preparing for months for this moment; there seemed to be pitfalls every step of the way. Those that stayed behind watched quietly as the archers on the walls cut men to pieces as the spiked pits forced them into designated routes. Those on horseback, in an attempt to avoid the pits, trampled those on foot. Large projectiles seem to appear out of nowhere as every catapult, ballista and engineered weapon fired upon the invaders at will. The whole scene was one of chaos. It was only the battle frenzy and confusion that kept men surging forward amidst the shadow of death that was engulfing the lot.

Stragess grabbed Lockstan, who noticed the General was looking very pale, "Call them back, call them back now!" His voice was very strained and he looked as though he was terribly ill.

Lockstan had already signaled the retreat but he knew the damage was done and that few would make it back alive. He could only watch helplessly as men were dying in countless numbers. His only thought was wondering where this army came from. Perhaps the General was wrong again, but the woman had said Arxsolum's army was away in the north. What did it all mean;

was it all misinformation. He definitely would not put it past anyone that would attack without following the formal rules of engagement. He cursed the witch who called herself Aliondrae. His attention was turned back to his General upon hearing him gasping. "Sir, what is wrong? Are you hit?"

Stragess still holding his leg was actually impressed again, it seemed that these defenders would go to greater lengths than he imagined to win this battle. He grabbed his second in command, "find the healers let them know that the arrows are poisoned," he laughed nearly choking, "I can not believe it, it was all a trap, we did exactly like she wanted...she played me like a fool." He was beginning to lose consciousness but in his last words he uttered, "Lockstan, nothing is as it seems, believe nothing you see." His eyes closed as he silently called, "Caellestus?"

Lockstan had no idea what he meant but it was time to do things his way. The healers began tending to the General so it was time to regain control of his army.

Chapter Twenty:
Dissention in the Ranks

Sorcia watched the onslaught from her vantage point in the mountains; she felt strange, almost ashamed and quickly closed her eyes. She knew that she should not be so remorseful about the death of all these people because they brought it upon themselves, yet it did not seem right. Ever since she took the scout's life, she was fearful. It had never occurred to how easy it was for a person to die or how easy it was to kill. Now that the war had actually begun she was nervous for her friends and her family for they too were fragile. The realization was really beginning to weigh upon her and she opened her eyes in an effort to get those thoughts out of her head; she had to focus on why they were doing this. Her attention returned to the battle. Perata's plan worked to a far greater degree than she could have ever imagined and she just watched in awe the killing machine called Arxsolum. Perata was right about the first strike being the most crucial; they would never again see such a one-sided battle. The invading army was in complete disarray, a handful of their wizards were dead, their General seemed to be wounded, and they had no clue about the army that defended this city. She steeled her heart for now it was time for the second stage of their assignment; they would go on the offensive.

"Phillos, Tonagal," She questioned, "are you ready?" She knew she did not need to ask. The two men were already dressed in uniforms that once belonged to soldiers from the disarrayed army. It was there mission to plant the poisoned food and drink into the food stores, using the confusion and their own confidence as cover. All agreed that Phillos and Tonagal would be best suited for such an assignment. They both seemed comfortable, almost eager to do it. With quick good byes, they started off.

The two men made their way to areas that they previously marked. One contained the food supply and the other contained their store of water. With the retreat in full swing it was easy to shuffle into the mix. No one questioned why either carried what they did, because they did not try to hide it and they walked as if they had a purpose. It was a game both of these men had played before but this was much easier than either anticipated. The sheer chaos in the camp was unbelievable. The wounded seemed to be dropping dead right and left as the poisoned arrows began exacting their toll. Men were not obeying orders and in-fighting starting to begin.

Arriving at their destination, the two men planted their wares without anyone being wiser, now they just had to make their way out of camp. The man who they knew to be second in command momentarily blocked the initial escape route. He was barking orders at a group of Sergeants and his face was livid with anger. "You will get your men under control immediately or I will run you through myself."

One Sergeant had the audacity to question the order and was pleading, "but the men are scared this whole place is cursed and..."

The man did not have a chance to finish his sentence as Lockstan's sword entered his throat. The man died with a look of confusion on his face, but for the others who witnessed it there was no confusion; the message was loud and clear. "You have until dusk to stay your men then we meet in the command tent for your orders."

Lockstan knew that it was dire to regain control. Fear was spreading like a disease and needed to be stopped before it destroyed them all. "If they want fear I will give them fear."

He turned to his personal troops; they were all composed and awaiting orders. Their discipline and having seen enough carnage in their lifetime kept them from falling apart at the first sign of trouble. "Take your squads, split up, find any who are causing dissent and eliminate them. Get the rest of our army back to their tents and make sure those in charge are doing as they say. If not then you replace that man. If you need to make an example then make sure it is thoroughly understood." He eyed all of his men, "Are there any questions about this?"

It was clear that the men grasped their mission; the only question that did arise was whether or not they should retrieve their dead and wounded. Lockstan thought for less than a moment and then said, "No, let them rot, the stink will annoy those in the city and perhaps be a warning for those who do not wait for orders. In fact I want all the wounded who made it back separated to one area, with what we have seen so far many will not make it, for those who become a liability, kill them." Lockstan was in full damage control mode. "Also for those men whose squads were destroyed," he looked around at the lost look of many of the men in the camp, "make sure they are reassigned and any trace of the old squadrons, such as tents, standards, whatever…have them removed." As no more questions came in and he could not think of anything else that would be of immediate help he just said, "Go."

He himself was also going do what he could to restore discipline. The rumors of this 'curse' bothered him. Moral was one of the most important things an army could have next to discipline. He had to seek out the rumormongers and quiet them. It was his desire to just kill all of the weak links he had in the army, but then there would not be much of an army left. He would just have to make them more afraid of disobeying him than of attacking that damned city. 'A couple of days and a few examples should be enough to reign in even the most skittish of troops.' Even though he was not sure if he even cared whether the General lived or died, he would be damned before letting him awaken to find the troops out of control.

Both Phillos and Tonagal knew better than to be standing there when the meeting was over for neither wanted to be made example of. "We best be getting out of here before it is too late, I really don't want to be reassigned." Phillos stressed the last word and then said more to himself, "Or do I?" His mind was working fast; he could cause a lot of trouble, more trouble if he were in the middle of it all.

Tonagal caught on to what he was thinking, "Phillos my friend, that is a death sentence, at least out there," he pointed to the mountains, "we have the advantage, we have a chance."

Phillos had a crazy gleam in eye when he turned to the former thief, "Don't you see, I can easily slide right into one of these units, I can just tell them I have been reassigned. I will just say I have been instructed not to talk about my old unit."

Tonagal was shaking his head, "I just don't know; the team is not going to like it. We need to follow the plan."

"This is following the plan. You remember what Perata said, when you strike them where they think they are safe then their own imaginations will begin to work against them. They will cripple themselves in an effort to make sure it won't happen again. They will build safeguards to keep others out, but I will be hidden in the last place they would ever look." Phillos took a deep breath and then changed his tone, "I have done a lot of bad things in my life, I have a chance now, here in this place, to atone for those sins. It is as if my entire life were nothing more than training for this moment."

Tonagal was shaking his head no, "I understand your passion, but you are not thinking this through. What about food? You know you can't eat or drink anything. That would be placing your self at risk."

"You are right, you are right," whispered the assassin, "one day then, two at the most, then I will hightail it out of here and join you."

Tonagal knew arguing was pointless and the more he thought about it the more he agreed that the assassin could really cause some stress from within. "All right then, I will inform the rest." He then turned and headed for the fastest way out of this camp.

He did not bother to wish Phillos good luck, luck was nothing more than the extent of someone's skill and that man had plenty of it.

The wily assassin watched him go; now all he had to do was 'reassign' himself. He figured his best bet was to find a unit with new leadership, someone who would not question too much. As he was thinking he watched as some of Lockstan's personal troops hacked a man to pieces. "This is the one," he thought, "this will work." He laid low until a new sergeant was appointed and then just waited until dark. He was amazed at the efficiency, if not the brutality, of the tactics Lockstan used to regain order. By the end of the night the camp was a paragon of discipline, including the mercenaries. It was evident that all men were now part of Lockstan's new army whether they liked it or not and the majority of dissidents were quickly removed. Their disappearance was more than enough motivation for others with similar thoughts to keep them to themselves. The rest of the men stopped thinking about what happened on the battlefield and began responding to the more immediate danger; Lockstan.

Once the sun went down Phillos approached the new sergeant who was taking his new post very seriously. He was personally making sure that all of his men knew how things would operate from here on out. "Sergeant, I was told to report to you for my assignment."

Dalin studied this new man and seemed satisfied. He then questioned, "Name and old unit?"

"Phillos is my name, but I was told that my old unit was not to be mentioned and the only unit I needed to be concerned about was yours."

The Sergeant understood perfectly, the higher-ups did not want any old loyalties. He also liked the sound of 'your unit.' "Listen up; the duty roster has already been posted for this evening so you get a free night." He used his most authoritative voice and continued, "A new one will be posted daily, that means you will check it daily. You will also follow my orders to a tee or you will be joining your old unit, if you get my meaning." The Sergeant was pretty pleased with what he thought was a very clever threat. "Do you understand what is expected of you?"

Phillos responded with a resounding "Yes Sir!"

Dalin then instructed, "Now report to Corporal Cassida over there for your billeting. Then get some food, your going to need all your strength tomorrow."

Phillos went through with his instructions, feeling pretty good knowing he was not going to have to stand any sort of duty tonight. He could use that time for more important things. He cast a sidelong glance at the food storage wagons and wondered how long it would take for anyone to notice some of the food was bad. He could not take the chance of eating or drinking anything he did not bring with him so he would need to be about his business quickly. Again he was amazed as he looked around and noticed all the regiments were now aligned in similar fashion as Lockstan's troops; a vast difference from a day ago. He thought with a smile, "Well we will see how much stress this new discipline can take."

While Phillos made up his bedroll he over heard two soldiers talking in raised voices about their new Corporal. "I can not believe Cassida was promoted above me," said the first, "he is not half the soldier I am."

"Well," returned the second, "After the untimely demise of sergeant Shanu, Dalin moved into his place and he promoted his friends under him. I do not think he had much time to weigh his choices."

The first soldier was still seething with anger and nearly shouted, "If that is the case then maybe we just need the untimely demise of our new corporal."

The second soldier looked around at the other soldiers around the camp and then over to him, "I realize you are just venting, but you might be careful not to say such things in the light of all that has happened. People have been disappearing right and left for much less. Maybe you should just get some sleep; you will feel better about it in the morning."

The first soldier said something unintelligible and headed toward his sleeping area. Phillos marked where the man slept, a plan forming in his mind, it was not much but he would be able to exploit it.

As night overtook the camp, the patient Phillos waited for the majority of the camp to succumb to sleep. He watched the soldier on duty make his rounds, which predominately took him away from the billeting area, which Phillos was thankful for. He would have more than enough time to do what needed to be done.

Quiet as shadow he stole out of his bedroll and headed to where the angry soldier slept. He figured if anyone questioned why he was up he would tell him or her he was relieving himself, but since no one even stirred such a deception was not necessary. Upon arriving at the sleeping man he was pleased to note that he took his armaments off as he slept and Phillos felt that at least the first part would be easy. He reached out and found the man's dagger and removed it from its sheath. Then found the other man involved in the pseudo- argument and ran the blade of the dagger across the neck of the sleeping soldier. There was no noise, not even a whisper as the man's life was taken. As calmly as he murdered the man he just as calmly made his way to his second victim, Corporal Cassida himself. He slept slightly away from the others so Phillos would have his privacy, but he did not like the distance he had to travel in order to get there.

His fears were well founded for the sentry happened by at that precise moment. Even though Phillos's heart raced faster than normal, his mind worked even faster. He knew the man seen him and could cause problems in the morning, which meant he had to act casual or else the man might become suspicious. "I have been looking for you; I have something to give you from Sergeant Dalin."

Upon hearing the Sergeant's name the sentry quickly came over, "Well, what is it?" The sentry was nervously expectant, not real sure about what was going on but not wanting to get in trouble.

"It is a dagger," returned Phillos showing him the bloody dagger he had just used to kill the other soldier.

"What is that on the blade, it almost looks like blood?"

"It is blood," Phillos said nonchalantly to the confused sentry, "which is why I need to give it to you."

The matter of fact tone in Phillos's voice made the sentry instinctively raise his hand as if to receive the dagger and he did not react when the assassin expertly reversed the blade and plunged it in the unsuspecting man's heart. The guard did not even have a chance to raise an alarm. He only looked at his killer trying to voice one question; why?

Phillos felt no remorse for the man's death; he was in the wrong place at the wrong time and could have ruined everything. He then dragged the sentry all the way to where Cassida slept being real careful not to awaken the sleeping Corporal. Normally he would not have much difficulty approaching quietly, but it was not as simple with a dead man in tow.

Finding the man still fast asleep, Phillos made sure that he would never awaken again. He glanced at the sky and could tell that dawn was fast approaching and still he had to clean up and return the dagger to its owner. He took careful consideration in removing all traces of blood from his own body but let it remain on the dagger. He also soaked a small piece of cloth in the Corporal's blood.

The next stage of his plan was to get back to the area where he stole the dagger without incident and leave some evidence on the man without waking him. Replacing the dagger in its sheath went smoothly as did placing the bloody cloth into the sleeping man's hand. He watched for several seconds as the cloth brushed across the man's belongings. 'That should be enough to make for an interesting morning,' thought the assassin as he quickly removed the cloth and headed to his own bedroll. Before he went to sleep he double-checked to make sure that all traces of his little adventure were taken care of. He then closed his eyes, satisfied with his day's work and quickly fell asleep.

He was already awake when he heard the commotion. It seemed sergeant Dalin and his men were questioning others about whether or not they heard or saw anything. When they asked Phillos, the only thing he could think of was that he heard an argument and that someone threatened the Corporal's life, but he never saw a face. Others quickly corroborated this story and eventually faces were put to the argument.

"Sergeant, we found one dead and we have the other in custody" reported the soldier and then with a satisfied tone added, "We also found this." He handed the dagger to Dalin, "the blood is still fresh."

The Sergeant stared at the dagger and then turned quickly to his soldier, "I need him alive and I want him now. We have to take care of this before word gets out…"

He was interrupted by one of his men getting his attention "sir," he said while looking off across the camp. Dalin followed his gaze and swore. Lockstan and a group of his guards were heading this way. "Get me that man now!!"

Chapter Twenty-one:
The Best Laid Plans
are Plans Unmade

The devious assassin watched as the confused man was brought before the Sergeant; Dalin recognized him immediately and had known him to be a hothead. He had actually thought of promoting him to Corporal before this little stunt. The blood smattered all over his clothes was noticeable about the same time the Captain was arriving. It was pretty clear to Dalin that he was looking at the culprit and he was well aware of what Lockstan did to those who could not keep order. It was in his best interest to end this incident before things could get much worse. He called his troops to attention then pulled out his sword.

The innocent man stood in front of him still not comprehending what was going on and pleaded, "No, no, please…" the rest of what he was going to say was lost along with his head.

Lockstan saw the interaction and commanded, "Report."

Dalin snapped to attention and replied, "sir, there was an altercation…this man killed two others along with the sentry on duty. I was dispensing justice."

Lockstan's head ached but he was in a fairly amicable mood. He knew that there would initially be squabbling in the newly formed units; he was not concerned with that. He was far more concerned with how they were handled. In this situation he liked what he saw. The punishment was swift and it was seen by all.

"You say he killed three men in an altercation, maybe we could have found a different sort of punishment for a man that useful."

Dalin had to justify his actions, "Sir, he did not face them in combat; he killed them in their sleep. The sentry was killed when he tried to intervene. I have already doubled the watch so that this will not happen again and everyone in my unit understands the consequences."

Lockstan approved of what he saw when he studied the man before him. He needed more men like him in this army. "Killed them in their sleep? Cowardly dog, I expect you did the right thing and I also expect that this sort of thing will not be happening again."

"No sir!" was all he could reply

The Captain had much more important things to worry about other than this, "Carry on."

Dalin stayed at attention until the Captain was out of sight. He could not believe his luck; he thought for sure his career was finished the day after it began. "It seems I will need to be more cautious so that something like that does not happen again." He looked around at his troops. There were had a large number of men he did not recognize due to the assimilation of other units. He could see by the looks on their faces that they were distrustful of each other. The last thing he wanted was his unit to become divided. Unfortunately his unit was tasked with finding as much building material and useful resources as they could muster. He worried about breaking them up but felt the impression he made with the manner in which he disposed of the troublemaker should be enough that it would keep them in line for some time. "At ease men, as some of you may know it is our mission to gather materials. Another unit will be going back through the pass to bring up any remaining supplies and large lumber. We are looking for two things, boulders no bigger than one man can carry and no smaller than your heads. Luckily for us those will be easy to find. What will not be so easy to find is wood necessary to make long ladders. For this we will need men to forage into the mountains and bring back as much useful wood as possible. When I say useful, it needs to be tall, strong wood. This means climbing, a lot of climbing so I want only men suitable to the task. In all honesty I do not know where even to begin to look, but you will look and you will find what we need. I will assign you into squads and each squad will have a leader. This part is most important, if I hear that there was even the slightest bit of belligerence from anyone that man will lose his head. Do I make myself clear?"

The unit responded in a uniform "yes sir." Phillos wanted to make sure he was assigned to the unit that would leave the camp, the less people the better. He also did not want to haul boulders all day. "Sir, if it would help I noticed a nice grove of pine trees early through the pass. I did not take a clear measure of how much but I believe it would be well suited for our needs." He then waited hoping the Sergeant would take the bait.

Dalin looked at the man who spoke up, he remembered him joining last night but he could not recall his name. He did not want to appear uninformed in front of his men so he just went with it, "all right, you will be the leader," he pointed to Phillos, "take the ten closest men to you and grab whatever tools you need and start out. Do not fail in this. The rest of you get moving on those boulders."

Phillos was feeling pretty good with himself; he managed to take out four people and create a mood of distrust and somehow got promoted in the process. Now all he had to do was make sure no wood was gathered. Hoping that Sorcia and the others would be where he thought he gathered the men and tools and quickly headed that direction.

As they began traveling north instead of into the pass one of his crew questioned, "Where are we heading? Did you not say you saw this grove while you were heading through the pass and if that is the case should we not be heading that direction?"

Phillos stopped the entire squad and faced them. "I did see the trees while we were heading through the pass, however I do not think I can scale cliffs and I certainly cannot fly. That means that we need to somehow gain altitude. Now, I have a feeling that we can make our way over here and hopefully the terrain will be passable enough for us. I am guessing it will be difficult but who knows we may even get lucky and find a closer grove. That is unless of course someone has a better idea?" He knew no one would argue his logic because they all saw how steep the walls of the pass were and none of them would be able to ascend them.

He took their silence for acquiescence and started them out again, making a show of trying to find trails and passable areas even though he knew this landscape like the back of his hand. The ruse was to avoid suspicion, plus he needed time so that his friends could spot him. He did not have an actual plan to speak of but felt confident that when the opportunity presented itself he would be ready. After about half a day's trek they started to notice scattered trees here and there. Phillos knew that sooner or later they would be satisfied with these and not go any deeper. It seemed he was running out of time.

The only thing Phillos could do was to offer a suggestion that might stall them awhile longer, "all right gentlemen, I think this is a good a place as any to take a break. We have a lot of work ahead of us and we need our strength."

No one argued the point and they all made themselves comfortable, while Phillos listened for any sign of his friends. He needed to figure out exactly what it was he wanted to do with these men. He could not take them all no matter how much surprise he had, but he had to do something. They were already looking around at the trees deciding which ones to cut. The only option he could think of was to separate them and take them in small groups. Then he heard it; a shrill whistle that sounded like any other bird in the region, but he knew better. His friends were out there and it seems they were waiting for him. He stood up, "the trees look fairly good here, but I am going to scout ahead a bit to see if there aren't some easier trees to cut. I don't know about you but I am looking to make this as effortless as possible."

As he started to walk in the direction he heard the bird call one of the men said, "Hold up, I go with you."

Wanting to make contact with his friends alone, he did not want this man with him but he could not afford to arouse their suspicions. The more he thought about it the more hc like the idea. He could easily dispatch one guy whenever he wanted. He stopped to wait for the man and said in elated voice, "even better."

Phillos waited until he was out of earshot from the rest of the group before he slid his dagger from its sheath. He said to the man walking next to him as he extended his hand in greeting, "I just realized I don't even know your name. I am called Phillos."

The man automatically put his hand out in response and started to say, "I am…" but the dagger stuck through his ribs made it difficult to finish. Phillos had a knack for hitting the heart through the gap in a man's ribcage. He saw movement to his left but was not worried when he saw Lexis come into view followed by Marhran. They both seemed genuinely glad to see him. Lexis took a look at the dead soldier then gave Phillos a sly grin, "we weren't quite sure what your plans were so we just ghosted you when you entered the mountains, once you stopped we figured we would let our presence be known."

He smiled back at her and responded, "Well…truth be told, I did not know what my plan was either. I must say I am shocked that you have been on us for that long, you are getting rather good but I must say I am glad for it."

Lexis only nodded her head so Marhran who had been silent decided to speak up, "once Tonagal told us what you were doing we couldn't stop Lexis. Since she was going I figured I would tag along as did Tonagal." He stopped, feeling a little awkward when no one responded. In an effort to end the silence he continued on, "What is our plan anyway, are we waiting for the others?"

At those last words he removed his gaze from Lexis, "the others?" he questioned, "Are they coming here?"

Lexis answered with a dangerous gleam in her eye, "Tonagal left the moment we spotted you guessing that we could use their help. I on the other hand don't really think we need 'em, we could probably handle this ourselves. In fact why don't you go back and ask a couple of them to give you a hand. Me and the giant over here will do the rest."

At that moment the rest of the unit strolled up and Sorcia answered. "Actually that is an excellent idea. What is not an excellent idea is showing the enemy the trails that we use and leading them toward our camp. I guess what I would like to know is what you were thinking, not only with leading them here but with your crazy idea of staying with them. That was not part of the plan."

Phillos took a good look at Sorcia who seemed to have matured. She no longer looked like a child and she was all business. He did not like the tone in her voice especially after the sacrifice he was making for the greater good. "It is good to see you as well your highness. As for what I was thinking…I was improvising. I believe it is our mission to disrupt the enemy and I am doing what I can. Last night I was able to remove four without raising any suspicions and this lot is not expected back until tomorrow so we create opportunity."

Sorcia heard the inflection he used on the title and realized she may have come across in a confrontational tone. She took a deep breath and steadied her words, "When we started this we determined all plans would be based on group decisions. I realize that you are doing what you can to make a difference, but I am asking you that in the future you do not do so at the risk of your life."

Phillos understood that her experience with the scouts changed her way of thinking and that she was concerned; she would make a good leader yet. "Sorcia, this whole operation is a risk to our lives; we need to take any advantage when we can. I cannot promise that I will not act in a similar fashion in the future, but I can promise I will give you a chance to talk me out of it if you can. Fair enough?"

Sorcia reluctantly nodded her head in agreement; she was indeed concerned and believed that the responsibility of these individuals rested on her shoulders; any wrong decision could end badly. "Fair enough, so what should we do with your friends in the glade?"

"Just as Lex said, I will separate them up and we can take them out individually."

Sorcia waited for everyone's agreement then added, "Rammel, you and Tonagal circle around in case they sound alarm, cut off their retreat. Marhran you stay up there in case anyone gets through. Lex and I will wait over here to set the trap and Phillos, good job." She added the last with a wink knowing that any damage they could do was good. She had remembered something Perata said about being cautious, but never to the point of paralysis. She watched Phillos walk away making as much noise as he believed a soldier would. She knew it was unnatural for him and actually laughed to herself. She then readied her bow and waited.

It did not take long before she heard the assassin's familiar voice say, "It is right over here, we just need a hand moving it."

She had no idea what type of story he concocted to get them to follow but it seemed to be working. She made a hand gesture to Lexis letting her know she would take the one on the left. They were well within bow range so she gave the signal. In one motion the two women spun from where they were hiding and launched their attack. Each hit their mark and was readying their second volley, but neither had the chance to fire because Phillos finished them off.

"All you could bring was two?" questioned Lexis in a half serious manner. She had the lust for blood and was not satisfied by merely shooting from a distance.

Phillos understood her desire; he had been just like her when first started in his profession. "Well, it just so happens there are seven more back in the glade. I think it may get a little suspicious if I invited more of them to lend a hand....so I figured we take what we can get."

Sorcia breathed out a sigh, "Do you actually have a plan or are you improvising again? It is just us three unless you want to call the others back."

"No," replied Phillos, "I think we should be fine if you two just communicate who you will be taking out. I will walk into camp and can take two before anyone is aware. Add in your two and we have even odds. What do you think?"

"I think there has to be a safer way, maybe it would be better for me to use my magic to subdue…"

Lexis quickly cut her off, "No we take them now, we have the element of surprise."

"I agree," added Phillos with a knowing look toward her.

Sorcia hated being outvoted, "OK, but we will be careful… oh and Phillos this time try not to go right where I am firing my arrows."

The two women quickly stationed themselves in an area that afforded them clear shots. They watched as the assassin nonchalantly walked back into the glade. A couple of men looked up as he entered but other than that they seemed relaxed. He pulled out his sword as if he was examining it and said something to one of the men. The man took the sword to get a clearer look at it as well and called over one of his friends. After a brief debate the weapon was handed back to the owner. Phillos grasped the pommel and then struck with blinding speed. Both men were dead before they hit the ground. The two women took that as the sign and unleashed a deadly barrage of arrows toward their intended victims as Phillos engaged a third man.

One of the soldiers reacted quicker to the attack than anticipated and immediately recognized that he was set up. He left his gear and sprinted as fast as he could, not caring where he was headed as long as it was away. A couple of arrows whipped past him but none found their mark. He believed that once he gained a lead no one would catch him, but he needed to know if he was being followed. His head turned to look and saw nothing a feeling of relief came over him; with his speed safety was only a matter of time. Something large sprung out from behind a tree and seized his head. The man's upper body was stopped cold, but momentum kept his lower body moving resulting in a near somersault.

Marhran kept his one hand over the man's mouth and slid the other to the back of his head. Using his massive strength, he twisted until he heard a distinct crack. The giant of a man released the now dead soldier and quickly turned as he heard another person running in his direction. He relaxed as he saw Sorcia. "Hey," he said in his quiet voice, "you all right?"

Sorcia un-notched her bow looking at the heap that was her quarry, "I'm fine, you?"

"Fine, will there be others coming this way?"

"No, when I left to follow this one," she stated pointing to the dead soldier, "Phillos and Lexis had the remaining soldier surrounded, so we can safely assume he did not last long."

The two made there way back to the soldiers impromptu camp and found that Rammel and Tonagal had arrived upon hearing the skirmish. Rammel seemed a little disheartened that he was unable to participate, but was in good spirits. Sorcia shifted her gaze to the rest of her unit, realizing just how deadly a bunch they had become. "Well, let's go do what we do."

Chapter Twenty-two:
Forging a Leader

Aliondrae grip loosened on her bow as she looked across the once beautiful landscape; it was littered with corpses of the enemy. She could hear her people cheering but it seemed distant, almost foreign. Her heart was pounding so loudly that it was drowning out everything else. Her only thought was that they had won, they had defeated these invaders easily; none of them even came close to the walls. Three months of stress, apprehension and fear culminated in this short period of time. It did not seem real; it could not be real, she desired to feel the jubilation that she knew she should.

Her gaze came to rest on Perata, who was watching the retreat with interest; he never seemed nervous, scared, or for that matter happy. If she did not know better she would swear he had no emotions; that he was not human, but she did know better, they had become close in these last couple weeks as close as two people could become. Even though she loved him more than any man in the world, she knew in her heart that it would never work. He was not destined to stay; not content to become a husband. He was meant for something more, perhaps greatness, whatever that may be, but she knew it did not include her and it was not going to be in Arxsolum.

Aliondrae flinched inwardly as Perata turned and met her stare. More than once she wondered if this man could read her thoughts. He was first to break the silence "Now begins the hard part, you need to get your people to rest. The next attack will not be like this."

Aliondrae did not hide her confusion, "Next attack? But we won…they lost so many men and the rest are running away. We have defeated them"

"They are not running away, they are retreating, and only those that did attack. Their army is far greater than the number we saw here today and they will come." Perata was not lecturing he was just saying it how it was. "You and your people did great things today. We have dealt them a painful blow but the battle has yet to begin and now you must ready them for the siege." He grabbed both her shoulders in his hands and then emphasized his word, "no matter what happens you must act as if you expected it to happen. The most important thing now is keeping their hope alive, keeping the possibility of victory within their sights. They must always feel as if they have a chance to win."

These words crushed her as she was emotionally drained, she grasped for any chance that he was wrong, "Do you really think that they will come back…I know that Stragess was hit, I saw him being dragged away, from what Discere said even a small hit from those poisoned arrows should kill a man. And the wizards, look at all those spell casters," she pointed to the main road where Stragess and his party demanded their surrender. Perata could see a host of black robed bodies lying dead. She continued, "They lost today and they lost badly. You told us that if we could take away their leadership and their magical advantage that we could win this battle." Aliondrae fought back her tears, "we did that today, we cut them to pieces and now you are telling me it is not enough."

Perata understood her pain; he knew that she did not revel in killing men. She did not want war; she did not want to see suffering; she only wanted peace and safety for her people. What she did, what her people did today was a test of the human spirit and yet it was only the beginning. He did not try to sugar coat his response or attempt to comfort her, it was necessary that he did not. This was a crucial moment; he needed to forge her into a leader and that meant constantly pushing her limits. If she broke now then this city was lost, but if she could find the strength, the courage to endure then hope remained.

"Yes, I did tell you that in order to win this battle that we needed to take away their leadership and their wizards, however," he emphasized, "I did not tell you that was all that was needed. Open your eyes Countess; we have spent three months training civilians not just to fire a bow but how to fight a war. They have done countless hours of close combat drills. They cleared miles of forest and flushed away all the game. They have basically cannibalized their own city and to what end? Why do you think we did that?" Even though he paused for a response he proceeded to answer it himself. "We did it to prepare for a war, which means that the enemy will breach these walls and they will engage your people in battle. You need to listen to what I say and not hear what you want to hear. For example, I believe I told you not one minute ago that the most important thing you can do now is act as if everything that is going to happen is because you planned it to happen. Breaking down and crying now because you do not want the invaders to come back is not the best way to demonstrate that." Perata's voice turned even colder than usual, if that was possible. "Know this Countess, if you break, this city breaks. So it is time you prepare your people, prepare them for the stench of decaying bodies, prepare them for the dread of waiting, prepare them for weeks of hardship and suffering; prepare them Countess, for a siege." With that he turned his back and walked away.

Stunned, Aliondrae stood there like she was just slapped in the face. It was difficult for her to catch her breath. She wanted nothing more than to lie down and cry because it felt that the one person she could lean on just abandoned her. Her head was swimming, she needed support but there was no one or nothing she could hang on to. She thought to herself how easy it would be to just give up, leave these people to their fate, and allow them to fend for themselves. Why not, why should she make these horrible decisions for people, who was she? Her eyes were closed and she was immersed in complete darkness. The only sound she could hear was a welcoming voice repeating those same questions over and over. She did not have an answer. Her body began to give in to the darkness trying to find some peace. It was almost in her grasp except for a defiant single voice that seemed a league away. She could not make it out. It was not asking questions like the one drawing her down but it seemed it was answering them. As annoying as it was, she, for some unexplained reason wanted to hear those answers, but the voice was distant; too distant. If she wanted to hear she was going to have to go back, she would not be able to rest, because if she went any further she would never find the answers. She stopped her descent and focused on the voice. It was her only beacon and it was familiar. Her desire was growing and she desperately wanted to understand the words. She concentrated harder all the while trying to place where she had heard it before. It was getting closer now and she knew it to be a woman's voice. It was repeating something; it was still quiet but it was a strong voice, a bold voice. She centered her entire being on that voice, that voice belonged to someone that could tell her what she needed to do, someone who could lead her. She started to make out the words, "I can not lie down, I will not rest, I make the decisions for these people for they are my people. I am Aliondrae." Realization crashed around her like an avalanche, she stumbled in order regain her balance, she looked around and saw Perata walking away, she saw the carnage outside her walls, she could hear the cheers of her people, but most importantly she could hear own words repeating over and over. She was Aliondrae, these were her people and she knew now that she would not lie down, not now, not ever.

Gryffyn witnessed the exchange between Perata and the Countess even if he did not hear the words. He had been around far too long and trained too many soldiers to not realize what Perata was doing. He did not envy his task; in fact he realized he could not do it, he would not be able to set aside his protective instincts. He knew that she was a good leader, very compassionate, very intelligent and very strong but what Perata was doing, if successful would make her a great leader. If he failed he would ruin her and Arxsolum along the way. As he approached he saw Aliondrae's face drained of blood, she was saying something but he could not make it out. She looked as though she would pass out at any moment. "She is not strong enough for this, not for this" he thought to himself as he rushed forward to catch her from falling. His gesture became unnecessary when her eyes snapped open; she did stumble slightly but regained her bearing quickly. She turned toward him as he approached and said, "Gryffyn, we had a great victory today, largely in part to your training of the people, so far we have done exactly what we needed but it is a long road that we travel and we must ready ourselves for what comes next."

Gryffyn paused for he did not expect those words, "my lady, are you all right? I saw you stumble"

She thought about his words for a moment, "sometimes the stumble is the only thing that will prevent the fall, and yes I am all right. As right as I can be in this situation." She gave him a confident smile, "make sure all supplies are restocked, such as arrows and bows if necessary. Get the catapults loaded so that we can be firing at a moment's notice…and Gryffyn let the people have their moment but not for too long. The enemy is in disorder now but they will be back and our people will need to be kept informed. Keep a force on the walls but have all others assemble in the Hall tonight at suppertime. I would also like a moment with you, Jaxen, Discere and Perata prior to that meeting to discuss our next steps. I will be in my chamber."

"Yes…yes your highness," stammered Gryffyn. Although he understood her words he did not expect them for she sounded more like a General than a Lady. "I will make sure the people of Arxsolum are ready and assembled at the appointed time. I will also inform the others about our meeting and we can meet in the war room in half and hour. In the mean time why don't you get some rest as well?"

Aliondrae nodded in agreement but decided she was not really tired; what she really wanted was to freshen up before the meeting.

She thanked the old weapon's master for his concern and sent him about his tasks. He looked very tired himself but she knew there was no way to make him rest. He was the self-appointed guardian to her and her family and nothing she said or did would change that. A solitary figure in the distance caught her attention, she knew from the stance that it was Perata and he was watching her. She was beginning to realize that everything he did was for a purpose, the last was to make her understand that she had the strength to stand on her own. She knew now that she could and that she would continue to fight no matter the odds, but it was nice to know that people she could count on surrounded her. She gave him a wave and proceeded to her chamber.

She noticed the healer exiting Discere's quarters looking fairly worried. She stopped and questioned, "Lineaus, what is wrong?"

"My lady, you know how he is. He doesn't know when to quit. I am hoping it is nothing more than exhaustion but at his age it is hard to tell." His face was very concerned, "Whatever magic he cast today took quite a toll, I'm afraid it will be some time before he will be up and moving around."

Aliondrae heard the worry in his voice and started to enter Discere's room. She had to make sure he was all right. Lineaus stopped her with his words, "he is sleeping now and it is vital he gets his rest." The healer put a comforting hand on her shoulder, "I will alert you when he wakes and you may see him then."

The truth of his words was the only thing that stopped her from entering. She had first met the wizard when she was a child and he was old then. In fact, she had no idea how old he really was. He always seemed capable of anything and it was hard to imagine him in any other state. She decided he was in good hands with Lineaus but made a point that she would come back after supper.

She finished washing up anxious to be doing something; waiting was always harder than doing. She heard a knock at her chamber, 'just in time' she thought as she opened the door.

Gryffyn proceeded to escort her to the war room. A large table dominated the room, which was actually one large map that showed the surrounding areas all the way to the pass. She quickly greeted everyone present while her eyes hesitated slightly at the seat usually occupied by Discere.

Jaxen noticed his mother's pause and started to explain that the wizard was not feeling well. She nodded in understanding, "Please everyone have a seat. We should get started."

Once everyone was comfortable she began, "I have requested this meeting to find out our next move. We have made it through the first couple steps and now it is time to ready for what is yet to come." She directed her comments to Perata, "I imagine you have already set in motion your plan, I would just like to know what we can expect. So far I have only heard portions of the plan and in truth that is all I wanted to hear, but now I wish to know it all. I need to know it all."

Perata took that as his cue and stood up. "So far we have completed stage one, preparing the city and stage two, initial defense. In fact our plan worked better than I could have expected. They were in a hurry and they got sloppy. It seems they felt they would be able to run through us and we caught them by surprise. This is a mistake they will not make twice. Now according to the reports from our scouts we only saw a portion of their army, which means we are far from victory." He paused to take a drink from his goblet, "Victory however is achievable. Right now they are thinking we were lucky, and yes we were, but it was our boldness that created that luck. Now we must continue to be bold. We must take the fight to them."

Aliondrae gave Perata a puzzled look, "what do you mean take the fight to them, do we not have the advantage behind these walls?"

"We do have the advantage behind these walls because they can not engage us without passing our barriers. They on the other hand have no such walls and we need to exploit that. A small force of horsemen will exit the city before first light in two days time and attack their camp. The attack will be quick and it may not cause much damage, but it will let them know that they are not safe."

Jaxen spoke up, "Commander, I understand such a plan but my men and I are ready now, why do we wait two days, why not attack now while they are still in disarray."

Aliondrae's heart skipped a beat when she heard that her own son would be leading the charge, but she kept silent knowing that it is what had to be. Jaxen was raised as a warrior and no one would be better suited for this type of engagement. Still it was hard to take as a mother knowing that both her children were going to be in harm's way."

Perata was watching Aliondrae's reaction, when he realized there was no argument forthcoming he answered Jaxen's question, "We are waiting two days time because right now they may be in disarray, but everyone is on edge and on high alert. An attack directly after would have been effective in the amount of men that would be killed but it would have shown our capability. If we let a day pass they will begin to relax, combine that with the previous day's emotionally exhausting attack they will be extremely vulnerable. I will get word to Sorcia's team so they can coordinate. This plan is not aimed at hurting them physically, because they have so many men they will barely register it, but it should hurt them psychologically. They will know defeat twice since coming here and that can have a profound effect upon their willingness to fight. Understand, this maneuver…just like our last will only work once, but once is all we need, because then they must defend against the threat."

Aliondrae never would have thought down that far, if she were to attack she would have done so as they retreated just as she would imagine any other commander. This means they were probably looking for it, confusion or not. "You mentioned getting word to Sorcia, I do not know if you are aware of Discere's condition. I am assuming that is how you planned to communicate."

Perata chose his words carefully so as not to insinuate that he had a plan in place for when either her daughter or her friend became incapacitated, "We have worked out a series of signals in case of contingency. The team also knows to be ready for such a move and do what they can to assist."

She nodded her head in understanding, "What then, after our incursion? What happens then?"

Gryffyn answered, "Then we wait, we play defense, and if opportunity presents itself we seize it."

She did have a final question, "Do we not need to worry about them attacking us in this time frame, before we attack them?"

Perata took a moment to answer, "The possibility of attack is there, but unlikely. Our show of strength in the initial attack will prompt them to be much more careful in the future. This means they will need time to prepare. I feel confident that we are safe for at least a couple of days. Of course watch will still be posted and we still need to be ready."

"Of course," Aliondrae was glad for this information, she was already formulating her speech to her people. A few days respite will do them good, especially if their raid goes off as Perata planned. 'Victory is achievable,' she thought to herself. "Thank you for your time gentlemen," she said as she stood to leave the room. "I will inform our people of the ongoing situation." She noted Perata's concern and finished with, "only, of course, what pertains to them."

Perata waited for her to leave the room before turning to Jaxen, "Prepare your men."

Chapter Twenty-Three:
A Long Way Home

Edward had been instructed by Tallox to make a lot of noise while leaving the camp so that anyone watching would notice. Of course he did not believe that such theatrics were necessary, if their enemy could elude detection for this long it was highly probable that they were aware of every move the Eastern Alliance was to make. Either way it did not make much difference in fact it made him laugh as he thought about the King and his ideas of trickery. Well, he was about to show him a few tricks of his own.

His troops were packed and ready to go before first light. Edward studied his map one more time trying to figure out what was fact and what was not. If what the old wizard had told him was true then Arxsolum was in grave danger, the question remained as to what Aliondrae was up to. Based on Discere's estimate that it would take approximately two months for the invaders to get through the mountains, which was one month ago and the fact that at their best pace it would take him approximately two more months to get his cavalry back to Arxsolum that would mean that his city would be taken long before he arrived. If they then continued north Edward would then encounter them somewhere in the forest of Nemorosus. That was of course if there truly was an army opening up the pass, he was no longer even sure his meeting with the Discere took place. Was it possible that their enemy was so crafty that the mage was only a part of their plan or was it more likely he dreamed the whole conversation? He wished he had a way to know the truth, and then berated himself for not leaving the second he heard the news, but of course he had to follow the orders of that fool Tallox who did not believe a word of it.

The difference in speed of travel was also a concern for the Count. It was time to make a decision whether to keep his army together in case he did encountered the enemy or let the cavalry ride ahead. Having a full force would be most beneficial if he was to run headlong into an advancing enemy, but then again speed was an issue. Ever so shrewd, he decided to split his force; if he happened upon news of the alleged invaders he would have some time in which to turn back and regroup. This made the most sense because he knew he would not be able to restrain riding at the infantry's pace. Plus if the rumor was false then his return to Arxsolum would be that much quicker and he would have time to regroup and formulate his final plans.

....

The majority of the ride was uneventful, yet Edward pushed his men hard and any travelers on the road quickly moved aside. They ate and slept in their saddles only stopping to minimally to spare the horses. Within a week and a half they reached the remote city of Aedulica. Edward was curious to find if there was any news, but it was quickly apparent that no one there knew anything of an impending invasion or of any cities evacuating. Most of them did not even know there was a war going on at all. No news was worse than bad news at this point, he was relieved because there was still hope his city stood, but then again Aedulica was such an isolated city that they would be the last people to know anything. This lack of information only reinforced Edward's desire to hasten his troops even though he was already driving the horses to the brink of exhaustion. They were bred for endurance and strength, able to carry hundreds of pounds of man and armor many leagues, but sustained speed was not their forte.

Andwer, Edward's lieutenant echoed his thoughts by commenting. "Sir, if we continue to the drive the horses in this manner they will become lame. I believe it would be wise to allow them time to rest or else we will lose them and any advantage we have gained in time."

Edward knew the words he spoke were true, these horses were no good dead and they were the only guaranteed thing of value he had left. "You are right, as always, you are right. We will allow the horses and the men a day of rest when we reach Quinvium. No senses in killing ourselves when we do not even know if it is necessary. Let us just hope this next city is not be such a dung heap and that they will have at least some idea what the outside world is doing." He spit on the ground, he had always had a disliking for the poor, small towns and with this experience dislike was now turning to hatred. When he became king he would do something about this rabble.

His lieutenant replied, "They will sir, Quinvium is a much more traveled city then Aedulica and it is nearer to Arxsolum. If there is news they will have it."

Edward already knew that it was a much larger city; in fact he had been there often. It was a meeting point of all the main roads in the region and a good resting point for travelers. Even though he knew it to be true it was good to hear the words, "You are a good soldier Andwer and a good friend. I thank you for that. It is just that I am anxious for some tangible information, nothing more. I cannot finalize my plans until I know what is truly going on." He paused slightly, "It seems these days that information is more valuable then the whole Eastern Alliance."

Andwer nodded in agreement, "I understand, plus it will be good to see home, to see your family."

Edward did not bother to correct him; it was not concern for his so called family that drove him. It was his desire to be king, and then he would happy. He looked at the location of the sun. By his calculations they should arrive in Quinvium before tomorrow's night fall, there he would be able to set his plans.

The men made good time and still had daylight as they rode into the city. It was immediately apparent that all was not right. Upon seeing mounted men, some people cheered while others seemed nervous and frightened. It was obvious they were preparing for battle, a defensive battle. He noted that they had plenty of manpower and remembered to his ire that they never sent troops to help with the Northern front. It seems they were only concerned about their own affairs. These preparations were an obvious sign that the rumors were true unless the story had spread and they were just over reacting. He needed some concrete information.

Edward found the nearest city guard, "I wish to speak with your Commander straight away, let him know that Count Edward from Arxsolum wishes an audience."

The guard motioned to another to send word ahead. He then turned to Edward, "My lord if you will follow me I will take you. The rest of your men can find lodging and stables down the second street to the East."

Edward instructed Andwer to take his mount and to meet him later at the Stray Wolf Inn, of which both men knew the location. He then let the guard know he was ready.

As he followed the guard through the city he once again took notice of the preparations. If this were his city and their was an army coming from the south, he would have sent his army down to Arxsolum, which was a much better defensive position, plus it would save his city from the scarring of war. It seemed so logical to him, but then again he reminded himself that royal blood did not guarantee intelligence. If an army big enough to clear a pass came this direction they would roll over this city no matter their number of troops.

He entered the small castle and was led into an adjacent antechamber that contained a table with food and drink waiting. His guide offered, "Count Grafor will be in shortly, please make your self comfortable and help yourself to some refreshments."

Only a few minutes passed before the door opened and Grafor entered, "My lord Edward, how good it is to see you. We all believed you to be up North with the King." He made the pretense of respect, but neither man was fond of the other; one because he was royalty and one because he was not.

Edward responded, "I actually came seeking news of Arxsolum, is it true…the rumors about the Pass?"

Grafor tried to be as political as possible, "Unfortunately it is, by this time the West should already be through the Pass and Arxsolum most likely under their control. We had a few of your city's inhabitants come through here awhile back with all their worldly possessions alerting us to the news."

Edward was floored; this was the first real evidence since he first heard the words from Discere. He barked at Grafor, "Yet here you stand, why did you not send your troops down there? You could have saved both cities."

Grafor shook his head as if he were talking to a child. "Edward," he replied, "you must understand that the number of people that sought shelter from us was a surprisingly small number that even when Aliondrae first sent an envoy to ask for assistance we…my advisors, thought it was just the request of a scared woman. We did not believe an army was coming through; it seemed such a ridiculous rumor. Now had we seen a full scale evacuation then that would have been something." He paused trying to make Edward understand, "By the time we learned the truth it was too late. We could not send any troops down there in time much less prepare the area for a battle. We hardly have time to ready our defenses here. Depending on how fast Arxsolum falls, they could be here in short order."

Edward stood up, anger building with each second he listened to this pompous man. He knew that no help would be found here, "I need to go."

Grafor stood as well and blocked his path, as he implored, "My dear Edward, do not be so hasty. It is good that you are here. Do you not see that it is providence you are here? With your men and my men we could route these attackers and chase them all the way back to the hole from hence they came." He tried to restrain Edward's shoulder, "It would be in your best interest to stay here."

Edward pulled free of his grasp; he could hear the desperation in his voice. Grafor was scared, as well he should be. His city was about to suffer the same fate as Arxsolum, but that was not Edward's problem just as saving Arxsolum was not Grafor's. His reply came in an icy voice, "My best interest or yours? I must attend to my men." With that he walked out of the room. Over his shoulder he could hear Grafor, "Sleep on it Edward, you know it is the right thing to do and your only hope of regaining what is rightfully yours."

Edward entered the inn and noticed his lieutenant had a table waiting. Before he could speak Andwer let out, "I heard the news, I am sorry." He was a career military man and did not have any loved ones in Arxsolum, but believed Edward would be grieving for his wife. He waited for a reply but when one was not forthcoming he continued. "What are our options? Do we wait here for the rest of our force or return to the Alliance for assistance?"

When Edward finally spoke, his voice was one of acceptance, "Grafor believes we should stay and try to stave off the enemy here with the strength of both our forces."

"I hate to say it but that does not sound like a bad idea," countered Andwer, "hopefully our remaining forces will be here before the invaders and it would be good to have a wall to stand behind."

Edward looked Andwer directly in eyes, "It seems like the best course of action, but what of the unknowns?"

"I do not follow?" he answered a puzzled expression registering on his face.

"The unknowns, such as how big is this invading army," returned Edward. "Consider this scenario for example; what if there was no large force attacking in the North and the entire army of the Western Dominion is coming through that damned pass? Would our combined forces stand a chance, here in this un-defendable city or would we be wiped out city by city until

Tallox finally turns his attention this way. By then it is already over, the entire Southern Dominion is compromised and there are no defendable positions left."

"Sir, they had confirmed reports of a large army massing up north. I cannot imagine the logistics of that just to be used as part of a ruse, no matter how conflicting those later reports were. No, I have to believe they divided their force to trap the Alliance in the open."

Edward laughed, "I am under that same impression, but that still brings up another unknown. Will our infantry get here before them? It all depends on their progress. I am guessing that if Aliondrae did not surrender immediately that Arxsolum would fall in less than a day. I am also under the belief that the invaders will realize word will travel fast and they will likely attempt to do the same in an effort to take as much ground as possible before we unite. So we can assume Arxsolum has fallen already and that the invaders are already heading this way."

As soon as he uttered that last sentence they heard a large guffaw from the table next to them. The old man sitting there was staring right at them. "What makes you assume that Arxsolum will fall at all? It has never fallen before and it has faced much worse."

Andwer put up a calming hand toward Edward and replied, "Spare us the history lesson old man, you know not of what you speak or to whom you speak it."

The old man countered, "I know more than you think and it is you that does not know to whom you speak."

Edward was slightly surprised with that comment, "Well then since you know so much then you must also know that Arxsolum has no army to defend its walls and even if they did they would have no one to lead them, which would lead an intelligent man to believe Arxsolum will fall, if it has not already." Thinking the conversation was over he turned back to his own table, but the old man was not quite through. He broke out into a fit of laughter bordering on madness. During his outburst he uttered,

"It seems I know more than you, for I know that Arxsolum has yet to fall and it is indeed defended by an army," at this point his face turned very grave and he lowered his voice, "an army led by a witch who resides in death's shadow." He ceased his ranting and looked around suspiciously as if what he said may have conjured an evil spirit.

"Silence your tongue, old man or I will silence it for you," growled Andwer. He turned to Edward, "We do not have to suffer this fool, he is obviously mad." He stood as to throw the old man from the inn himself but was quickly stopped by the Count who seemed interested in what the man had said.

Edward watched the man just sit there and nod his head back and forth waiting for him to offer more on the subject but it seemed he needed a little prompting, "You do indeed know more than us, tell me more of this army and," he paused slightly emphasizing his words, "and this witch."

With those words the old man seemed to return to reality. He situated himself as if getting ready to tell a tale. He began with a deep breath and then uttered, "She calls herself Aliondrae and Arxsolum is her city; a city left defenseless due to the vanity of her husband. She alone was responsible for its welfare and its people. Knowing that if nothing were done then she would lose both, for an evil force is threatening from the West." The man paused in a dramatic fashion to make sure his listeners received the full effect of his words. "Aliondrae besieged others for assistance but no one would listen and no support was sent. The Countess was running out of options and running out of time. In a desperation move the witch turned to the dark forces for a solution. In exchange for her soul the underworld would provide a commander for her forces a commander unlike any other. It is death himself who shall hold Arxsolum and Aliondrae's soul."

Both listeners were taken in by the old man's ability to tell a story, as it unfolded they both found they were paying close attention. It occurred to Edward that this man was probably a bard in his youth. It was amazing to him how a slight spin could be placed on actual events to create something that would be forever enduring and possibly become legend; a legend where he was not the hero but only a footnote along the way. He should stop this story before it spread because he did not want history to remember him as the vain husband who left his wife to be massacred, but strangely he first wanted to hear how this story, for it is all he believed it to be, ended.

The crazy old man continued, "The forces surged to attack a city they believed to be unguarded. A city that should break at first contact, but the city did not break. On the walls could be seen the man who could only be death and he defended those walls with reckless abandon." The old man ceased his story, stood up and began to hum. The tune was hauntingly familiar to them both but neither could place it. While Andwer was trying to figure out where he had heard that ghostly tune Edward, amazing himself, questioned, "How does it end old man, tell us that much."

The old man was making his way to the door; he stopped his humming and spun spectacularly to face him. "My dear Count Edward, I can not tell you something that has yet to happen." He began his mad cackle again; do I look like a seer?" With that he resumed his song this time using the words, words that they both knew. The song was something neither had heard since they were children. The old man was singing the tale of Arxsolum before the first war of the Dominions. The legend spoke of the bravery of the people who defended the walls and how against all odds they never fell.

Edward was so caught up in trying to remember the song that he did not realize the old man used his title until Andwer brought it to his attention. They both made a move for the door at the same time knowing the old man could not have traveled far. They burst into the night in an effort to subdue him, to get answers, yet there was no sign of him anywhere. Edward did not know if he wanted to kill him or question him, either way he wanted to find him, yet the man was nowhere to be found as if he vanished into thin air.

There was something eerie about the whole encounter and it affected Edward greatly, he grabbed Andwer, "Alert the men, we ride for Arxsolum at first light!"

Andwer did not argue and he did not hesitate for he had similar feelings, "Yes my lord!"

He did not know which was crazier the old man's story or the old man and he did not know what to make of either. He did believe him though, at least the part about Arxsolum still standing, but he did not know why. The only way to find the answers was to ride to the source.

Chapter Twenty-Four:
Jaxen's Raiders

The crisp night air felt good against Sorcia's skin. She glanced toward the keep; it was still dark but dawn was fast approaching. Sorcia felt a presence near her that she knew to be Tonagal even though she could not see him. It did not matter, they were both ready just as she hoped the others would be. Signals from the city notified them that they were readying for an attack. It was scheduled just before sunrise most likely in an attempt to catch the enemy while they were still half asleep, but other than that there was not much detail. She was disturbed that she was not able to make contact with Discere; she had tried several times to no avail. "What had happened to him?" she questioned herself. She hoped it was out of caution that her attempts to communicate with him had not been successful and not for something more sinister. Her imagination could easily start running wild, but this was not the time to let emotions cloud her actions. She chased away the negative thoughts and went over their plan again. Phillos and Lexis should be in the enemy encampment by now. They were going to take out the men who guarded the slave holding area. Sorcia was not sure if the captives would be in any condition or even have the desire to fight, after awhile people in slavery tend to lose the will, but Phillos was sure he could convince them. If not to fight at least to run then they would have a chance at freedom even if it cost their life. Either way Sorcia needed them gone, either dead or fleeing, an uprising at the precise moment of Arxsolum's attack would definitely be a thorn in the side of the invaders. She knew she was using them, but the morbid truth was that they were aiding the enemy albeit against their will. Anything that helped the invaders hurt Arxsolum, which means it had to stop. She knew that even if they did fight the majority would die, but that had to be better than enduring their lives they had now. She trusted the assassin's judgment and he was determined that they would at least try to run. Sorcia had to figure he was gauging that prediction on something; he always seemed to see the angles. The man was amazing and his resolve second to none. She had yet to figure him out, an assassin who lived for himself, yet was willing to die in defense of the very city he preyed upon.

The familiar sound of the city's gates being opened surprised Sorcia and her eyes immediately snapped in that direction. Even though her eyes were accustomed to the darkness she was not expecting to see much. To her astonishment she had no problem identifying who or in this case what that came out of the gates. She may not have had extensive details to the city's plan but she had expected more of a stealth mission. Instead Jaxen's horseman tore out of the city gates, their entire ensemble including their mounts covered in a ghostly white substance. They screamed as they charged into the invaders camp like undead ghouls. The few sentries who were up and alert were summarily ran down or cut to pieces.

The snap of a Tonagal's bowstring reminded her of their mission; to disrupt the enemy from organizing any sort of resistance. She quickly followed suit and chose her targets carefully making sure every shot counted. The commotion in the site below was mesmerizing; it seemed Jaxen's raiders would be able to run through unchallenged; it was a frightening scene of carnage. She started to understand the idea of pretending to be spirits because it was disabling the soldier's reason. They had no idea what was happening, they were being attacked, when it was them who should be doing the attacking.

All was progressing well until she felt something. It started out as a tickle on the back of her neck as the hair began to stand; someone was drawing magic and a lot of it. She searched frantically to identify where it was coming from and spotted the source immediately as a large ball of fire appeared and flew straight at the horsemen, then a second then a third.

War wizards had joined the fray. Other attacks were directed at the ground on which the horses ran and the very land began to shake and tremble causing the cavalry's formation to break. If they separated they would be vulnerable. She knew she had to do something or else her brother would be killed and the attack would fail. Never using her magic in a destructive way or even against another person, she was not sure what to try. She thought about the fireballs she had just witnessed but was unfamiliar with how to conjure them. She knew if she had time she could figure it out, but time was not on her side. She did know something similar that might work. She quickly found her center and concentrated on her favorite thing; she called forth a ball of blue energy. This time, however, she did not attempt to limit it in size but was going for something more. She drew as much power into her as possible and right when she felt she would burst, unleashed the torrent in the direction of the wizards. The energy flew straight through the camp gathering size and speed as it traveled. It consumed everything in its path from tents to men. Sorcia tried to hold on to consciousness but she had never allowed the magic to enter her on that level and her strength was slipping. She reached out trying desperately to hold on but the blackness was surrounding her with every second that passed. She hoped it was enough to give her brother the time he needed.

Jaxen dove out of the way as a fireball flew past his head, Perata warned him that they would be wielding magic but never being in a real battle he was not sure what to plan for. He was definitely not expecting balls of fire to appear out of nowhere and did not know how to defend against it. "Hold the ranks!" he shouted desperately to his men. The ground began to pitch causing the horses to fight for footing. He watched helplessly as one of his men went down, he could not tell who it was. In an effort to aid the fallen man, he changed his heading. There was buzzing all around his head, arrows he figured but there was no time to retreat. He needed to get his men out of there, Perata made it perfectly clear that it was necessary to pull all his people out no matter the cost. He saw a handful of black-cloaked figures near him. He knew enough about magic to realize that two were shielding and the others were attacking. He also knew they had him in their sights. There was nowhere to hide as three fireballs arced toward him. Jaxen prepared himself for the blow wondering if he could lower his shoulder and run through them or if they would knock him back. Yet the fire never reached him, instead of being hit from the front and knocked backward as expected, something ripped him forward toward the wizards' location. The unseen force was more than enough to send him reeling. He hit the ground and lost his air, but he knew he had to move. He scrambled to his knees gasping for breath that would not come. He tried to remain calm while at the same time looking for the wizards, but they were nowhere to be seen, nor soldiers for that matter. Everything that was in front of him a moment ago was now gone. He regained his horse that seemed to be as shocked as he and quickly found his man, unconscious but alive; probably just knocked out from hitting the ground. He lifted him onto his horse; seconds later more of his men were around him using him as a rallying point. They were all screaming something but he could not hear a thing, just a loud ringing in his ears. With a final look around completely amazed that they were not surrounded by thousands of enemy soldiers, they made a mad dash back to the safety of the city.

....

Lexis and Phillos both could tell that the attack began but they still waited for the right moment. That moment presented itself when the guards moved to investigate the sounds of battle, the assassins responded simultaneously. Six guards lay dead before even one of them comprehended the danger. The two killers looked at each other, both knowing they were a lethal combination. Their efficiency gave them a small window of opportunity in which to gather as many of the captives as possible. It was still early so many of them were half asleep. They did not have time to explain the situation and decided it was easier to shove weapons into the hands of any that looked capable and tell them they could reach freedom if they fought. Many of them had no idea what was happening, but it was apparent that they had a chance to escape. The lot of them were not fighters and did not know where to go, but after the last couple of months being worked to death it seemed anything was better than staying. A few of the more cognizant slaves did not hesitate and began running back in the direction of the pass and more importantly, their homelands. Those in the back followed without much thought as to why, but they trusted the ones in front. Phillos was aware that even if some of them made it through the camp they would die long before they reached their home, but if he were in their place death would be a better option than to remain a prisoner. Their was hope, they did not have the look of people completely beaten, some of them still expected to regain at least a semblance of their former lives. He was sure that when they surrendered initially that they never imagined they would be treated as such. The look in their eyes was one of desperation and it was that very desperation that he was counting on. For the moment all was working like he thought it would.

Sgt. Dalin, who had been alerted to the sounds of battle, noticed that the slaves were out of their containment area. He barked orders to his men to recapture them; he was already on thin ice because his men failed to return with the necessary supplies he was tasked to find. He did not even know where to look; his failure had him relegated to standing guard over the prisoners. If he lost them also then his life would quickly follow. His soldiers understood the situation and reacted swiftly to close of their escape. It looked as if their uprising would end before it even began.

Phillos recognized the threat and altered his original plan, which was to blend into the confusion like last time and disappear. He instead charged into the soldiers shredding several to pieces before they could put up a resistance. They did not expect an attack from one they assumed was one of their own and did not realize the danger until it was too late. The slaves, upon seeing that they had capable fighters on their side followed his lead and began to attack the soldiers with anything they could find. The guard's confusion and lack of numbers allowed the slaves to carve quite a path through their ranks and kept their hope alive. However the dream of freedom quickly faded as more and more soldiers entered the melee. The slaves were poorly fed, near starvation; mostly civilians who did not have military experience and their initial momentum was soon stopped. It was apparent that they would not be able to make it. The majority of them just threw themselves on the ground to surrender and those that did not were instantly killed. Phillos and Lexis fought back-to-back trying desperately to return to where they entered the camp. The problem was that the soldiers were all keying on them. Their only hope was to get back into the mountains where they knew the terrain and could hopefully lose pursuit.

Rammel and Marhran heard the commotion near the front where Sorcia and Tonagal were stationed but they were posted to cover Phillos's and Lexis's retreat. They were both fighters and hated having to wait while battle raged; luckily they did not have to wait long as they saw their two friends sprinting toward them with dozens of enemy soldiers close behind. The two men began to unleashed barrage after barrage of cover fire. They needed to create distance between them and the pursuers or else their friends would be overrun. The soldiers were quick to return fire, but the higher ground and cover made them difficult targets. Phillos and Lexis began the ascent into the mountainous region, narrowly avoiding the incoming arrows. The pre-chosen route had many twists and bends allowing their cover team above full range of sight. To their surprise several groups of soldiers still followed.

Both the giant man and the dwarf soon ran out of arrows and then somewhere along the way Phillos was struck in the back. Lexis saw him hit the ground, but could not assess the full extent of the damage right then and there. She struggled with his weight knowing the pursuers were close but not willing to leave him behind. She did not make it far before she could feel the presence of her assailants. Setting Phillos down, she drew her blade. After one last look at him believing this to be their final moment she turned to wait for the onrush. She was no longer afraid to die; she just wanted to make them pay for taking away the only thing she ever cared about. The first man to arrive caught the tip of her blade in the face and he stumbled back into the others. Several more rounded the corner and hacked mercilessly at the smaller woman. They were upon her instantly; her only tactic was to fill the narrow area with as many dead Westerners until she could no longer move her arms. She was a fair enough swordsman but no match for the strength and numbers that came against her. The hold on her blade was lost at the same moment she felt her shoulder get crushed. She was dropped to one knee but defiantly pulled her dagger as another blade swept toward her unprotected neck. The deathblow never arrived as something darted from behind her and crashed headlong into the oncoming soldiers. Before Lexis could decipher what she was seeing something powerful seized her and threw her back. As she lay on the ground stunned by the turn of events she realized quickly that it was Marhran that had moved her. He needed room to swing his axe and she was in the way. The other must be Rammel, She could not see him in the mix but heard his gravely voice yelling obscenities as he fought. She was amazed at how the two worked as a team. Marhran's size and reach allowed him to stand behind the dwarf and still attack while Rammel stayed low and kept the invaders off balance. The two axe-wielding fighters were holding their own against the superior numbers, but for how long could they last? Lexis scrambled over to Phillos and ripped his sword out of its scabbard with her left hand. She then darted back into the fight vowing to go down swinging. She heard the distinct sound of arrows whistling above her head, however they were not aimed at her but at those she fought. The remaining soldiers still held the advantage in numbers but they had no idea where the arrows were coming from and how many others their might be hidden in the mountains. The soldiers witnessing many of their comrade's deaths were quickly losing the will to fight and began retreating.

When the area cleared; Marhran scooped up Phillos in one arm and gave Lexis a concerned look. Rammel followed the look toward her shoulder and questioned as they were running, "Lassie, that be your blood or theirs?"

Lexis's entire right side was numb, she knew she was hit badly as she replied, "A little of both I think."

"Aye lassie, I think you be right, you took quite a blow but you stood your ground."

They raced through the trails; Lexis was rapidly losing her strength. She started to fall but the gnarled hands of Rammel caught her. He easily hoisted her over his shoulder and continued the flight. Tonagal joined them when they got closer, both Marhran and Rammel noticed that he was carrying Sorcia in the same fashion they were carrying their wounded. Neither said a word or slowed down even though they were fairly sure there was no further pursuit. They reached one of their hiding places and darted inside.

Rammel began checking over the wounded. Lexis had a bad gash on her right shoulder but she would definitely survive. He pulled out a brown colored salve from his pack and instructed Marhran to apply it to her wound. He then moved to Phillos who still had a piece of arrow sticking out of his back. He must have broken the shaft so that he could continue to run. He also had a nasty cut on his head from when he went down. The dwarf knew the injuries in themselves were not that bad but the tip of the arrow seemed lodged between his ribs dangerously close to his heart. Pulling it out without a healer was not a wise move. He took out some rope and strapped the man down under the questioning stares of his companions. "If he moves he may injure himself more, we need a healer." His attention then went to Sorcia. She was as pale as a sheet and her breathing was shallow, but did not seem to have any wounds. The dwarf gave Tonagal a perplexed look.

The thief, understanding his confusion responded, "Your guess is as good as mine. All I saw was her drop her bow and her entire body tensed. Then an eerie blue light shot from her hands. It raced through the camp devastating everything in its path. I really don't know what it was but it sent the enemy wizards running, which saved our attackers from Arxsolum." He stopped to feel her forehead with his hand, "Then she collapsed and has been like this ever since. I was bringing her back here when I came across your little scuffle and did what I could. As for her, I just don't know."

Rammel swore an oath, he knew quite a bit about many things but he did not know how to help her. "I guess we just make her comfortable and hope she wakes." He pointed over to Phillos, "we are going to need her magic to help that one. I am no sure how far that arrow penetrated, but it no looks good."

Tonagal had a good grasp of the situation, "You two are exhausted. Try to get some sleep. I will keep an eye on these three."

Chapter Twenty-Five:
Change in Tactics

Lockstan walked out of Stragess' tent with the healer. "I am sorry to say that I do not believe he will pull through this, in fact I am amazed he is still alive at all. His symptoms are similar to all the others and none of them survived…I am familiar with several different types of poison and he…" The healer went quiet upon seeing the General's personal guard listening to their conversation.

The large Captain noticed his look, he had instructed the healer not to speak of the poison that was not only on the defenders weapons but now seemed to be in their food and drink as well. It was the healer's duty to inspect all their stores and destroy anything that was suspect before the soldiers stopped eating all together. "Well, I will leave you to your duties; I expect you will be finished before supper. Assign anyone you deem worthy to assist you but hold them to the same rules. I do not need soldiers who are too weak to fight. I expect a full report in the morning."

Lockstan watched him leave; he had hoped for better news… anything that could lift the morale of the men. No matter what he told them it was apparent that they were afraid to sleep, afraid to eat, and afraid to stand watch. He was facing a very clever and very dangerous adversary. The worst part of it was that his men felt that the woman who stood on the wall was responsible like she had access to unknown magics. He knew better but still control of his men was slipping. Looking in the direction of the city he quickly spotted her figure, watching him, as he liked to watch her. She was always nonchalantly walking the walls and doing what seemed to be nothing, but always watching. It seemed impossible; day and night she would be on those walls, never sleeping, like some supernatural being standing guard over her domain. It was a trick; it had to be, she was just a woman and certainly nothing more than a figurehead. Lockstan scanned the rest of the city looking for the real threat; the large man who also prowled the walls. He was very rarely visible, but he was always there, waiting, planning, this man was the enemy. Lockstan swore to no one in particular; he needed to find a way to overcome his men's fears and let them know that the things that were happening were manmade and not the results of some curse. It was time to take some drastic measures to keep his men motivated for the fight. His gaze wandered over to where the slaves were held, contempt rising like bile, he should kill them all after their little uprising but something told him they could still be useful. He laughed to himself, an idea occurring to him that just might solve his problems.

"Excuse me sir?" Lockstan turned in the direction of the voice and noticed that Stragess' personal guard was speaking to him. He realized he probably seemed a mad man by laughing while everything was about to collapse. His food stores were tainted, his soldiers were dying or becoming sick, he had lost more war wizards, and his men believed they were cursed; yet he laughed. As the man approached his laughter subsided and his voice seethed "What is it?"

The guard, not normally the timid type seemed reluctant to voice his question. He knew that the Captain was a busy man and was losing his patience so he just spit it out. "I overheard the healer speaking about the General. Is it true, is he not going to make it?"

"People die in wars all the time, he will not be the first nor will he be the last."

"Sir, I understand about death, it is just that I thought he was a favorite of Caellestus." He hesitated not really comfortable at speaking the God's name. "I am surprised that he would allow this to happen."

Lockstan too was surprised, not at Stragess' condition, but at the guard's fearful question. Religion always had a strong effect on fools, which gave the Captain a second idea. Calculating his words carefully, Lockstan did his best impression of the clerics he had seen, "He was one of his favorites, but then he questioned the God's master plan. He lost his faith and his belief that we could win. Caellestus is not merciful to those who do not do as he bids." He watched as the man took in his words. It was time to spread some fear of his own. "Have you not noticed many of the soldiers becoming sick and dying for no apparent reason?" He waited for the man to nod his head, "It is because they have angered our god and he is punishing them all. He came to me last night and said that it was I and those who were unwavering in their belief of this invasion that would come to glory. It is only those who believed that would live."

"I had no idea…I, I thought it was the witch's doing."

Lockstan continued on embellishing his lies with every word. "I too thought this place was cursed until he visited me. He said the witch's power was nothing compared to his and we need not be afraid, for that is where her power comes from, from fear, your fear. He told me that we were destined to win this war, but there was no place for cowards. He will end the existence of all cowards so that the witch's power would fade." He gave the guard a strange look, "You are not a coward, are you?"

The man almost relieved himself right then and there, he stammered, "Of course not Sir, I know that we will be victorious. I am a true believer."

Lockstan looked around conspiratorially, "It is important for you not to be afraid especially when the attack begins." He left the man with those words knowing that they would spread like wildfire; the soldiers would soon believe that it was their own fear that killed these men. It would not alleviate all his problems, but at least his army would have the illusion of not being afraid, which could snowball into real courage. He took a last look toward the city and the familiar figure on the wall. "Two can play your game princess."

He laughed again, perhaps he was going a little mad and with what he had planned next people would definitely begin to think just that. Heading directly to the holding area for the remaining slaves, he turned to one of his pages and ordered him to have his chief engineer report immediately. The page ran off to do as he was bid while Lockstan examined the slaves. They still looked like they could work, well…at least some of them. A few had been worked over pretty viciously. His men were not overly gentle in their quelling of the uprising. It could not have happened at a more inconvenient time, but no matter for it now, it was in the past. He instructed the guards to round them up so that he could address them as a group.

When all the slaves were accounted for Lockstan began, "I am going to forgive you for your indiscretions and will give you a chance to earn your freedom."

The slaves all perked up at that, most not believing him but all definitely interested in hearing more. They figured that the man who spoke already had them under control and did not need to promise anything. They would already do as they were told or they would be killed; simple as that, but now he was offering freedom. It seemed such a foreign concept, but also the greatest thing they have ever heard.

His chief engineer arrived and began delivering his report. He was nervous because he was behind schedule and the Captain had been in a foul mood as of late. He did not want to be the next example of incompetence.

Lockstan waived off his report. "I want all your engineers that specialize in dealing with the pass, more specifically ones who can close it back up and I want them started immediately."

"I don't understand," stammered the engineer.

Captain Lockstan grabbed the smaller man and lifted him off the ground as if he were a child. "What do you not understand? I want you to assign some of your engineers to close the pass behind us and I want it done now!" His last words came out as a roar as he threw the man to the ground.

"Sir, with all due respect we would be cutting off our own escape and supply routes," he saw the look in Lockstan's eyes and realized that it would not be wise to continue.

"Do not think for a second that your belligerence is going unnoticed. First you cannot keep schedule with the siege engines and now you are questioning an order. What you should be questioning is what I am going to do with you if you do not do as I say and do it without delay."

The engineer did not miss his leader's tone, he swallowed the lump in his throat and out of pure survival mood stood at attention, "Yes sir, it will be done." He did not want to mention that it would slow the remainder of his projects down; in fact he did not want to mention anything other than another robust 'yes sir.' It was time to do as instructed; if he failed then his life would be forfeit.

"That is more like it," he pointed to the slaves, "these belong to you, use them as you see fit." He then raised his voice so that they could all hear. "Any of you that work hard and succeed in this task will be given your freedom. If you do not work hard, if you cause trouble in any way, or if you fail in this task I will kill you myself. I can promise that it will not be enjoyable, well…at least not to you." He grabbed his engineer, "I will also need some engineers who specialize in tunneling, and in fact I want your best tunneler."

The man thought quickly and spit out the first name that came to mind, "I can fetch him this second if you wish."

"I do wish; have him report to my tent. I will be there in short order, tell him I do not like to wait."

Lockstan then ordered his page to find Aloster, one of the more capable wizards that was still alive and a list of several more warriors that he thought would be able to undertake his next plan.

Making his way back to his tent he thought more about his plan and began to feel better. It was time to engage the enemy face to face, but in order to do that he needed to get past their defenses. He strolled through his camp noticing the camp keeping up its discipline. He still had them in an iron grip, but he knew it was slipping with everyday they waited. It was time for action.

Before he reached his quarters a small gathering of people were already there. The fact they did not waste any time assembling boded well for the quality of men he selected. He ordered them into his tent and warned his guards they were not to be disturbed and no one was allowed near the area. He pulled Aloster aside; the wizard whispered a few words then looked back to Lockstan, "It is done."

Lockstan always believed in being open with his plans, but lately he learned the less people knew the better. He had the feeling that his enemies knew far more than they should and he did not want to take any chances. "What we talk about here today stays within this group, no one, not your best friend, squad leader, nobody is to be told. If anyone gives you a hard time direct them to me. Our wizard has put a spell that will keep out all eavesdroppers, which means if this information gets out it came from one of you. This mission and your life depend upon stealth; I would recommend you keep your mouths shut. You have been hand-picked because I know all of you personally and I trust you." He waited so that if anyone needed to protest they could. "In order to breach these walls we are going to need some people on the inside to hold position. Those people are going to be you."

Not one of the men said a word yet they were all wondering how such a feat was to be accomplished. Finally Aloster spoke up, "What is your plan, how do we get inside."

Lockstan gave an eerie smile, "We tunnel, come up on the inside before they even know we are there."

One of the engineers embarrassedly spoke up, "Sir, with all due respect, I have been studying this city and I can promise that they have built those walls to counter that very plan. I would guess they have another 10 to 15 feet of stone buried beneath every section of wall. We could get under eventually but it will take some time."

Lockstan did not seem upset after hearing the news. He just nodded his head, "10 to 15 feet around every portion of the walls, I agree with your assessment, but I did not say we are going to tunnel under the wall." He then asked the confused listeners, "Where is the only place that it will be unlikely to have block underground?"

Mikon spoke up again, "Sir I would believe all the sections would be blocked and even if some were not we would have no idea where to begin looking."

"We do know where to begin looking, it is so obvious you and everyone else will overlook it. We will tunnel right under the main gate. Aside from the road leading in I would doubt they fortified the ground underneath the gates. Do you think that to be true?"

The engineer answered carefully, "Sir you are probably correct, I have never seen a fortress built that would spend the time or materials to do that. The reason is that towers on both sides guard it…it would be suicide. Our men would be cut to pieces before we cleared a foot of soil."

Lockstan replied, "Only if they knew you were there. They will never expect it and will not defend against it."

"How could they not know we were there, the walls are always manned. It would be hard enough to do it on some secluded section of the wall but there is no way they will not notice us starting a tunnel right under their noses. The only way we could do that would be to start back here, but again that would take a very long time and more than just us. We would need to get started immediately."

"If we had time, I would agree with you that a tunnel from back here may work, but since time is not on our side…we are going to go right up to the gate." Lockstan looked directly at Aloster, "You see our wizard friend here has a few tricks up his sleeve. He will use his magic to mask your noise and cloak your actions."

Aloster quickly caught on to what the Captain was planning, "Sir, I have only the strength to hide myself and maybe one other, I have never done a group of people."

"You can and you will. You will only need to do it for a short period of time and you will not have to cloak a large area. The enemy has done quite a bit of work for us already. Those death pits they dug, as a surprise for us will turn into a surprise for them. Once you are inside Aloster will cloak the top and it will appear as if it is empty. You will need to clear the spikes, but after that you should have free reign to work undisturbed."

Lockstan noticed the look of concern on Aloster's face. It seemed the young wizard did not feel as confident in his abilities.

"You will also have the cover of darkness to aid you, not to mention the sheer audacity of it. You start now, go and gather your supplies. I expect by morning that you have made some progress. Work in shifts so that when you are not working you are sleeping. We attack in four days time," his tone changed slightly, "you will be through by then and will hold the other end while we send troops to back you up."

The little group did not argue; to argue was to die. In fact the more they set their plans the more conceivable it became. They just had to get past the first night. Mikon gathered all the excavating supplies he thought they would need. The hardest part would be removing the soil and getting rid of it. The pit they were heading to was further back than they initially wanted but Lockstan was right, it was a good start to a tunnel; all they had to do was remove the pointed spikes with in it. During the nighttime hours they could clear the dirt and during the day there was enough room to store excess dirt unnoticed.

The team waited until night fully engulfed the land and when they received word from Aloster, started off. He assured them that no one could see or hear them but it was still a bad feeling being wide open and unprotected. They reached the pit without a sound of alarm or any arrows and began breaking down the spikes. The hardest part was removing the few bodies that had unfortunately fallen in, but the up side was that the dead bodies actually broke many of the spikes so it was not quite as precarious to climb in. Aloster put his cloak around the hole as the others set to work and found it was not too difficult to hold. As each section was excavated Mikon would reinforce it. Switching off between digging, dirt removal, and resting was making for a fast paced excavation. With the pace they were going it seemed they might actually keep to the schedule of four days.

. . . .

The sun rose the next day, it was the first good night of sleep Lockstan had since arriving on this side of the pass. He was not worried about another attack from the city. In fact it was that attack which gave him the idea. It was unprecedented, unexpected and extremely successful. Lockstan knew it was something that would only work once but it did work and he learned from it. It was time to forget everything he was taught about traditional strategy and go with some unconventional tactics.

To the surprise of the vast majority in the command tent, the chief engineer reported that the collapsing of the pass was going well. Lockstan listened to their grumblings but did not feel the need to explain further because it needed to be very obvious to everyone that there was no turning back; it was through the city or to the grave. He waited for any news of commotion on the main gate road but when none was mentioned his spirits lifted even more. Things were starting to go according to plan and even his men were in better spirits. His plan would work; it was so simple, so obvious, but exactly what was needed against this type of adversary. "Three more days," he thought to himself. Then there would be a battle.

251

Chapter Twenty-Six:
Misdirection

Four days had passed since Jaxen's attack and Lexis was moving around fairly well spending most of her time trying to keep Phillos still. He swore up and down that if they did not pull the arrow out of him soon than he would do it himself.

Rammel replied for what seemed the 100th time, "I understand your need, but we must wait for a proper healer or we may damage ya more than help."

Phillos met the dwarf's gaze, but pointed at Sorcia, "Well now we have a proper healer, so let's get on with it. I feel like it is beginning to poison my insides."

Rammel already knowing what the answer would be countered, "Just so ye know, the lass is still a little weak and may not be able to do what is necessary. We could wait another day to be sure."

"Put your self in my position, I have been lying on my stomach for several days. It is time to take a chance. Sorc can you do this?"

As Sorcia nodded her head positively Rammel gritted his teeth, "Damn ya, but you are right. Steel yourself cause this is going to hurt more than a little."

The dwarf made his preparations while Lexis found some clean water and bandages. Sorcia positioned herself near Phillos as best she could, a little nervous because she did feel incredibly weak, but she agreed with the assassin the longer they waited the worse it would be.

Rammel had Marhran use his big body to hold the injured man as still as possible. He needed to move slowly and it was going to be extremely painful; one reflexive jerk at the wrong time could easily bring the assassin's death. His stubby fingers felt the area around the wound. There was barely any shaft left for him to grab, but with his strength it was enough. The initial pull was straight and the arrow slid slowly a quarter of an inch until it met resistance. Rammel swore in his native language, which sounded more like a grunt. When he noticed the strange looks from the others he explained, "The tip is barbed and it is caught on his rib. I need to push it back in and rotate it. If I go too far I could enter his heart. If I no go far enough then I will only lodge it worse. The barbs on some of these arrows are meant to tear up a man's insides; this could be one of them."

"Do it dwarf, I trust you," gritted Phillos through his teeth.

Rammel did not hesitate; he pushed the arrow back to its original location and rotated it with his powerful fingers. He did not know what the barbs looked like but by closing his eyes he could imagine its design. Moving ever so slowly, he used his other hand as a probe to feel for any changes. He then pulled back again this time with less resistance, when he felt the moment was right he gave a quick jerk. He heard Phillos gasp as the arrow scraped past his ribs and tore his flesh, but smiled as it came free. "I think you be needing some rest after that."

Phillos did not answer; he just lied there trying to take the pain. He began feeling a warming sensation as Sorcia applied her magic. She did what she could but in her condition it was not much before she nearly passed out. She leaned back against the wall of their cave, "That is all I can do for now, I do not think he is in any danger. I will get some rest and try again later." She then reached out to Lexis, "Then I will take care of your shoulder."

Lexis smiled as she applied some of the dwarf's healing salve to Phillos, "I am fine for now, but when you are ready I will take you up on your proposition."

Phillos sat up for the first time in four days and gingerly felt the area around his wound. His hands were slapped away by Lexis's good arm as she began to dress the wound. In an effort to take his mind off the pain, he asked, "Any change of events?"

Marhran answered, "Tonagal is out keeping an eye on things, but so far not much has changed, neither side has made a move. The invaders are preparing for their attack but they don't seem to be in much of a hurry. They have made some good progress closing up the pass behind them, which I still don't understand why. I know you said that it will make his men fight harder, but I don't know how."

Phillos laughed as well as he could without racking his whole body with pain, "Lockstan is one shrewd individual; I can promise a lesser man would not be able to do what he is doing. The reason he is closing the pass is to take any option of retreat away from his men. The reason they will fight harder is because they will have only one way to go and that is through Arxsolum. Basically it is victory or death."

"So that really does not bode well for us then," joked Marhran.

"No my large friend, that is not good for us at all."

Tonagal entered and he looked worn out, "I don't think it will be long now, they have the look about them like they are going to attack any moment. Their men actually look very optimistic and they are on the move, with the vast majority heading east. My guess is that they do not want to navigate the pits in front of the main gate. They have built large enough siege towers that they could reach the top of the walls if they use ladders as well, but I really don't know." He took a look at how pale Sorcia was, "I am thinking we need to somehow alert those within the city."

Sorcia understood the comment, "I can try, but the last couple times were unsuccessful. I just need to rest for a while then I will give it a shot. I need to know what is going on with them." Her thoughts went to Jaxen; she needed to know if he was all right.

....

Jaxen stood on the wall surveying the enemy in front of them. It had been four days since he led his cavalry into their encampment and he was just now getting his hearing back. The first thing he heard was the story of how he was thrown from his horse by the force of an explosion that took place amidst the enemy spell casters. He wondered if maybe Sorcia had something to do with that. Whatever or whoever was the cause saved his life and his brigade. Mortality had been on his mind since that day, he should have died, but he did not. With a quick nod of his head he greeted the approaching Perata, "What are your thoughts, Commander? Is there anyway they will just give up and let us be or if not do you truly think we can win?"

Perata took a moment to answer, "We can win, but I think it is more of a matter of cost. By the looks of their preparations I would doubt that they would just give up. They still need to get past our outer wall, and if that happens we will retreat to the castle. Unfortunately, we do not have the ability gain it back, so we should do what we can to hold it, but not yet to the point of losing more men. We have options and are in a strong position. The only thing I know for sure is that a lot of people will die."

Jaxen sighed, "That is what I am afraid of."

Perata placed a comforting hand on his shoulder, "There is no shame in being afraid to die. We must do what we must for the benefit of others."

"You miss understand me, I am not afraid to die, I am afraid to live," Jaxen gathered his thoughts. "I am afraid that everyone, my family, my friends, even every single Westerner who stands before the city now will die, and I will be alone in what is left of Arxsolum holding on to the remnants of our flag." He turned to meet Perata's gaze, "That is what scares me; you tell me what am I to do if that happens."

Perata met Jaxen's stare, "You want to know what to do if all your loved ones are dead and the enemy lays defeated at your feet. I will tell what you will do. You will unfurl the remnants of that flag and you wave it. You let any and all know that you still stand and because of that Arxsolum stands. You hold your head high and you remember that your loved ones died so that you could do just that. You do anything less and those that died did so for nothing. Do you understand me?"

Jaxen stood there not saying a word. He wished he had Perata's resolve, he just remembered that the man he spoke with had lost everything and yet remained strong. Jaxen knew at that moment what it meant to be a man. He squared his shoulders and affirmed, "Yes, I do understand." He too would be strong, no matter what the outcome.

Perata gave him one last pat on the shoulder and told him to ready the people for tonight, "Have everyone on the walls...all shifts."

"You think the attack is coming tonight?" question Jaxen wondering how he could be so certain.

"Their encampment seems to be prepared, our scouts have not said much but communication is not as precise as I wish. The fact remains that time is against them and they will need to make a move soon. From what I could gather up here, they are well disciplined and will be ready soon. If I am wrong then some people lose some sleep but it is far better than them losing their lives." He stopped talking when Discere joined them.

Jaxen was first to greet him, "Good to see you out and about, you had us worried for awhile."

Perata smiled as well, not only because he liked the old man but because they were going to need him in the upcoming battle, 'It is good to see you, how's your strength."

"Well," replied the old wizard, "that is why I came looking for you. I was finally able to make contact with Sorcia, she is not in much better shape than me, but we were able talk for a bit. She said that the invaders are ready to move and that the attack could come any time."

Jaxen silently looked at Perata still amazed at the man's instinct when it came to war.

"If they are ready then they will come tonight, that is what I would do."

Jaxen asked, "Wouldn't the darkness hinder their movements and if they use light then won't they be easier targets for our archers. I would think they would wait until dawn like we did."

Perata explained his thought process, "When we attacked them you needed to see, more importantly your horses needed to see where they were going. They do not need to see that well and the darkness will mask much of their movements. To get past our defenses; stealth and force will be their two best modes of attack. They will throw everything they have in an effort to overrun us but I guarantee it is also a diversion to get some men into the city." He stopped talking to gather his thoughts, trying to figure out where they would try to gain access. "We will need to keep sharp eyes all around the city walls; this will significantly reduce our force for protection but is essential to keeping them out. We will also need to keep the cities sewers flooded at all times."

Jaxen quickly left to relay the message to Gryffyn and the others. Discere planned to take care of the sewers, not surprised at all that this man knew about them.

Perata watched them leave but remained at the wall doing his best to figure out the invaders best moves, desperately wanting to keep them out of the city. The moment they figure out that the defenders are merely civilians, it will be the turning point of the entire siege. The sun began to set and it would not be long now.

....

The city's inhabitants all crouched in their assigned positions. They were warned that the attack could come at nightfall but hours have passed and no alarm was sounded. Many were too scared to sleep, but the late hours and the quiet was making them tired. The majority of them had been stationed at the east wall after the scouts had warned that the enemy was circling around. It seemed that they were going to stay away from the gates completely.

Perata finally heard what he had been waiting for and gave Discere the signal. The wizard had not regained all of his strength back but the spell he was about to cast was fairly simple. He stood at the wall with his hands outstretched and then clapped them together. The result was instant, several orbs of light descended upon the approaching army illuminating the area around them. Perata then gave the word and his archers made their presence known. This time was much different than the last. The attackers were not running out in the open. They hid behind and in large wooden structures that protected them from the incoming arrows. Those who did not have the protection of the siege engines worked in teams of shield bearers and archers making them difficult to hit while allowing them to return fire. Even with the elevated position the skill of those on the wall was becoming apparent. Without their distance markers and practice on this side of the city, many of them were just firing blindly hoping for the best.

Perata ducked his head just as a fireball crashed into the section of wall where he was standing. He swore an oath, he needed to find those blasted wizards and neutralize them. More fireballs crashed into the wall, it was obvious there were several magic-users still involved in this attack. He watched as Discere scanned the area looking for an opening and then launched his own volley of fireballs into the approaching masses. The old wizard ducked back down breathing heavily. Perata realized that without knowing the location of the wizards that he was helpless against them. Before the mage could rise again to send another volley Perata stopped him, making him promise to save his strength until his magic could have the most impact. Discere understood the request but remained at the walls; he was not going to miss his opportunity.

The first tower hit the wall and ladders were being raised from the platform while archers hidden in the tower covered their men's ascent. The early warning allowed Perata to have his people bring over as much pitch as they could carry and they began putting it to use. It was directed toward any towers within in range and was followed by torches and flaming arrows. The first tower was instantly ablaze and not one invader made the wall. Perata ran as fast as he could to where the second tower had been sent.

The invaders made sure there was plenty of space between each so that the defenders would need to separate to defend against them. Several of Arxsolum's people had already been hit and Perata arrived just in time to engage a soldier scrambling over the wall. He promptly ran him through, just as Jaxen arrived to throw another invader back over the wall. The sheer number of defenders on the wall dispatched the men who did make it over, but more and more ladders were springing up.

Jaxen and Perata were relentless in their efforts to repel the invaders. For the moment they seemed to have the advantage but only because they knew where the attack was going to be. If his people were spread out any thinner, they would be undone.

The pace was becoming difficult but Perata felt they might hold the night, until above the clatter of swords and curses the main gate alarm could be heard. It was only to be sounded if they were breached. There must have been a secondary attack. If there was a breach it would not matter how long they held this section, they would still lose the advantage. The right thing to do was sound retreat while they still had a chance. Things did not always go to plan, but Perata had hoped to hold the wall much longer than a day. His discipline overrode his frustration and he sounded the retreat.

All the defenders knew the routine and headed toward the stairwells. Once through, the heavy iron doors were shut and locked. The reinforced doors would not hold for long, but it would allow the defenders time to reach their next position.

Perata separated from the others and headed in the direction of the main gate where he found quite a battle going on. The more experienced fighters were effortlessly slaughtering the civilians who engaged them. After assessing the situation, he calculated that even if he and Jaxen moved at their top speed those defenders would soon be lost and they would be in a difficult situation. He had no idea how the breach occurred but it did not matter, now was the time to ready for the next wave and attempt to regain control of the battle.

He alerted Jaxen to sound the retreat again so that maybe a few of those at the gate could be saved. He and Jaxen raced down to the battle in an effort to create enough of an opening to his men time to draw back down the winding streets. Perata had noted in his first tour of the city how the streets could be used to his advantage and assigned archer units to roofs of buildings to slow the invader's advance. If they did it right each unit would allow the previous unit time to escape while causing quite a bit of damage to the enemy.

He spotted Gryffyn surrounded on all sides and rushed to his aid. At the same time the first unit of archers reached their mark and began their deadly hail of missiles.

The addition of Jaxen, Perata and some cover fire allowed a few of the main gate guards to escape. They raced down the streets fighting periodically along the way. The archers were much more effective in this area because they each had their assigned practice areas and the invaders were not carrying shields.

Perata and Gryffyn were the last to race through when the make shift gate closing off the alley slammed shut. It would not be difficult for the Westerners to pass the gate but it would slow them. He noted that they did not pursue right away, but were holding their position until more reinforcements arrived. Perata waited for Gryffyn to catch his breath and asked, "What happened, how did they get over the wall?"

Gryffyn took a large breath of air, "They didn't, they tunneled under, I don't know how, but they came right out in the main square. They completely passed our defenses and had almost no resistance when they came up. I saw their Captain, but I couldn't get to him. They just poured out of that hole like cockroaches. We did all we could to contain them."

"Damn, but that is clever, they tunneled right under the main gates." Perata watched as the next wave of archers took their positions, "Well then, we will make them pay for entering this city. Run ahead to the castle and make sure everything is ready, I will take command here and bring them to you."

Gryffyn nodded his head; he would do as he was ordered.

Perata turned his attention back to the battle; the invaders were doing their best to find protection from the incoming arrows. Their numbers did not seem to be diminishing because more and more found their way into the castle unhindered. He found a bow and joined the archers, but did not unleash. He was looking for certain targets, officers, wizards and more importantly, the large man who gave the orders. It seemed he was quite clever and it would be in Perata's best interest to remove him from this battle altogether.

The soldiers in the street began their charge of the makeshift gate. They took heavy losses in the process but hit the gate with the force of a battering ram. The wall was not meant for a sustained attack, it was only meant to create a choke point. This one would not last much longer; Perata sounded the withdrawal and ordered his men to the next checkpoint, where another unit of archers would be waiting.

The invaders passed the first gate only to encounter another further down and again suffered heavy losses. The run and cover technique was utilized all the way to the castle and cost the invaders plenty, but man power was the one thing they had in excess. Perata and his defenders were forced all the way back to the castle and once he had his people behind those gates it was time to make the final stand.

Chapter Twenty-Seven: The Final Barrier

Lockstan glanced over his latest report; only slightly amazed at the amount of casualties they took advancing through the city. The defenders had created lanes of death in five different areas en route to the castle walls. Each time they got a little closer they would run into another makeshift blockade, albeit not overly difficult to push through, but the non-stop arrow fire caused plenty of damage. Eventually their sheer numbers were sufficient to overwhelm each location and breach the barriers but many men were lost along the way. The exact number of deaths did not really matter to Lockstan; he would kill every last man under his command to take this city. He knew now that this was a defining moment in life; when he pulled this off it would just be the beginning of his greatest triumph.

His head turned ever so slightly as he listened to the commotion outside on the streets; his men were finally able to bring what was left of their original siege towers in from the eastern wall. Two of them were still fully functional, while a couple of others could be easily repaired with the amount of materials now at their disposal. He laughed to himself, a habit that had been increasing lately. He rubbed his hand over the smooth mahogany table at which he sat, 'enough material indeed.' His thoughts strayed back to his strategy, simple but effective, he would attack the walls right in front of him. Looking out the window of his makeshift headquarters he locked his eyes on a section of wall located on the western side of the castle in a very affluent part of town. This would be a quick battle; he, as well as his men, noted the defender's inability with close combat and doubted there were more than a handful of real soldiers hidden behind those walls, which made the walls the only true obstacle. To no one in particular he voiced, "It seems old Stragess was actually right about their army being gone, just underestimated their resolve." Clasping his hands behind his back, he admitted to himself that the inhabitants, even as limited as they were, put up quite a fight. Toward the wall he uttered, "None of that matters now. This time tomorrow all that you know will be mine."

He proceeded to step out on to the balcony ignoring the beautiful day; he cared only for his vantage point. This residential area must have belonged to nobles or wealthy business owners who lived in a manner most men would never know. The homes were stripped of anything of value…monetary value, but they still offered the much-needed materials and also happened to make very nice accommodations for his men. Some food stores were found but due to recent events he warned his troops not to eat or drink anything that was left behind, being more likely than not poisoned. The reasons he liked this spot were numerous. The streets offered easy smooth ground in which to move his towers, his men had many areas from which to advance and he could place his archers on the high roofs of these homes to offer cover fire. This side would more than likely not be a commander's first choice when deciding on a way in which to assault the walls, but that is exactly why he chose it. It was an unorthodox tactic, but the enemy he faced seems to have adjusted their defenses to the traditional tactics and would most likely have prepared for an attack on the east wall. He would not fall for that trap again. He rubbed his hands together in anticipation, he had moment's thought about letting his men rest and condemning the defender's to live on whatever supplies they had in their city, but it was only a brief moment. He was not the waiting type, and this city was only the beginning. This would be his launching point for the rest of the invasion and he would sweep through and flank the Eastern Dominion's main forces. He smiled, he knew that he would be part of something great when General Stragess handpicked him to be his second in command, and now he was in charge. This is how he would be remembered, as the man who conquered the East.

He focused his thoughts, "first things first," he needed to take this castle, not just to catapult his full invasion, but now it was personal. He also had to take in account the look of this city, it was apparent that they knew what was coming, which meant that other cities could be preparing as well, including the Eastern army. It would not be beneficial for his forces to get trapped between an attacking force and these walls if the Eastern Dominion decided to turn their attention this way. What he needed was a foothold in this Dominion and Arxsolum would do nicely. That meant that there was no time to dig tunnels or build more siege engines; no time to starve them out, no time to wait. He was not worried, his plan was one of the finest he could think of, he always believed that brilliance would come to him in the moment and so far it had not failed him. He would utilize all his assets in a single spot to take away their defensive advantage, and then once a hole was opened his men would flood inside. From what he witnessed near the city's walls, they were by far the superior fighters and would easily take control when it came to a face-to-face confrontation, which was inevitable. The plan was decidedly simple, but that was the beauty of it. He remembered countless hours of discussion with his mentor Stragess about the intricacies and complexities of proper strategy and how to engage an enemy. All of it boiled down to one truth; if you had an advantage then you needed to press it. His advantage was the amount of men he could throw at one spot and after his ingenious way of bypassing the cities walls those in the castle would be wary of leaving any spot unguarded. This meant they would have to spread their forces while he focused his. It no longer mattered to him how many men guarded the castle, he would capture this city, his city. He cursed the slow trek of the sun across the sky for he planned to attack this very night.

As the sun finally abandoned the sky, the army of the West launched their assault. Lockstan's troops incorporated the same tactics as before, using the towers and additional ladders to gain the necessary height, but this time they fashioned angled coverings fitted from the shields of the numerous dead to force the burning pitch to role off. . The archers stationed in the defender's former homes and shops were far more effective then when firing from the ground. They used the built in cover of the building to take their time and aim, with less distance due to their elevated position, the skilled shots were devastating. The mass of men on the ground did their best to use grappling hooks, but if one did crest the wall it was quickly cut. The progress of the battle was fairly slow, the defensive position of those on the castle wall was still an advantage, if only a small advantage, but the sheer numbers advancing was beginning to ware on them. Lockstan watched in amusement as his men died in droves but it was not important because like last time they were merely a diversion from the real mission.

Only a few war wizards remained able to effectively fight so he had to make sure they were used properly. He felt that their earlier attack on the top of the city's walls was ineffectual and wanted to use them in a different way. He again couple engineering and magic with the goal of weakening the base of the wall. The wizards would use their magic to soften the rock itself, shifting the blocks that no tools could touch giving the engineers something to work with.

Their effort went pretty much unnoticed as the defenders were doing everything they could to contend with those trying to scale the walls. Staying hidden under the cover of shanties, they were able to stay protected from most of the carnage the blazed around them. The shanties were also used to house large battering rams the size of oaks and fitted with steel heads. When the time was right these battering rams would slam into the weakened walls. The engineers used their hammers and spikes to exploit even the slightest of cracks that the wizards could provide; the sheer relentless pounding of the rams then compounded their efforts. The walls were thick but their labors were unrelenting; sooner or later something would have to give.

The night was unusually bright and seemed more like a foggy day due to the amount of objects that were ablaze. Bodies littered the ground and were becoming nothing more than stepping-stones to those that followed. Lockstan was gauging the progress and could see that the defenders were tiring; it would only be a matter of time. He looked to the East and watched as the sun was beginning to make an appearance on the horizon once again, amazed at how quickly the night had passed. Then he heard it, a noise different from the sound of battle, a noise he had been waiting for. It was a slight cracking noise that came from the area where his crews were working.

It started as a small fissure in the base of the wall, slowly spreading outward. The second crack came shortly after and this one sounded like the very planet split asunder. From the assailants to the defenders, everyone heard this one. Seconds later the wall began its collapse amidst a chorus of cheers and curses. Many responsible for the collapse were trapped under it and those who were stationed on that section of wall were thrown about like rag dolls. A portion of the wall itself remained but it opened a fairly large passage gap and more importantly gave the incoming soldiers a rubble stairway in which to reach it.

The climbing was difficult as the invaders had to scramble but the area was momentarily undefended due to the collapse, which allowed for handfuls of invaders to achieve more defensible areas. In a matter of minutes the entire area was teaming with bloodthirsty soldiers. Lockstan could not believe his luck, it was his time now. He turned to his Sergeant and ordered him to send in the men he had in reserve for just this moment and then raced for the gap himself.

The faithful of Arxsolum led by Perata and Jaxen met the initial rush head on, throwing them back down what was left of the wall, but more and more kept scrambling up. Archers on both sides did their best to hinder the other and bodies littered the area. The battle at the downed section raged for nearly an hour with both sides taking heavy casualties. Perata was a perfect killing machine as he set himself in the middle of the hole and killed anything that came near him. The one thing that fueled him was the fact that if the enemy got through it would all be over, there was nowhere left to retreat; he would never answer the questions that plagued him. He shrugged off his gloomy thought as he figured this was as good a place to die as any. His sword darted into the pit of a man's stomach at the same time that he brought up his dagger anticipating that the next victim would be on top of him instantly. To his surprise he had time to ready his sword before engaging another attacker. It seemed the tide was slowing. He had been so deep in the trenches that he did not notice the confusion of the attackers; something was happening in the rear of the invader's forces. He parried a low strike and kicked the man in front of him into those behind. Using the moment to assess the situation, he noticed the surge of invaders had subsided drastically. Perata did not know what was happening exactly, but he knew he had to capitalize on the opportunity. He quickly found Master Discere waiting near by; the aged wizard was a man of his word and had conserved his strength. He heard Perata screaming, "Now, now is the time to use your power."

The mage followed the pointing arm of Perata to where the wall had given way and understood immediately that it needed to be shored up. Discere had been waiting for this moment, in a thunderous voice he boomed, "Clear our people back, I do not know how long I will be able to hold it." He pulled out an old spell book, one that he rarely ever opened. The spells contained within were very complex and extremely difficult. He stepped forward into the melee without his mind focused. Raising his staff high he pointed at a section of wall that was still standing; he then made an arc like movement so that the end of his staff stopped moving at the other section of the wall. He let loose his spell with every amount of resolve he possessed.

Perata watched as a wall of blue energy shot between the two points. The magical wall cut into anything it touched including men. The wall trapped a significant amount of invaders inside the castle, but kept far more out. Jaxen was wildly engaging several of those men and Perata ran to join him. As a team they spearheaded Arxsolum's counter attack against those left inside. Perata spun around looking for another opponent when he noticed two figures engaged in battle high on the wall opposite where he was. He recognized them both immediately. Gryffyn had done what he promised to do; he sought out and engaged the large Captain of the enemy forces. Perata wanted desperately to assist the old weapon's master, but he was quickly engulfed by a surge of attackers. His thoughts raced to the Gryffyn, all he knew about swordplay he learned from that man, but still he worried; anything could happen in a fight.

Lockstan barely parried the quick thrust and took an elbow to his face for his efforts. This confrontation was not going anything like he planned. In an effort to create some distance he threw himself backwards and drew his second sword while he rolled to his feet. He knew he was not the fastest swordsman in the world, but he was damn fast. That mixed with his strength and his intelligence made him a match for even the most experienced warriors, but this grizzled old fighter standing in front of him was an enigma. The young Captain could not believe a man of his age could so easily deflect his powerful blows much less have the position and bearing to strike and strike repeatedly.

He cursed inwardly, his heart told him that he would not be able to beat this man; nothing was as it should be. The whole campaign was riddled with problems. It should have been a fairly easy passage through a mountain range, then a quick surrender of an unguarded city, which should have led to the destruction of the whole Eastern Dominion, but such was not the case. Now this, he should be able to just cut this old man to shreds, but as it were he was outmatched and there was nowhere to run but through him or back over the wall and he would be damned before ran like a coward.

His mind work furiously as he attempted to find the old man's weakness yet no matter what angle he approached the problem, he always came back to the same conclusion; he was going to lose this fight. Utilizing two weapons and every dirty trick he could think of was only buying him time. Lockstan had never met a man that could best him and the thought of it was paining him more than the several wounds he was receiving. It was at that moment that he had a startling realization. He could accepted that he would not be remembered as a great conqueror, he could accept that he would not be the man who swept the Eastern Dominion, he could accept that he would not be the man who took Arxsolum, and he could even accept that he would die here today. He would not, however, accept letting some man brag that he had bested him. He formulated a plan no longer with the idea of winning but based on the idea of not losing; there was only one way he could rob the old man of his victory. He turned his sword edge slightly to the right in order to position his attack. Against anyone else the move would have been negligible but against this man it was everything because he was good, too good. Due to that fact he would never suspect what was to happen next.

Gryffyn was surprised at the skill of this young warrior, he had faced countless men in battle but this man was different. He was incredibly strong but did not rely solely on strength. His technique was flawless and he quickly changed tactics to fend off the attacks. His conditioning was superb and seemed that he would never tire. The old Weapon's master knew that the young man would not be able to hold him off forever but he was growing weary himself and needed to make his move. Then he saw it; the large man angled his sword slightly to the right. It was his only the slightest of an opening, but it would be enough; he would attack on the man's left first high then low, and finish with a reverse spin for what should be the beginning of the end. That small movement should be the catalyst that would put the young warrior further and further down the path toward defeat.

His sword moved like a bolt of lightning arcing high aimed directly below the defender's shoulder. Gryffyn knew this blow would be blocked so he had only a fraction of a second to anticipate the trajectory of the man's sword so he could slide right into the next sequence. To his surprise the giant of a man did not try to block this attack at all and in doing so created an opening of his own. The man set him up, it was suicide, but it was genius. Gryffyn could only hope that when his blow struck it was enough to kill the big man instantly or at least decrease the force of the blow he knew would be coming.

The strike was perfect and penetrated the lacings of the young warrior's armor and entered the man's ribs, but he did not see pain on the man's face only a smile for at that instant both his swords came crashing downward between Gryffyn's neck and shoulder with a force that was overwhelming. The blades coursed through the armor protection and bit deep into the old man's upper chest. The force of the blows was enough to embed the weapons solidly into his torso and knock him to his knees.

Gryffyn never expected to live forever, but never did he imagine one so young would be his undoing. He locked his eyes on the invader, who was looking back at him. Gryffyn was in awe of this younger generation, the commitment of Jaxen, the power of Sorcia, the ability of Perata and now this man, a boy who matched a master. He realized there and then that this invasion was far from over; it seemed that fate had been waiting for this time in history to let loose upon the world warriors equal to the greatest of legends. As his life force drained from his body he summoned up his last remaining bit of strength and saluted the man in front of him. He knew that this moment in history may have started as just an invasion of a city, but it would become a war of epic proportions.

Chapter Twenty-Eight: The Return

Edward and his cavalry had been riding hard ever since they left Quinvium, resting only enough to keep the horses alive. Their approach was uninterrupted as the roads were empty and the horses were familiar with the trails. They arrived at the outskirts of Arxsolum just after daybreak with enough light to see the large plumes of black smoke rising in the distance and they were beginning to smell the putrid stench of burning bodies. The signs were both a blessing and a curse as they all wrestled with their imaginations, was Arxsolum still standing, was it in ruins, or in the hands of the enemy? None of them had an idea of what they were riding into, but no matter what it was they were riding hard. As tired as the horses were, the familiar area kept them moving even though the landscape had changed.

The alteration was astonishing, what used to be acres and acres of forest were now nothing more than a barren patch of land. The open countryside, although disheartening, gave them an excellent vantage point of the city where a large black flag proudly flew high above the castle walls giving the men hope. It was a flag that the men recognized immediately even though few had ever seen it. They knew it from legend and it meant that Arxsolum still stood, that their countrymen still lived. Upon seeing the standard flying all the fatigue vanished from their bodies, the only thing they could think of was their home. They raced down the North road approaching the city and to a man could hear the sounds of battle from within. Upon seeing the traps and obstacles scattered about, Edward gave strict orders to stay on the road but to make all haste toward the gates. The entire countryside was beset with rotting corpses and remnants of a gruesome battle. The deserted enemy encampment could be seen in the distance but was ignored in their desire to reach the battle. The gates were thrown wide open and the streets behind them barren; the fight was well inside the city. Edward and company barely slowed as they sped toward the castle. Many of the men took in the change that overcame their city, but gave little thought as to how it came to be. They passed through the many makeshift blockades doing there best to avoid the number of corpses that littered the streets. On the Western side of the castle they found what they were looking for, the flank of the invading army. Edward gave the signal and the warhorses nearly a hundred strong thundered into the unsuspecting soldiers. The attack created instant confusion within the ranks; their thoughts were concentrated upon the walls in front of them.

The army of the West immediately turned to confront the new threat giving those in the castle a small respite. Edward's men were tired from the journey but the men they faced were equally exhausted from the fight and they were on foot. Fighting in the streets was not the ideal place for a cavalry yet they were still impressive in their ability. Edward signaled his lieutenants to separate into smaller groups to be more effective and they crushed those that stood against them. The defenders on the walls fired volley after volley into the Westerners; reinvigorated as they realized their army had returned.

The onslaught continued as the leadership within the Westerner's began to dissolve. The cavalry of Arxsolum used their momentum to scatter the larger number of invaders into distinct groups. The horses moved in an out of the streets they knew so well giving the impression of a much larger host.

Even with the fight going their way Edward knew he could not keep up the pace much longer. He was aware of the condition of the horses and his men; most were on the brink of collapse and would eventually begin to falter. If he did not act now he and his men would be fighting on foot; he signaled for his men to break contact with the enemy and make for the castle gates. Those that manned the gates did not hesitate with the opening them upon seeing the return of Edward and cheered as he and his men entered. The gates were quickly slammed shut as the last Arxsolum man passed through.

Edward's attack had severely hindered the invading forces; they were still significant in number but were without direction and out of position. Many of the units who still held discipline began ordering retreats after noticing they lost much of their cover fire and that their flank had been compromised. They did not know what type of force was attacking their rear and without higher orders did what they thought was the best way to consolidate their forces. They began making their way back toward their encampment, which only furthered the confusion of the other units. More and more men quit the battle and concentrated on their own survival.

....

Sorcia's team followed the invaders into the city and once inside it was not difficult to disappear. This was their city and with their collective knowledge they easily avoided detection. Making their way closer and closer to the castle none of them were really sure what they were going to do once they arrived, but it was better than doing nothing. Sorcia voted to find a way back into the castle so that they could help defend but since the invasion all possible entrances had been blocked off. She thought to out loud, "One would little secret gate sure would be useful right about now." The other could only nod in agreement as they watched the Westerners prepare for battle.

Tonagal pointed out that they were stationing archers in homes and on the rooftops of building adjacent to the castle. "From those positions their archers would be able to do quite a bit of damage."

"Well, I guess that settles it, we take out their archers from behind. Once the battle is joined we should be able to move fairly unhindered." The immediate threat was apparent and their plan was simple, they would enter as many of the buildings as possible and neutralize the archers.

Phillos spoke up, still moving a bit gingerly from his wound, "Normally I would prefer to do this sort of thing with one maybe two-man teams, but I do not know how many warriors they will have stationed in each building. I think our best bet would be to stay as a group just in case we find ourselves fighting a substantial amount." He stretched his back a bit and added, "Besides, I am not sure just how useful I am right at the present."

The others acknowledged the idea as a good one and if they found themselves in a difficult situation at least they would die with friends. They silently waited for the initial attack to make their move, which did not take long. They heard the enemy horns blaring and knew it was time to move. The first building was entered and it housed nearly fifty men on the bottom floor, but it appeared that most of them were trying to catch some sleep before they were called into action. Sorcia theorized that these were probably some of Lockstan's personal reserve; he was not going to waste them by flinging them against the wall. These men were probably much more able and would be utilized once the wall was breached when they could do real damage. This meant that the team wanted to avoid a confrontation with them and quietly but confidently bypassed them without incident. They quickly made their way to the higher floors; fortunately there were only archers and just a scattering of men who were looking for quieter places to rest.

The plan hinged upon the ability of the group to remain silent enough so as not to alert those down stairs or in the other rooms. The method was simple; sneak up while the archers were distracted and inflict as much damage as possible before they knew what hit them. They each agreed to assigned targets so that they would not waste efforts. Phillos, Lexis and Tonagal all stayed back and readied their bows. It was their job to keep watch for any soldiers who happened to wander by while the other three were ready to silence those in each room. The additional sound of the group's bow strings snapping never even registered in the rooms where the only thing heard was that sound. When an archer went down others assumed they were hit from the archers on the castle walls, an attack from behind never even entered their minds.

They continued their simple and methodical approach, building by building, and floor by floor. The extermination was going rather well with only a few times having to engage in physical combat. Marhran and Rammel seemed to be having a contest to see who could pitch more soldiers off a roof than the other. Both Lexis and Phillos wanted to get in close as well but due to their wounds Sorcia limited them to covering with their bows.

As the sun broke over the horizon, their cover of darkness lifted, making moving from building to building more difficult. While they were waiting for an appropriate moment to hit the next building they heard the crack. They did not have to see it to know what made that noise. The castle wall was being breached. The next thing they heard was a chorus of horns blazing and they watched as a mass exodus of troops followed. They were all being ordered to the direction of the breach.

Each member felt an overwhelming sense of helplessness knowing that rushing in and helping hold the wall would only end in his or her deaths. The only thing they could do was keep taking out the archers and hope that those on the wall could hold. With the majority of ground troops out of the way, stealth was no longer an issue. They attacked each house with reckless abandon; their fury was unrivaled. They rushed each consecutive house with only one thought in mind, to kill anyone in it. They believed that if this was their last stand then they would take out as many of the enemy as they could before they went down. Above their curses and battle cries, above the din of the battle another more distant sound was nearing. At first it sounded like a rapid drum beat but it was quickly turning into deafening thunder.

Sorcia's head snapped toward the direction of the sound, she knew that sound, she knew the sound of riders when she heard them and anxiously found the nearest window to locate where it was coming from. Her eyes were drawn to the banner racing up the streets and she was stunned when she realized what it was. It took her a couple of moments before she could tell the others what she saw because she was not quite sure she comprehended it herself. "It's our army, our army has returned!"

The shock was evident on all their faces, but before anyone could celebrate Rammel spoke up, "Your army may have returned but this fight is far from over, we best find a proper place to hold up while we still can."

The rest of the group nodded in agreement their strength and resolve returning with the good news. There was hope yet. With all the chaos in the streets and the invader's attack being broken for the moment the suggestion was brought up to attempt to re-enter the castle. They did not foresee too much difficulty in reaching the gates, however the problem was then gaining entrance, no one was really sure what to do then.

Their flight to the castle was hampered by only a few encounters of mainly men retreating plundering but the majority of the fighting was still on the western side. They kept to the shadows as much as possible and when needed ran like hell. By the time the team reached the gates they were all exhausted but it did not appear they had anyone on their tale. The next step was hoping they could get the attention of those inside without catching an arrow for their efforts.

Sorcia shook her head in disappointment, "I can't reach him with my magic, I don't know if I am just too tired or worse, but I don't know what else to try." The others understood that attempting to reach the old wizard by way of magic was a long shot since he was more than likely fighting for his own survival on the western side.

"We need to get their attention somehow," she said again aloud and she ran from their spot of cover directly in front of the gates and started shouting. She was not sure if she was going to be shot before she was recognized but desperation was sometimes the best plan. To her astonishment the gates opened almost instantly and her team was ushered in.

The first person she saw was her mother, or at least the women her mother had become. She was dressed like a warrior and shouting orders at the newly arrived cavalry like a seasoned strategist; readying them for a counter attack. She already had fresh horses brought up for the men who were not injured and was marshalling them back through the gates. Edward tried to intervene but Aliondrae cut him off with questions, "Where is the rest of my army? How much time until they arrive?"

Edward was stunned; he had ridden into the middle of chaos and now was being told what to do. "Aliondrae, we must stop for a moment and assess our next move. I don't think you understand the situation at hand."

Aliondrae spun around, her eyes blazing, "I understand the situation far more than you for I have been in it for the last couple of months, much more time than was needed for you to return. The situation at hand is that the enemy is momentarily broken and we must seize that advantage. We must take back enough of the western part of the city to that we can re-fortify the wall. Now," she said in a voice colder than ice, "stand aside or I will have you removed."

Without knowing how else to respond he just moved aside. As he did so she marched past him to meet Perata and Jaxen followed by many of his raiders. She pointed to where the mounts and cavalry were preparing, quickly seeing what Aliondrae was pointing at. They had more men than horses. Without even a moments hesitation Perata took charge of the situation ordering the men to be divided into two teams, those on horse and those on foot. He spoke with such authority that the cavalry instinctively responded to his commands. He then spotted Sorcia's team and without even a question as to how they were doing sent them without Sorcia back out the gates to assist those on foot. He pulled Sorcia aside and directed her to the west wall to assist Discere as best she could.

The newly combined force flew out of the gates with the goal of taking back the city so that they would once again have a defensive position. As the gates closed, calm settled on the courtyard. Edward was standing in disbelief irritated that his men were just taken without his permission. He also had time to regain his bearing after Aliondrae ordered him out of the way. He put his hands on his hips as he waited for an explanation, "Just exactly is going on here?" he questioned with a growl. Aliondrae did not waste time explaining, she did not even look his direction, she just grabbed her bow and began her ascent to once again man the walls. Edward stood there a moment, as everyone went about with a purpose, and with nowhere else to go followed after his wife.

The remainder of the day was a route of the invaders. Many of them losing the taste for battle as several different men tried to take up the reigns of leadership. The mercenaries were the first ones to flee the city when they looted as much as they could carry. The men who were forced into fighting for the invaders readily gave up leaving only small pockets of resistance within the city. The majority of invading army heard the rumors that another army had reinforced those inside the castle gates and thinking themselves at a disadvantage made their way into the countryside. Without any real leadership and no common direction the battle that seemed an eternity to the faithful of Arxsolum was finally over.

Chapter Twenty-Nine:
Forever Changed

The meeting room was quiet as the names of the dead were being reported. The list seemed endless and when Aliondrae spoke she was on the verge of tears. "We must find a way to honor all of our fallen, for they stood with us and without their sacrifice we would not have saved our city. Unfortunately, we must tackle some more looming projects first. Most importantly is the issue of the dead; what are our options?"

Lineaus spoke up, "I understand that many of our people will not feel overly compassionate for the invaders but we must also consider the risk of disease. Our best course of action is to cart the bodies east toward the Irritum Sea and burn them as quickly as possible. As for our own, well…I know that some families have traditions that we should abide by but for the most part I think we should establish a memorial cemetery."

The Count began shaking his head, "No, no we do not have time for that nor should we waste good land. This city is in financial ruin, for whatever reason you decided to destroy all of our fields, which will take time to come back. This city exists because of agricultural trade and we are going to need every ounce of land if we wish to return to that trade. It would make more sense to just burn all the bodies and be done with it. We can then move on with our lives and hopefully try to save what is left of this city."

The others at the table were not happy with what they heard but Aliondrae did not bat an eye, "That is not going to happen. The men and women that died in defense of this city will get a proper memorial. They will not be burned and forgotten."

"Aliondrae, I do not think you understand what is best for the future of Arxsolum, now I have made a decision and that is final. I do not need this lot of advisors to instruct me on how to fix my city that you decided to devastate. You are just lucky I came when I did."

Discere stood up out of his chair, as exhausted as he was he was still an imposing figure, but it was Perata who spoke first. "I had heard you were a shrewd man, but so far everything that has come out of your mouth is nonsense. You do not know of what you speak. Your forest, your fields, and your finances will come back, the dead will not. They gave the ultimate sacrifice for what they believed in and should not be forgotten, for if it was not for them then there would be no Arxsolum."

Edward eyed the large man who spoke to him still irritated that everyone around seemed to follow his lead, "First off, who are you and why are you speaking to me as if you are my equal? I..."

The Countess slammed her fist on the table, "Edward that is enough, you forget your place. You have no authority to make decisions, this is my city and I will decide what is best for it. Now we are grateful for your return and will be even more grateful when the rest of our army arrives. You may not have noticed but we are still out numbered, the only reason we are still not under attack is that the invaders are no longer working as a unit. We will not fall into that trap. As for the man who sits across from you, he is the reason that we are all still here. He is in charge of everything, including the cavalry until I deem otherwise. Is that clear?"

Edward noted the dangerous tone in his wife's words. She was as changed as the city he rode into. He had tried to fall back into his role as the aggressor but this time it was not going to work. He knew enough to check his response and wait for a better moment. "I apologize for my remarks, it has been a long a difficult journey and I am only thinking of what would be practical. Of course the deceased should be honored and remembered for their actions, but we must also think to the future as well."

No one at the table truly believed his sincerity but none of them had the desire to call him on it. Sorcia cleared her throat to gather their attention, "I have an idea, one that will honor our dead and also return Arxsolum to some semblance of its former self. I was thinking that with so much of the forest leveled it would give us plenty of land to properly bury our dead. With each grave we could plant a tree in remembrance of what happened here. I know if I had not made it, that is where I would like to be, forever a part of Arxsolum."

Every one at the table agreed that it was an excellent idea, a way in which to rebuild and remember those that gave everything. When the details were sorted out, the topic shifted and Discere began to speak, "we still must face the fact that we are not out of danger yet. The Council has contacted me and it seems the Eastern Alliance is not fairing well, in fact they are barely holding their ground. If they are defeated we could face another invasion, this one from the north. The pass itself is also a priority even though it has been partially closed. By the accounts of Sorcia and her team it can still be traversed, which means the possibility of threat from there as well."

"Perata, what are your thoughts?"

"The Countess is right, we are still outnumbered and the first thing we must do is gain back our advantage. That means we must first clear the city as there may be some resistance left. Sorcia, you and your team will round up some of the more able fighters and cleanse the city, house by house, street by street. In the mean time we will begin work repairing our defenses from the inside out." He motioned toward Jaxen, "you and your raiders will be tasked with those on the outside. I do not expect you to route them all but it is imperative that you do not allow them to regroup. It is still quite dangerous out there so you will need to travel in force. Once the remainder of Arxsolum's regular army returns we can then methodically push them further and further from the city.

Keeping them from regrouping will give us time to re-establish our defenses. Once that is accomplished we can then decide what must be done about the pass as well as a possible invasion from the north. I will oversee the repairs until your ground forces return then you will have the means necessary to properly reclaim your territory."

Aliondrae understood the meaning in his words and all though he did not say it he was intending to leave. "Where will you go, with a war going on you will find very few welcoming areas. Perhaps now is not the best time to be traveling, and there is still so much to do, we could definitely use your expertise."

"No, it is time. I will head north."

Jaxen cleared his throat and corrected, "We, we will head north." He met Perata's questioning gaze, "You will need a guide and there is safety in numbers."

"Make that three; there is no way you are leaving me behind," added Sorcia quickly.

Edward seemed amused and waited for some sort of outburst from their mother but instead saw something in her eyes; understanding. Things had definitely changed, before he left Aliondrae hated to let her children out of sight, now she is seemingly letting them head straight into a war. He shook his head; he would need to revisit his plans.

Aliondrae spoke directly to Perata, "Well then, I guess we have a lot of work to accomplish in a short time, we should get started."

Perata made his way over to the twins, "I am fairly sure that a couple of months ago neither of you would be chased from your home yet now you are telling me that you want to leave."

Jaxen cocked his head, "There is a vast difference between choosing to leave and being forced to leave. Besides, if the Eastern Alliance is truly in trouble then Arxsolum will never be safe. Maybe we can be the difference?"

"Do you think the three of us will have that much impact on a war?" questioned Perata in his usual way.

"Indeed we will," replied Sorcia, "but just so you know I told my unit that when you leave, I leave…they all decided to tag along. So all said…there are eight of us and all rather capable."

"Well, actually," interjected Jaxen, "…many of the raiders are under the impression that with the return of the regular army that the unit and their ranks will disappear. In an effort to alleviate their fears, I have given them the option to come with us as well. A few that have families opted to stay behind, but the majority will follow."

Perata eyed the twins, "You have already made these plans? What if I had made the decision to stay?"

The twins looked remarkably similar at the moment as they both smiled. "We knew that it was only a matter of time, and to answer your earlier question, yes, we do believe that we can make a difference."

Epilogue:
Clawing and Scratching

Stragess found himself walking; his sight was greatly diminished by the fog. He had no idea where he was but always the realist it occurred to him that this may be the afterlife. "Am I dead?" he jokingly questioned not expecting anyone to answer.

"I cannot yet allow you to die, there is far too much work to be done!" came a hard reply.

Stragess jumped slightly at the voice, yet it sounded familiar, a voice he had not heard in some time. It only took him a moment to realize that it was his God speaking to him. The General flung himself onto his knees and began to beg forgiveness for his failure.

"What makes you think that you have failed?" The booming voice pained Stragess ears, " Do you presume to know the plans of a God?"

"My lord…," pleaded Stragess.

"Silence!" returned the disembodied voice. "Silexunatra once again attempts to thwart my control. She has a new champion, you will do whatever it takes to find him and kill him. Do you understand?"

General Stragess did not understand, and he could swear he almost heard desperation in his God's request.

The slight delay in answering nearly cost Stragess everything. His body was ripped from the floor and effortlessly held aloft by an unseen force. He began to feel his muscles tearing as each one of his limbs were wrenched in different directions. Gritting his teeth through the pain he yelled, "My Lord, I will do as you bid."

The General's body was unceremoniously dropped to the floor, "Then it is time to rise and fulfill your destiny."

Stragess awoke with a splitting headache and a crushing weight upon his body. He was weak, but he was alive. He caught just the shimmer of light of to his side and with everything he possessed pushed, pulled, scraped and clawed to get to it. When he reached his goal, it took a moment to fathom where he was. The weight that was on him was dead bodies, scores and scores of rotting bodies piled around him. He laughed, 'they left me for dead.' He quickly noted his surrounding but there seemed to be nothing but his dead companions. He tried to make his way across the sea of dead but found he was too weak. He realized he must have been here a few days, a few days here and no telling how long without food. He would need nourishment if he planned to survive but in his current condition there was no way he would be able to hunt even if game were available. His left hand moved in an attempt to push someone's leg off his mid section, but before he finished he stopped. He took a look at the leg and swore, 'I must survive." Without any more hesitation he ripped open the pant leg and tore into the dead man's leg with a ravenous hunger he had never felt before.

In between bites he could hear sounds of isolated battles but definitely nothing that would indicate a full scale invasion. It did not take long to ascertain the fate of his army, they were broken and on the run. He did not have time to ponder the events as he heard the distinct sound of hoof beats nearing. He just stayed where he was and did not move a muscle. His caution was rewarded as he watched the cavalry of Arxsolum sweep past in pursuit of, more than likely, remnants of his army. He may have lost this battle and even though he felt a small pang of defeat it was no longer his concern. His concern was the present and he would do whatever necessary to fight another day.

.

Made in the USA
Middletown, DE
01 March 2022

62001974R00182